THE HIDDEN VILLAGE

IMOGEN MATTHEWS

ISBN 13: 978-9492371256

Cover design: Leo Johnson

Copyright text © Imogen Matthews, 2017

Publisher: Amsterdam Publishers, The Netherlands

Introduction

The inspiration for this novel came from my Dutch background and frequent visits to Holland. My mother was Dutch, she was born in The Hague, grew up in Rijswijk (where I was born) and went to the University of Leiden. When I was a child I remembered how she often recounted stories to my two sisters and me about her youth and the deprivation and difficulties she and her family suffered during the Hunger Winter in 1944/45 whilst "under the boot of the Germans". Despite these extremely challenging times, she revelled in the adventures she and her friends had, such as when one time a group of them stole out at the dead of night and cut down a large lime tree outside her house and chopped it into pieces for fuel. 'I can't imagine how we dared do it,' she said, smiling at the memory. 'We were fortunate there were no Germans patrolling in the neighbourhood, because the noise we made was enormous.' She remembered doing her fair share of sawing and finding an inner strength she hadn't realised she possessed.

Towards the end of her life, when she was 91, I asked my mother to repeat her stories so I could get them down for posterity. I also had another motive, to write a novel set in Holland in WW2. Since 1990, I've been on holiday with my family to the Veluwe, a beautiful national park where we love to cycle through magnificent woods and across expansive heaths. One year, we came across a World War 2 memorial deep in the woods. It had been designated in memory of a group of Jews who hid from the Germans by living in underground huts in a purpose built village. Several of these huts had been reconstructed and I found it hard to believe that whole families could have lived in these gloomy cramped spaces for years on end. The alternative, deportation to a concentration camp, was too awful to contemplate.

Back home, I discovered a book called *'Het Verscholen Dorp'* by A. Visser on bol.com, a Dutch website. It was an account of the hidden village I had found and was derived from archive material, letters, photos and interviews which the author had conducted with people who had lived in the area at the time. The courage and tenacity of people determined to help others in the face of terrible adversity and prepared to put their own lives at risk was remarkable. I had a compulsion to retell this story as fiction, inventing characters from my imagination, some of whose experiences were based on what actually happened in this place, unknown to so many. As *The Hidden Village* is a work of fiction, I changed some of the place names to my own invention, but anyone who has connections with this part of Holland may find certain aspects recognisable.

Memorial stone for those given shelter in the Veluwe woods

On the 31st of October 1944 Jews were shot
by the Germans at this place

PART 1

CHILDHOOD INNOCENCE

Chapter 1

Jan's heart beat fast as he crouched, quite still, behind a huge beech tree. He'd been running so fast that in this new position his thighs screamed in pain. A rustling sound. Fast footsteps. Muffled voices. Then they were gone and he let out the breath he'd been holding and rolled back so he could stretch his legs out. All the while he kept his eyes firmly on where the footsteps had passed close by, just in case they came back. Adjusting his position so he was more closely hidden, he began counting slowly. At fifty he allowed himself to take crouching steps in the opposite direction and hearing no further sound, broke into a run. Twigs snapped, leaves crunched and his breath came fast and loud again, but he didn't care. He'd beaten them this time.

When he reached the sandy path he looked quickly left and right, then slowed, swaggering and sniggering to himself.

Without warning, two shapes emerged from the trees, one on either side, shouting out in victory. They jumped on Jan, wrestling him to the ground and suddenly they were all laughing as they rolled over and over.

'You bastards!' Jan yelled, furious he'd been ambushed after all.

'Thought you could escape us? Never!' taunted Nico.

'Serves you right for getting me last time,' said Lex, the smallest of the three friends.

'Race you back home.' Jan struggled free and stumbled to his feet. He was off down the path towards the houses at the edge of the wood. The thought of his mother's pea and ham soup, bread hot from the oven and creamy milk spurred him on. He'd make sure he wouldn't tell her where he'd been as it would only worry her. Lately, she'd been fretting at the rumours that Germans were patrolling the woods. Not that he'd seen any, and even if he had, he was sure it'd be no different to the games they played. A shiver of excitement snaked through his body at the thought. Calling back to his friends, he said that he'd see them later at the usual meeting spot deep in the woods where few people went.

***

'Oscar!' Time for lunch!'

His mother stood at the bottom of the staircase, craning her head, even though she knew Oscar kept his door firmly shut. He'd been in there since breakfast and Sara couldn't help herself from worrying. It wasn't natural for a boy of his age to take his studies so seriously. But she didn't want to discourage him in case he decided not to study at all. It had taken all her powers of persuasion to keep him on the straight and narrow after his argument with his father. Sara tried to shield Oscar from him, but it didn't always work. Max simply didn't see that shouting at his son never had the desired effect.

Oscar's door flung open and he thundered down the wooden staircase two steps at a time. Sara noticed the shadowy bruises under his eyes and how he pursed his mouth into a thin line.

'I made your favourite soup,' she said brightly, scraping her ladle into the black saucepan she used for all their cooked meals. She filled two bowls with the thick steaming broth and placed Oscar's in front of him.

'Where's father? Where's Jan?' he said, frowning into his soup.

Jan burst through the door and kicked his shoes into an untidy pile in the middle of the floor before plonking himself down at the table.

'Jan! Must I tell you every time to leave your shoes at the door? Now go and wash your hands!' His mother fixed him with a piercing glare.

'Why always me and not him?' whined Jan, playing football with his shoes till they came to rest behind the door, then dragged his darned stockinged feet over to the sink.

It was true, she never asked Oscar, whose fingers were stained with graphite where he'd been moving his hand across the page.

'Oscar hasn't been mucking about outside picking up heaven knows what,' she said. She resumed ladling the soup in the bowls, then glanced at the clock striking the half hour above the kitchen range.

Shoes being scraped on the outside doormat announced Max's arrival.

'Quick, sit down. And properly,' Sara scolded Jan, who was holding a finger under the tap to make it spray in all directions. He turned it off, rubbed his wet hands over his face and through his tangled fair hair and took his place opposite Oscar who stared at him impassively.

Max, a tall upright man with a stern expression, walked over to Sara and pecked her on the cheek she'd turned towards him.

'So, Oscar. Good work this morning?' he said, sitting down at the head of the table, shaking out his napkin.

'Mm...' said Oscar, through a mouthful of bread.

'Speak up, boy.' Max picked up his soup spoon and brought it down hard on the table.

'Yes, father,' said Oscar, without looking up from his bowl.

Satisfied with this response, Max turned his attention to Jan who was swinging his legs back and forth, making his chair rock. 'Jan, I hope you've been helping your mother today.'

'*Ach*, Max, leave the boy alone. He's been playing with friends. It's not a school day.'

Max waggled his spoon at Sara. 'You're too soft on that boy. He'll grow up out of control. Just you see.'

Sara didn't answer back, just pursed her lips and shot a quick glance at Jan, who was oblivious to his father's remarks and was engrossed in shovelling down his lunch.

'I bumped into Dick Foppen today,' said Max after a couple of minutes eating in silence. 'The situation's not looking good.'

Sara looked up in alarm. 'How many?' she whispered.

'It's hard to say, but it could be hundreds,' said Max, a deep furrow appearing between his eyes.

Sara gripped the edge of the table. She left the remains of her soup in front of her. Oscar looked from one parent to the other and opened his mouth to speak when Max got there first.

'He thinks things will be fine for the moment but will let us know as soon as anything changes.' He carefully laid his spoon in his empty bowl. 'In the meantime, we need to prepare for difficult times ahead. We may need to provide shelter to people unable to defend themselves.'

'Do you mean Jews?' asked Oscar. 'Why are the *moffen* singling them out? They're no different to anyone else. It's not fair.' His cheeks flared red as he thought of Sofie.

'I agree. It isn't fair. But it's the way it is and we may be able to help. But all of you need to know that if we do, you must not breathe a word to anyone. If we are discovered sheltering *onderduikers*, they will show us no mercy.' His stern gaze moved from Oscar to Jan, who began jiggling in his seat with excitement.

'Will I know them? Can they share my room? I can let them sleep in my bed and I…'

'Shh, Jan. This is a serious business. It will need a lot of planning. If we take anyone in, we will have to make provisions to make sure that no one knows they are here,' said his father.

'But we've only three bedrooms, so we'll have to share,' Jan persisted, but was silenced by another look from his father.

From the outside, the house was large, with a deep roof that sloped all the way down to the first floor windows. It was spacious enough for the Mulder family who had lived there since Max's father had died and left it to his only son. The kitchen took up most of the ground floor, so the family spent their time in there, warmed by the old black range that Sara kept stoked up with wood, chopped by Max with help from the boys.

At the top of the narrow wooden stairs were the three bedrooms. The walls were really part of the sloping roof, so an adult could stand up straight only in the middle of the room. Above Oscar's room was a hatch leading to the attic which they had started to use for stockpiling dry food.

Finishing his soup, Max wiped his mouth with his napkin, then folded it and stood up. 'I must go back to the shop. Remember, don't mention our conversation to anyone.' For the first time since he arrived for lunch he smiled, then left the house.

'Father's so serious. Is it really that bad?' Oscar asked his mother.

She wished she could pretend. 'Let's look at it as if it's a big adventure. None of us knows what's going to happen, but at least we're all together.'

She forced a smile, but was unable to ignore the sense of foreboding creeping through her body.

Chapter 2

Sofie couldn't concentrate on the algebra her teacher had set the class. The x's and y's swam before her eyes as she tried to remember the formulae they'd been taught only moments before. Everyone else's pencils were moving quickly and the more she imagined how the others had got it, the more she panicked.

Two minutes left. Blindly, she scribbled something down hoping that Mevrouw Klein wouldn't ask her to speak out in front of the class.

'Pencils down,' barked the teacher.

Sofie obeyed, keeping her eyes on her exercise book.

'Oscar, please tell us the answer to the first question.'

Sofie exhaled as quietly as she could. If she kept her head still, she could see Oscar two rows forward out of the corner of her eye. He scraped back his chair and spoke in a quiet but confident voice. A voice that suggested he knew the right answer.

'Well done, Oscar, as always,' beamed Mevrouw Klein. 'Now please choose someone to answer the next question.'

Sofie's heart began beating fast. Oscar knew maths wasn't her strong point, but he'd do anything to attract her attention.

'I'd like Sofie to go next.' Oscar tried to meet her eye but she still wouldn't look in his direction.

'Sofie? Did you hear? Oscar is asking you to tell us the answer to the next question.'

Sofie felt Mevrouw Klein's eyes bore down on her. Slowly,

she got to her feet and forced herself to look up. 'I think it's...' she paused, delaying the inevitable ridicule she knew was coming her way. 'Twenty one squared,' she said softly.

'Does anyone else think that's the right answer?' asked the teacher, prolonging Sofie's agony.

Oscar's hand shot up. For a moment, Sofie softened, knowing he was on her side, defending her from the teacher's wrath.

Mevrouw Klein relaxed her stern features. 'Yes, Oscar, you are right. That was the correct answer. Sofie.' In a louder voice, 'You may sit down.'

Sofie's cheeks burnt with indignation. How dare she praise Oscar and not her? The earlier warmth she felt towards him vanished. But at least she could melt into the background for the rest of the lesson.

One by one, students were asked to call out the answers and Sofie was surprised to see that despite her earlier panic she'd managed to answer them all correctly. And when asked by Mevrouw Klein who had achieved this seemingly impossible task, she was the only one to raise her hand. Not even Oscar.

Grudgingly, in Sofie's view, Mevrouw Klein acknowledged her achievement with a curt, 'Good work, Sofie. Let's see if you can keep it up.'

The end of school bell rang out. Relieved to be released from the class, Sofie hurried out into the yard where she bumped into Liesbeth. Although they were both fifteen, Liesbeth was in the year below Sofie by a fluke of their birthdays being in different months. They were neighbours and had been friends as long as they could remember.

'You OK?' asked Liesbeth. You look as if you've been given a hard time.'

Sofie shot her a look, irriated at her friend's uncanny knack of reading her mood. 'You could say that. I hate maths and I'm going to give it up as soon as…'

Sofie hadn't seen Oscar come up behind her.

'But you were the best in the class,' he said, gazing at her.

Sofie tossed her bag over her shoulder and made to go. 'Was I now? It certainly didn't feel like it. Coming Liesbeth?' She turned on her heel, anxious to get away from Oscar. Liesbeth shrugged in his direction and hurried after her.

'Why are you so mean to Oscar?' she said with a quick glance to make sure he couldn't hear. 'I thought you really liked him.'

Sofie was walking ridiculously fast leaving Liesbeth trailing in her footsteps. Sofie wouldn't reply till they reached the turning to their street where she stopped dead. 'Forget anything I said about Oscar. He's, he's such a wimp.' Sofie pressed her knuckle into her left eye and rubbed hard, leaving red marks on her cheek. Liesbeth knew better than to challenge her. At least once a week Sofie would 'go off' Oscar only to forget about it the next day.

'Come and have some milk and cookies,' said Sofie as they drew level with her house.

'Are you sure? Looks like you've got visitors already.'

Behind the net curtains the shapes of three people were just about visible.

'Oh, Mum never mentioned anything. Let's go in through the

back and let them get on with it,' said Sofie, slamming the gate behind them. They squeezed past the clutter of bikes, rusty buckets and stacks of wood Sofie's dad had chopped ready for winter. The kitchen door was ajar, as always.

'Where are the cookies?' said Sofie, surveying the kitchen before dumping her bag on the floor.

They heard the front door bang shut and her mother came through into the kitchen. Like Sofie, she kept her wiry chestnut hair tied back with a piece of old ribbon. In repose, her face looked harsh and Sofie often took it as a sign of disapproval. Today was one of those days, so Sofie decided against mentioning the cookies just yet.

'Who were those people?' she decided to ask.

'That was Mr Foppen and his wife. They've been calling on everyone in the street and telling them to take care when going out. Earlier this morning, Mr Foppen was in Harderwijk and saw German soldiers on the street. He left immediately to come and warn us that they may be on their way to Kampenveld.

As her mother had forgotten to pour them a drink, Sofie went to the larder and helped herself to the big blue jug covered with a square of muslin. She wasn't particularly bothered by her mother's news which was hardly new, because she'd told the same story about the soldiers coming a week ago and still they hadn't materialised.

'Want some?' She held out a china cup with milk to Liesbeth who was standing very quietly as if she wished she weren't there. She gulped her milk down as fast as she could.

'Thank you, but I'd better get home. See if my mum's had a visit too.'

Mevrouw Steins's face softened. 'Yes dear. It would be best. Let's hope it's just another false alarm.

After Liesbeth had gone, she was back to her worried self. 'Sofie, I have something to tell you. Come, sit down.'

Sofie didn't really have time for this. She was beginning to regret she'd been a bit harsh on Oscar and wanted to cycle over to his house so she could say something. Reluctantly, she perched on the edge of a kitchen chair, ready to flee.

'I didn't want to say in front of Liesbeth, because it wouldn't have been fair,' began her mother, smoothing down her faded floral apron. 'Mr and Mrs Foppen have kindly offered to help us if it becomes necessary. They have a large attic where the three of us can sleep safely until the danger passes.'

'But there have been rumours about the Germans for weeks and nothing's happened. What makes them so sure something's going to happen now?' Sofie was irritated and just wanted to escape.

Something in her mother's expression made her stop. She'd never cried in front of her daughter but her eyes were full of tears. She blinked and then almost as quickly they were gone. Had Sofie imagined it?

'We don't need to do anything just yet. But we have to be ready, just in case.'

'What about school? I've got my exams in two weeks?'

Sofie wasn't usually concerned about such things but they represented stability in her life that she felt was in danger of slipping away.

Suddenly, her mother was back to her old self, planning and

organising as if their conversation hadn't taken place. 'Is it just two weeks away? Then we must stop chattering and you must go to your room and revise. Go, hurry.' She clapped her hands. 'I'll call you when supper is ready.'

***

Sofie sat at the little wooden table where she'd worked for all her exams. It was quiet, apart from the occasional thump and clatter as her mother moved around the kitchen. After a while, the familiar smell of fried potatoes and onions wafted up, but today she didn't get her usual warm, hungry feeling. How could she revise, knowing all this could be taken away from her? What was the point if the Germans were really going to march in with their heavy boots and arrest people like poor old Willem van Dijk? No one knew what had happened to him after he'd disappeared walking to the shops one morning three weeks ago. He lived on his own, so there was no family anyone knew of to kick up a fuss. Sofie shivered and pulled her thin cardigan tight round her middle. She'd always found Willem a bit odd, the way he talked to himself as he shuffled down the street. She and Liesbeth would walk by with straight faces, then burst out giggling after they'd gone past. Secretly, Sofie was pleased he never seemed to notice. But now he'd gone, she wished she'd been a bit nicer towards him, even saying hello.

Scraping her chair back, she went to the window. Turning into the street was her father on his old bicycle which had almost flat tyres, but somehow managed to get him from A to B. He caught sight of Sofie and waved, his cheeks rosy from his exertion. Sofie let out a sigh of relief when she heard the front door slam and ran downstairs to greet him. Halfway down she stopped. Raised voices reached her ears. Not her father's. Not her mother's, but foreign male voices. She crept back up a few steps, straining to hear. She heard her father cry out and the scraping of a chair on floor tiles, then his protesting voice in faltering German. From her hiding place she saw two tall uniformed men, both with crew-cut blonde hair and set jaws. One was pushing the butt of his rifle against her father's forehead. She could tell her father was trying hard not to react and was whispering quietly in response to the soldier's barked questions. Suddenly, she could bear it no longer and came rushing down the stairs, shouting 'No, No!' at them.

Surprised, the soldier lowered his gun and looked her up and down with a sneer. 'So. What do we have here?' Sofie could make out what they said only because it was similar to Dutch.

'My daughter. Please don't harm her,' her father said.

Sofie caught sight of her mother almost invisible on the other side of the kitchen. Did she really think they wouldn't notice her, Sofie wondered in irritation? But the soldier was more interested in Sofie. He came and stood one step away from her, appraising her. He said something to his colleague and they both laughed, harsh mocking laughs that left Sofie in no doubt of their meaning.

'What right do you have to come in here and treat us like we've done something wrong? My father's just come home from work. That's all.' Her quavering voice tailed off, betraying her rising fear. The two men stared at her, smirking.

'Shh, Sofie. They don't understand. You're wasting your time. Let me deal with it,' her father said, hunched in his chair, looking defeated.

'*Papiere!*' snapped the one with the rifle, lifting it in her father's direction again. Her father slowly got up, went to the dresser and pulled open a drawer, whose contents spilled out onto the floor. Sofie rushed forward to help, but the other man stepped forward, blocking her way.

Her father's hands shook as he rifled through the old newspaper cuttings, balls of string, odd nails and all sorts of other paraphernalia carelessly shoved in the drawer over the years. After several painful minutes when Sofie was bursting to help, her father pulled out the document he'd been searching for.

'Here.' He looked the rifle soldier in the eye for the first time.

Sofie's heart was beating fast. Her father couldn't help his dark features and the size of his nose. If they didn't believe him, she was sure they'd arrest him, or worse, shoot him right here. And then once they'd dealt with him it would be her turn.

A small whimpering sound could be heard from a dark corner of the kitchen. Her mother was obviously thinking the same thing.

The German spent a long time examining the ID card, turning it over and over, as if he was searching for something. Then he suddenly shoved it back at her father, snapping: '*Alles in Ordnung!*' He jerked his head at his colleague to move towards the door. But he must have caught sight of Sofie's mother, as if he'd only just noticed her and growled out an order to see her ID.

Sofie had never seen her look so scared. Her strong, capable mother, who'd always been there to protect her, had been replaced by this snivelling, pathetic creature.

'I'm not a Jew!' blurted out her mother, rooted to the spot.

'*Papiere! Sofort!*' shouted the soldier, who was clearly losing what little patience he had.

'Mother! Just show him!'

The soldier must have seen her looking in the direction of the cupboard under the sink and marched over, flinging the door open and began pulling stuff all over the floor. Her mother's handbag was tucked away at the back, where she always kept it. She'd had it as long as Sofie could remember. It looked dilapidated and forlorn in the soldier's prying hands. With a wrench, Sofie was reminded of all the times she'd begged her mother for a few cents to buy this and that, sweets, a magazine, a colouring-in book. At every request her mother had agreed with a sigh. Sofie used to feel a momentary wave of pity as her mother had fiddled with her ancient purse with the broken zip and counted out a few cents into Sofie's hand. Now her mother seemed detached and just stared, waiting for the inevitable.

Shaking the sorry contents of her bag onto the draining board, the soldier fished out her crumpled ID card and again spent his time examining it.

'*Pah*!' he exclaimed, tossing it aside. '*Komm!*' to his accomplice, before striding out of the door and away.

Slowly a smile spread across Sofie's father's face, but he held a finger to his lips before she could say anything.

It was her mother who seemed to spring to life. No longer the victim, she resumed her role bustling around the kitchen, tidying up the mess left by the two intruders and ticking off Sofie for not helping. Softly whistling, her father began laying the table for supper as if nothing had happened.

'Dad…' she began, but he gave her a penetrating stare.

Confused, she ran back upstairs. But she knew for certain this wasn't the end of it.

Chapter 3

Jan couldn't wait to get back to his friends. He was bursting to tell them the news but his father's stern face kept clouding his mind. Surely Nico and Lex could be trusted to keep a secret? After all, secrets were the glue that kept this little group together. Like the time that Nico told them how he'd spied on his sister, Bettie, who met Peter the baker every Wednesday at seven in the alley at the back of his house. They all knew that Peter was married with a two-year-old son whom he proudly trundled in his pushchair down the centre of the village on Sunday afternoons. But Nico had seen Bettie and Peter kissing and after telling his friends, swore them to secrecy. Whenever Jan went round to Nico's house he'd search Bettie's face for clues, but was always disappointed. Why was it that grown-ups could keep a secret so well?

This was different and perhaps he'd better keep his father's word, for the time being anyway.

Jan whistled to himself as he skipped along the path framed by enormous beech trees, just coming into leaf in the warm sunshine. He knew the path well, the patch of bilberries the three of them would raid later that summer as soon as the tiny green berries turned purple and sweet and the big rock covered in moss where they took a sharp right. There was no path here but the boys used the rock as a marker, before plunging into the leafy undergrowth till they were hidden from the path. After a few yards, Jan came to the gnarled oak tree and resisted the temptation to climb to the upper branches. It was more fun doing that when the others were there.

Where were they, he thought impatiently, and began scuffing his feet through the dead leaves that always covered the woodland floor. Straight ahead, the trees thinned to reveal a clearing surrounded by some straggly bushes. Jan dropped to his knees and began crawling through, knowing he was completely hidden should anyone come up behind him. He'd sometimes bring his father's garden scissors when the branches and twigs became so entangled that they scratched their arms and legs. They definitely needed a trim now, he thought, stopping to suck his stinging hand. Then, a rustling sound.

'Nico? Lex? Are you there?' he called in the direction of the sound, but guessed the low moan came from a much older person. He held his breath and crept forward an inch, parting the foliage to get a better look.

At first he felt indignant that someone had discovered their hiding place, then realised the man lying in front of him must be hurt.

'Hello?' Jan pulled himself through the gap and stared at the man lying quite still, his foot at an odd angle. He grunted something Jan couldn't quite catch. He wore a grey uniform, trousers torn at the knee and it looked as if he'd been rolling in the dirt. He had short, dark, cropped hair and the beginnings of a beard. His face broke into a smile. Trying to hoist himself into a sitting position, he slumped back onto the bed of leaves and bracken he'd made for himself. 'Can you help me?' he said in a low voice. 'Do you live nearby?'

Jan crawled on his hands and knees towards the man so he

could examine him more closely. 'Are you English?'

The man laughed. 'Yes. My plane came down over there,' he pointed vaguely in the direction of Farmer Janssen's field.

Jan's eyes grew wide. 'You were in a plane?'

Again the man laughed and seemed to forget his injured ankle for a moment. 'You speak good English. Do you learn it at school?'

'Yes, but my mum's English. She speaks it to us at home. But what about the plane? Did you fly it all the way from England?'

The man's face clouded over. 'It was only my second sortie. But I suppose I'm lucky to be alive.'

'How did you find this place? No-one knows it's here except me and my friends.'

'I apologise for breaking in like this, but if I'm honest, I didn't realise it was a den.' The man's eyes twinkled.

'A den? What's that?'

'A place to hide. Which is exactly what I wanted. I needed a place to hide so the Germans wouldn't find me. I thought the best place would be in woods where I could regain my strength.' He pulled a small hip flask out of his jacket and took a swig.

'Are you hungry?' asked Jan, enthralled by his new companion. ''Cos I can run home and get you some food.'

'Would you? I haven't eaten since we set off from Kent. It must be two days ago. That's where I came from in England,' he said, in response to Jan's puzzled look.

Jan scrambled up and was about to go when he remembered his friends. 'Nico and Lex are meeting me here.'

A look of alarm passed over the man's face and he tried to get to his feet. 'I mustn't let anyone else see me. Don't tell them about me, please.'

But it was too late. They both froze as they heard the sound of voices and undergrowth being trampled underfoot. Two surprised faces poked through into the clearing.

'Who's this?' said Nico, banging the dirt off his shorts as he pulled himself up.

'He's English. His plane was shot down and he's hiding from the Germans,' Jan said quickly in Dutch.

'Is he a real soldier?' asked Lex, staring at the man's uniform.

'Yes, stupid. But you mustn't go telling everyone. This is secret. Promise?' Jan held the palm of his hand and waited for the other two to slap it.

Lex copied Nico, though Jan worried that he didn't understand why it needed to be a secret.

'C'mon back with me to the house. I'm going to get some food and drink for him and we can discuss what's going to happen to him.'

All the while, the man sat back on his makeshift bed watching them through half closed eyes. It was obvious his ankle hurt badly as it was so swollen that he wouldn't be able to put any weight on it. Nico saw his discomfort and pulled a fallen branch over so he could rest his leg on it.

'You need to keep it lifted up,' he said in Dutch, gesturing to the man who gave him the thumbs up. Jan smiled too, enjoying this real-life adventure.

'You remember all that stuff?' he said to Nico.

'Only 'cos my dad twisted his ankle out in the forest just after that first aid lesson we had.'

Lex was hopping from foot to foot. 'I thought we were going to fetch stuff for him,' he whined.

'Will you be OK here for a while? Oh, I'm Jan, by the way, and this is Nico.' He nodded at Nico. 'And this is Lex.' He slapped him playfully round the head.

'I'm Nigel. I'm very pleased to meet you all.'

They grinned at each other for a moment, then Jan led the way out of the clearing, the other two scrambling after him. They chattered, laying plans for what to do with their fallen pilot.

'We'll bring him some bread and sausage. Mum won't notice if that's gone missing,' called Jan over his shoulder. 'C'mon you two, we need to hurry.' He was almost running now, anxious to get onto the path and back home.

It was the smell of a cigarette that stopped him in his tracks. Then he saw the shadow stretching towards him from the base of the oak tree. Jan turned to Nico and Lex and put a finger to his lips. They tucked in behind him. No one dared to move.

A man wearing a grey belted coat stepped out from behind the tree, barring their way.

'So,' he said, grinding his cigarette with his boot.

Chapter 4

Sofie left the house five minutes earlier than usual. She took the path that snaked round the back of the village, ending up in *Boslaan*, almost opposite Oscar's house. She hung back as she watched him come out with his brother Jan and was puzzled to see them deep in conversation. Normally, Jan would skip off, kicking loose stones down the road, stopping to stroke the neighbour's cat, while she and Oscar walked side by side on their way to school.

Oscar looked over his shoulder and caught sight of her, calling her over. He said something to Jan in a low voice who didn't need an excuse to run off and swerved off down the road, making aeroplane noises with arms outstretched. 'Have you forgiven me then?' he teased, waiting for Sofie to catch up.

Sofie furrowed her brow. 'Oh that! You know I hate maths and...let's forget it.'

It wasn't like Sofie to come round so quickly, but Oscar didn't mind. He looked forward to walking with her to school each morning. It was probably best he didn't mention the conversation with his father the night before. Maybe his father hadn't meant to worry them but he'd suddenly become so angry about the Germans and then made them all promise not to tell anyone about the meetings he intended to have at their house.

'Oscar. Something awful happened last night. We got a visit from two German soldiers who demanded to see mum and dad's ID. It was so scary. I thought they'd drag dad off, but they seemed to accept his papers. I can't see how, you know the way he looks and everything. Then after they left, mum and dad refused to talk about it. Just acted as if it hadn't happened.'

'You were really lucky. And they left, just like that?'

'Not after pressing a gun to dad's forehead and searching through mum's handbag.' Sofie shivered as she remembered. 'Oscar, we're going to have to go and stay with the Foppens. It'll be hell.'

Oscar took her hand and squeezed it. 'Because of this? When was this decided?'

'The Foppens were there when I got in from school.' Sofie stopped dead. 'Wait, do you think those *moffen* might have caught wind of us having to leave?'

'Not possible. The Foppens are far too careful.'

'How do you know?' Sofie gave him a furious look. Oscar always had an answer. It was like he always knew what she was going to say next. 'I…' she began.

'Don't say anything. Just walk normally,' hissed Oscar, through his closed mouth. Sofie kept close to him, eyes wide at the scene in front of them. A windowless van was parked up ahead, its back doors open and two German soldiers were shouting at an elderly couple to get in. They were each carrying bulging cardboard suitcases as if they were going away for a few days. The man limped, which seemed to irritate the Germans, who kept on at them to get a move on, but wouldn't let his wife help him. Sofie caught sight of her eyes, wide with fright.

The two of them drew level but pretended what was happening was perfectly natural. Sofie pulled the scarf on her head slightly forward and stared at the ground as they passed.

'Hey, you!' shouted one of the soldiers in Oscar's direction. 'Close this door, will you?' He had an unpleasant smirk on his face. Oscar kept his face neutral as he turned back and stood by the van.

'Didn't you hear? Close the door. Unless you want to go in.' Both men laughed loudly. One raised his rifle and Oscar heard a click. He quickly put his hand on the door. Two pairs of round eyes stared out at him. He licked his dry lips, screwed up his eyes, then slammed it shut.

'Good boy. Now get out of it,' the rifleman said, who was lighting a cigarette as he leant against the side of the van.

Oscar caught up with Sofie who was waiting, her head averted. Walking quickly away, they could hear the van start up and pull away.

'I can't believe you did that?' Sofie shot at him.

'What was I supposed to do? You saw those two had guns. If I hadn't they'd have shoved me in the back too.'

'Or shot you,' Sofie said in a quiet voice.

'No, I don't think they would've done that. Just threatened me. They'd already got who they wanted this time.'

'Did you know that couple?' Sofie looked up at him and tried to blink away the tears that filled her eyes.

'By sight. They never go out much because he can't walk far. I sometimes see her going to the village with her shopping bag.'

'Why them?' Sofie wondered, innocently.

'It's obvious. They're Jews. That's why you've got to watch out.'

'But what use are they to the Germans? They're hardly able to work in those camps are they?' She glanced at Oscar, who was staring straight ahead as they resumed their walk to school.

'I don't know, Sofie. I wish I did.'

His comment chilled her. Perhaps her Oscar didn't have all the answers after all. He put an arm round her waist, but still didn't look at her. She leant into him, grateful for his warmth, even though the morning sunshine was beating down on them.

Chapter 5

'Good afternoon, Mr Hauer,' said Jan as nonchalantly as he could. Nico and Lex knew better than to speak.

'Jan. A surprise to see you here, hmm?' said Mr Hauer, squinting at him as he lit another cigarette.

'We're on our way home,' said Jan, not untruthfully. It annoyed him that he felt he had to justify himself to the forester who had a habit of popping up whenever Jan had something to hide. He knew that was his job, patrolling the woods, making sure nobody was doing anything they shouldn't, like lighting fires or stealing logs from the woodpiles he and his men had assembled ready for distribution to the sawmills. Why he was interested in the antics of a few boys was beyond Jan's comprehension. They'd never actually done anything illegal but whenever they crossed his path, Jan came over all guilty. All those times when Jan was only trying to prevent the forester from finding his den.

'What time is it?' asked Jan, desperate to divert the forester's attention. Voices carried in those woods, where normally the only sounds were birds chirping or the crack of twigs as bushy-tailed squirrels scampered from tree to tree. *Please don't make a sound.*

'Off somewhere in a hurry?' said Mr Hauer, his foot propped on a fallen branch. He clearly had no intention of going anywhere himself.

'We're on our way home. We'll be late if...'

'Then you'd better get a move on.' He stood aside and the

boys were forced to run off down the path leaving Mr Hauer, who could so easily have seen where they'd come from and decide to investigate.

'D'you think he'll...'

'Shh!' hissed Jan at Lex, who had a habit of not quite understanding the urgency of a situation. Once Jan was sure they were out of earshot, he slowed, but kept on briskly in the direction of home.

'We're going to have to be really careful. I don't think we should be going back until it gets dark.'

'But mum says I have to be back home before dark,' whined Lex.

Good, thought Jan, who didn't want to have Lex to worry about right now. 'It's probably best I go back on my own.'

'Hang on. What about me?' said Nico, stopping mid-path and stamping his foot theatrically. 'I don't have to be back any time soon. 'Sides, we may need two people if we're going to help move him.'

Jan hesitated. Nico was right; perhaps it'd be safer with two.

'Look, this is what we'll do. When we get home, I'll make sure the coast is clear and get some food and stuff. Lex, you keep guard outside. Nico, you chat to Oscar. OK?' Jan's heart thumped with excitement.

The house was quiet. Jan's father was at work and he could see the bent form of his mother, pulling vegetables from the garden, her back turned away. He mouthed to the others to be quiet as he and Nico slid in through the side door. Lex was told to tuck himself under the front window and keep watch.

Jan needn't have worried about Oscar. He wasn't in, though he might have turned up any minute. Jan whispered to Nico to keep an eye on his mother through the kitchen window, while he rummaged in the pantry for food. There was a newly baked loaf of bread and a potato pie, ready for supper, but it would be too obvious if he took either of those. He carved a slice of ham from yesterday's joint and wrapped it in a scrap of greaseproof paper, then took two apples from the top crate and a few biscuits from the tin on the sideboard. Nigel would probably be thirsty but Jan didn't know how to make coffee and anyway it would make a smell that would arouse suspicion. In the back of the cupboard where his mother kept the crockery he found a glass bottle and filled it with water from the tap. He was packing it all into a cloth bag when Nico suddenly dived onto the floor.

'Your mum's heading back in,' he said in a loud whisper.

'Quick. Out through the front.' Jan pulled Nico by the sleeve and the two boys tiptoed towards the front door. Jan jiggled the handle but of course it was locked. They only ever used it when they had visitors and his dad kept the key on a long chain attached to his trousers.

'Upstairs!' shouted Jan and they both shot out of sight to the sound of Jan's mother stamping her muddy shoes on the outside mat. She hadn't heard them, but now they were trapped on the landing. 'We're going to have to go down and tell her,' Jan whispered. He should have realised earlier that she'd be an ally, but he'd been so fearful of what his father would say, that he'd panicked.

'Jan? Is that you?' His mother's voice floated up the stairs. Jan poked his head through the banisters. 'Hi, mum. It's only Nico and me.'

'But it's only 4 o'clock. Is everything alright?'

His mother's anxious face peered up at him.

'Course,' said Jan, brightening up and thundering down the stairs, two at a time.

'So why is Lex sitting under the window? You haven't excluded him from your game, have you?'

Jan went to the window, opened it and leant out. Lex was sitting on the ground with his legs outstretched. He seemed to be asleep. 'Lex! I thought you were keeping guard!' he said in an annoyed whisper.

Lex leapt up, his head popping up above the window ledge. He saw Jan's mother and ducked down again.

'Come on, stupid. Game's up. Mum's already seen you.'

'Keeping guard? Against what?' said his mother, hands on hips.

It all came out in a rush. 'We found this man he was in our den in the woods he's a pilot he's English and his ankle's hurt so I said I'd get him food and…'

'Slow down. So this English pilot's hiding in the woods and needs our help, is that it?'

'No. Yes. He's not hiding really. Just doesn't have anywhere to go.'

'So you came home to get him food,' she said, eyeing the bag he was trying to hide behind his back. 'Why didn't you just come and tell me? You must have seen me in the garden.'

'I thought you'd say it was wrong or something,' mumbled Jan, shuffling from foot to foot. Nico had nipped outside and was playing ball with Lex in the road.

'No, you did the right thing. But it might be dangerous so I suggest we wait till your father comes back.'

This wasn't what Jan wanted to hear. 'Father'll be cross with me. He won't let me go back and Nigel will be all on his own.'

Sara smiled at the mention of the man's name. She rested a hand on his head. 'I'll speak to father. He'll understand. Now let's see what you packed in here for your new friend.' She peered in the bag, turning over the meagre items. 'No bread? He'll need bread to go with that ham. And what about a slice of pie?' Her eyes twinkled and Jan started to relax. 'Now leave it with me and you go and play with your friends, but don't stray into the woods again.'

Jan was relieved at his mother's response. But he wasn't sure what his father would say to having Nigel come back to the house.

Chapter 6

'You haven't told anyone else have you?' Jan's father stood in the doorway in his outdoor coat and shoes, his face like thunder.

'Only Nico and Lex but they won't tell a secret.' Jan looked pleadingly at his father's face.

'Then it's no good. We can't bring him back here. It's too risky.' Max peeled off his leather gloves, slid them into his coat pocket and shook the coat onto the waiting hanger. Sitting down on the little wooden stool by the coat stand, he began unlacing his work shoes.

'But he's hurt and he's hungry and has nowhere to go.'

Max paused, a pensive look flitted across his face. Then shaking his head, he said: 'No, Jan. You heard.'

Jan then did something he never usually did and burst into tears at which his mother came hurrying out of the kitchen. 'What is it, sweetheart?' and folded him into her arms.

'Do you know about this, Sara?'

'Yes, Jan told me and I think we can't leave the poor man in the woods. We can go after dark and no one will see us.' She stared hard at her husband.

'Did anyone see you?' Max asked Jan, whose heart began to thump.

'No. No one,' he said, still sobbing a little, while holding his hand behind his back with fingers crossed. 'Honest, it was just us three and I told them they mustn't tell anyone.' Jan waited till his father relented.

'He's English, is he now? Well, your mother will have someone to speak to.'

'Thanks father.' Jan hopped from foot to foot, not daring to rush at him for a hug in case he changed his mind.

'We'll treat it as a dry run,' said Max to Sara, ignoring Jan, as he eased his slippers onto his feet.

Jan didn't dare raise his hopes, so kept quiet as his father talked of his plans to get Herman, the local carpenter, to build a secure hiding place up in the attic. Of course there'd be no time now, so Nigel would have to stay in the shed at the back of the garden. It was hardly big enough for a man to lie down and was full of gardening tools, empty flower pots and bits of old furniture.

'I'll help clear it out and I'll bring down the old mattress from under my bed and some bedding,' Jan said eagerly.

'Oscar can help you. Where is he? I haven't see him today,' said his father.

'Isn't he upstairs?' said his mother, hurrying to the foot of the stairs. 'Oscar? Are you up there?'

'What's going on?' said Oscar from the landing. He came down and stood behind one of the kitchen chairs which he held onto tight.

'Ah, I'm glad you're here. Things are progressing a little faster than I hoped. Jan has found an injured English pilot who's waiting in the wood for us to help him. But first, we need to make provision for him here and I'll need your help,' said his father.

'There were Germans in the village today. The couple at number seventeen, they took them away.'

Sara's face became pale. 'Old Mr Bouwer and his wife? Surely not? How do you know this?'

Oscar sat down heavily on the chair. 'I was walking past and two Germans were herding them into a van. It was awful.' He wiped his forehead which had become damp. Sara moved towards him ready to give him a hug, but stopped when he turned his face away.

'Damn it!' his father barked, making Oscar start. Jan moved quietly out of sight behind his mother. 'We must prevent any more of this happening in our village. I didn't realise they'd started here already. We have no time to lose and must draw up plans to stop them destroying our community.'

'Max, it's dangerous...' began Sara.

'It's dangerous if we do nothing. I cannot stand by and watch. It's our duty to stand up to them and I expect you all to support me in this.'

Oscar looked at the floor. Jan barely moved behind his mother. Sara nodded slightly and pursed her lips. There was no point challenging Max when he was like this.

Max exhaled heavily causing his shoulders to droop. 'Alright. Let's get on with the business of helping this pilot. At least we'll be doing something worthwhile.' Issuing instructions to Jan, he forbade him to go back into the woods alone and outlined the precautions he needed to take in order not to be seen.

But Jan wasn't listening. His mind was racing ahead, back to the spot where he'd found Nigel and where his adventure had begun.

Chapter 7

Oscar agreed to go with Jan, who knew the woods like the back of his hand. This meant they would hardly need to use the little torch Oscar kept in his trouser pocket. It was a clear night, so there was a strong chance that their path would be visible by moonlight.

Jan was in his element, clearly enjoying being the one in charge. He'd obviously found the pilot and had promised to help. He knew Oscar would follow him as he had virtually no knowledge of the woods. Normally, Oscar tried to avoid the woods which he found a bit creepy, especially after dark. But he wasn't going to admit that to Jan, who kept running on ahead, much to Oscar's rising panic. He dared not call out. Oscar knew the whole point of this exercise was to conduct it in deathly silence.

He hurried to keep up with his brother who seemed to revel in each twist and turn of the path. He was convinced he deliberately ran ahead, making a point of waiting for Oscar who was less sure of his footing on the stony path. Drawing level, Oscar hissed at Jan to stay close in case they came across anyone they needed to explain their presence to. Their father had made them agree to say they were taking a short cut through the woods after visiting an elderly relative. Oscar was sure their cover would be blown if Jan scarpered off ahead of him, leaving him exposed.

The moon disappeared behind a cloud, so he flicked his torch on and off as he tried to memorise the direction of the path ahead of him. After a while, his panic subsided as he realised there was no one in the vicinity. Then a loud rustling up ahead gave him the shock of his life. He jumped behind a tree and crouched low, his heart pounding. Jan was nowhere in sight. The sound was like someone wrestling to get free from something. Oscar was torn between going to investigate and keeping well hidden. All at once a dark shape leapt from the bushes and bounded away through the undergrowth. Jan turned up and fell about laughing at Oscar who leant against the tree for support.

'What was that?' gasped Oscar.

'Only a wild boar. You must have frightened it. Or perhaps it frightened you,' laughed Jan.

'Me? I'm not frightened. It just gave me a shock,' said Oscar, regaining his composure. It wouldn't do to let Jan see how scared he really was. He'd had no idea it would take this long to get to Jan's den and he began to wish he hadn't agreed to come along.

'C'mon, it's not far now,' said Jan, as if reading Oscar's mind. 'See that tree? We turn off there. It's a bit of a scramble, but you won't mind, will you?'

'Course not.' Oscar cursed inwardly. He let Jan take the lead again but this time kept close behind him.

'He's gone!' shouted Jan in a too-loud voice, as they emerged into the clearing that was his den. The branches that the pilot had made for his bed had been pushed to one side and the only sign of life was the flattened grass under the tree.

'Are you sure he was here?' asked Oscar, who couldn't tell one clearing from the next, especially in the dark.

'D'you think I'm stupid or something?' flashed Jan and

disappeared into the bushes behind the oak tree.

Oscar was unsure what to do next. He didn't want to appear even more of an idiot than he felt. To his relief, he heard two voices, one of them Jan's. Emboldened, he parted the branches and saw a huddled shape which shifted slightly in his direction.

'This is Nigel,' said Jan in an excited whisper. He began pulling items out of the bag. Nigel grabbed the bottle, unscrewed the top and drank greedily, making Jan giggle.

'Thank you, thank you. I needed that so badly,' said the pilot, wiping his mouth, before swigging deeply again. 'I'm so sorry. I should have introduced myself.' He stuck out a grubby hand at Oscar.

'Oscar. Jan's brother. I hear you are hurt. Can you stand up?'

Nigel put both hands on the ground behind him for support and winced as he heaved himself to standing. 'It's still very swollen. Do we have far to go?'

Oscar wasn't sure if it was the moonlight that made Nigel's face look so pale. He decided to tell him a half truth. 'No, not far. Maybe 15 minutes.' He shot Jan a sharp look as he said this. At Jan's pace it would have taken 15 minutes but he suspected it would take four times as long. Oscar was nearly as tall as this Englishman and judged that he'd have to support him most of the way back. Jan would have to keep an eye out so they wouldn't be seen.

'Are you on your own?' asked Oscar.

Nigel sunk back down again. 'There were three of us when the plane came down. One minute I was trying to avoid hitting the village, then everything went black. When I regained consciousness, it was just me beside the plane. I was frightened it might explode so crawled as fast as I could to some trees at the side of the field. And then it did explode. I was lucky.'

'Here. You must be hungry,' said Oscar, nudging the food packages in his direction. Nigel began stuffing ham and bread into his mouth.

'Where are the others now?' asked Jan, eager to hear the rest of the story.

Nigel chewed in silence for a few moments before answering. 'I don't know. I'm hoping they managed to escape.'

'Did you see anyone after that?' asked Oscar.

'No one. But I made sure I didn't stay by the plane. It was engulfed in flames and the heat was terrible.'

'How far away is it?' asked Oscar, nervous that their hiding place would be discovered.

'It's hard to say. I don't think it's far as my ankle hurt too much. As soon as I reached the edge of the woods I looked for somewhere safe.'

'We need to get you out of here. My father says you can stay with us for a while.' He looked anxiously at Nigel's ankle.

'Don't worry about me. It's only a sprain.' Nigel said with an encouraging smile.

'Here, lean on me and try to take a few steps.'

Holding out his hand, Nigel managed to find his feet.

The wood was much darker now the moon had disappeared behind a cloud. Oscar ordered Jan not to go too far ahead but he repeatedly disappeared from view before skipping back to check on the faltering couple. Their progress seemed interminable as Nigel had to stop every few minutes and lean against a tree so he could take the weight off his foot.

'How far?' called Oscar in a loud whisper to Jan.

'Don't y'know? We haven't even got to the main path yet,' said Jan, clearly revelling again in his superior knowledge of the woods.

Oscar became more and more irritated by Jan, by Nigel's constant apologies for taking so long and with himself, for agreeing to come. He could be at Sofie's house now, listening to music on her little radio and trying to forget about yesterday. He just hoped she was safe indoors with no more unwelcome visitors. To make matters worse, it began to drizzle, fine droplets that rustled on the canopy and soaked their hair and clothes. It seemed to spur Nigel on and before long they could make out pinpricks of light from houses in the village.

All at once the night sky lit up, as if by lightning, followed by a deep crunching sound that shook the ground beneath them. Instinctively, Nigel threw himself down. Oscar and Jan went down too. High pitched voices and screams reached their ears. They stared at one another in mute horror. It didn't sound as if it came from the village, but Oscar knew it'd be risky if they were all to turn up just then. 'Jan, stay here with Nigel and I'll go and find out.'

Free from the burden of half carrying Nigel, he sprinted home along the eerily empty streets. It was curfew and there was no sign of life from the blackout windows. He felt encouraged as this was no different to normal.

His mother was waiting just inside the hallway. Her face broke into a smile when he walked through the door but crumpled on seeing that he was alone.

'Did you hear the bomb?' Oscar said, catching his breath.

'How could I not? But where is Jan? You haven't left him?'

'I told him to wait with Nigel behind the cattle grid. Where's father?'

'He went off on his bike to Kampenveld to see if he could help.' Her voice shook.

'Is he mad? Doesn't he see he's putting himself in danger?'

Sara wiped a tear that escaped down her cheek. 'He insisted he went. Said it's his duty to help.'

'But not towards his own family,' said Oscar in disgust. 'I have to go back and get Jan and Nigel down safely.'

Sara hung onto his sleeve. 'I'll come. I can help.'

'No, mother. You must wait here. Just in case father returns.'

The sarcasm in his voice cut through her. Kissing him lightly on the cheek, she let him go.

Chapter 8

Sara wished Max hadn't rushed off so impetuously. She was sure he had no idea what he was letting himself in for. Since his brother, Johan, had been arrested three weeks ago in the middle of Amsterdam, Max seemed to be on a vendetta against the Germans. Johan had been on his way home after a church meeting when he was stopped by a soldier who was pleased to turn someone in on that quiet evening. The soldier hadn't believed where he'd been and held him overnight in a police cell. When it came to his hearing the next day they had threatened him with deportation to a work camp in Arnhem. Johan, always a smooth talker, managed to wriggle his way out of the arrest with nothing more than a reprimand. His fluent German had helped him. But Max had become enraged at his brother's treatment even though Johan had come to no physical harm. The arrest had been a trigger for Max's anger and determination to fight against the injustices meted out to his fellow countrymen.

'If we don't stand up to them we'll be under the boot for ever. Can you imagine what life would be like? No freedom to walk the streets when we like. Forced to go to Germany to do the jobs they're too superior to do themselves.' Max kept on night after night round the kitchen table to his friends Bert, Michel and Gerrit, who all thought along similar lines. There were stories of people being arrested for no reason other than that they were Jewish. The Germans were also turning their attention to any young man who refused to go and work in Germany. Sometimes, it was difficult to work out from the whisperings in the village what was true. People were prone to exaggerate if the rumours weren't about anyone they knew. Secretly, Max feared for his own son Oscar, even though he was only nearly sixteen. If this war carried on like the last one, they'd be after him, he was sure.

As the situation worsened, they began to hatch plans to help people evade the Germans. Herman was a great ally and started to attend their meetings. He was in demand building numerous false walls and doors so that people could disappear into hiding at a moment's notice. But it was dangerous and sometimes noisy work, always accompanied by the fear that a neighbour would betray him to the Germans. The consequences would be terrifying.

Sara was permanently worried, but knew it was useless arguing with Max who always had to have the last word. She made sure she didn't join in their conversations, but would listen to their discussions while she went about her chores in the kitchen. Secretly, she admired his determination to make a stand, but trembled inwardly every time she heard another piece of bad news on the wireless set they brought out from its hiding place under the kitchen floorboards.

There'd been no time to think when the bomb went off. Although it happened nearly a mile away just on the outskirts of Kampenveld, Max was pulling on his coat and running out of the door before Sara had a chance to object.

'Wait here for Jan and Oscar. They'll be back soon and make sure the pilot isn't seen. Take him straight out to the shed,' he ordered, belting up his coat and pulling on a woollen hat against the chill night air.

'Be careful darling,' she cried, but he'd gone almost before the words were out of her mouth.

Max's cousin lived in Kampenveld so it was understandable why he rushed off. But it bothered her that he seemed more concerned for Fanny's safety than that of his own family. Fanny, a teacher at the Grammar School, was a good ten years younger than Max and lived on her own in a small townhouse by the canal. Max would find reasons to visit her at least twice a week and rarely asked Sara to accompany him. On occasions when they did go together, it would be so Sara could go to the shops while Max called in on Fanny for coffee. Sara would arrive at Fanny's laden with bags of flour, sugar, vegetables and meat. She always brought a little extra something for her, like tea in a twist of paper.

Only last week, she and Max were there and Fanny had invited Sara to come in for a coffee after she'd finished her shopping. She noticed how Max had been so much more cheerful than he ever was at home, jumping up to help Fanny fetch another cup and joking about the *ersatz* coffee that really didn't taste of coffee at all but everyone pretended was delicious.

Sara was tired after dragging herself round the shops in the market square and was grateful for a rest. Sipping her coffee, she listened to them chat and thought how he was never like that at home. Their conversations were usually fraught with one problem or another that needed dealing with. There never seemed time to just relax round the fire and chat like they used to.

'It's so nice she can come, don't you think?' Fanny was asking Sara, who hadn't been listening.

Max looked across at her, his face clouding over in irritation. 'What's wrong with you? Aren't you well?'

'Sorry, I was wondering when we might be able to get hold of some cheese. The grocer has run out. What were you saying, Fanny?'

'Bep is coming to stay. She thinks it'll be safer than staying in the town. I haven't seen her since *Sinterklaas*.' Her cheeks glowed.

That was last week and her best friend Bep would have arrived by now full of stories about the bombing over Rotterdam. She would have been so relieved to arrive in Kampenveld, which was not much more than a village with its 300 or so inhabitants. Compared to Rotterdam, nothing much ever happened in Kampenveld. Until tonight.

Chapter 9

The cup of tea Sara had made for herself had turned cold. She was exhausted but knew she wouldn't be able to sleep, even though the house was completely quiet.

Everything had happened in a rush. Half an hour after Oscar had left, he and Jan appeared with the pilot who was limping badly. She glanced up and down the street in case anyone had seen them, but there were no signs of life.

'Come in,' she urged.

'Shouldn't you be indoors?' A man's voice came from the direction of the street. Swinging round, relief flooded through her as she saw it was old Mr Visser, who never took any notice of the curfew and walked his black and white mongrel through the village every evening.

'I could say the same about you,' she quipped. Nigel and Jan must have ducked down in the bushes. Only Oscar stood at her side.

'There won't be any more disturbances tonight. Mimi needs her walk.' He looked fondly down at his dog which was straining at the leash.

'*Voorzichtig,* meneer Visser. Careful. You don't know who you can trust these days,' said Sara, eager for their conversation to be over. Pausing, she turned to look at him, noticing how thin he looked in his shabby brown overcoat. He'd lost his wife only last year. 'Mr Visser, please come and join us for a coffee tomorrow morning. You're welcome to bring Mimi.'

There were several gaps in his teeth when he smiled. 'I would like that very much,' he said and held up his hand in a wave as he continued his route back home.

'In, quick,' hissed Sara to Jan and Nigel, who emerged from the bushes.

Inside, Nigel held out a hand to her and politely introduced himself. 'Your sons have been so kind to help me. I had no idea how I could get out of the woods on my own, particularly on this leg.'

Sara felt the colour rise in her cheeks and hurriedly dragged a chair out from under the kitchen table. 'My husband is very pleased to help and has prepared a place for you to sleep where it's safe.' She realised how foolish her words must have sounded, but went on: 'Max is taking the war effort seriously which is why he isn't here. He's gone to see if he can help in Kampenveld. You know, where the explosion was this evening.'

'I've heard about people like your husband. They are very brave.'

'Or foolish,' said Sara, with a deep sigh. 'I don't think he realises what it's like for me when he goes off on his missions. He thinks he's invincible.'

Nigel smiled. 'It's surprising what people will do when faced with danger. Some crumble but others are inspired to face it against all odds.'

'And you? Which are you?' She wanted to know.

'Me? I'm not really sure. I did everything I could to prevent the plane coming down over the village, but whether that was because I wanted to save myself or others, I can't tell you. It all happened so fast, it was instinctive. But I wish I could find out what happened to the others,' he said, more quietly.

'Max might be able to help. He has contacts.' Sara stopped herself from saying more. It wouldn't do to say too much even to this stranger who was so clearly in need of their help. 'I'm sorry but you have to sleep in the shed.' Sara laughed at the absurdity of the situation.

Nigel laughed too and held her gaze for a moment.

'Come on, I'll show you where to go,' said Oscar.

Sara had forgotten he was still standing by the door. Jan was curled up on Sara's armchair by the stove, fast asleep.

'Wouldn't you like a cup of tea first?' They both laughed again, united in their Englishness.

'I would love one, but not if it's too much bother,' said Nigel, glancing at Oscar.

'No bother. I bet you haven't had a proper cup for ages.' Sara busied herself with the kettle and fetching cups from the dresser; best cups, not the normal chipped ones.

By the time they had drunk their tea and swapped stories about pre-war London, Oscar had disappeared up to bed. It was left to Sara to lead Nigel, limping, out to the shed her husband had cleared earlier. The old mattress from under Jan's bed completely filled the space between the tools, stacks of old flower pots and skeins of garden string. An even older sleeping bag had been spread out over the top.

'It's not exactly the Ritz,' said Sara, apologetically.

'It is to me compared to another night in those damp woods.

I'm so grateful.' He seemed to move towards Sara who stepped back in a moment of awkwardness.

'I can leave you the torch,' she said, holding it out to him. 'I must see if Max has come home.' She couldn't see his face, but he thanked her and said goodnight. She hurried back to the house, her heart pounding on hearing Max's key in the lock. With relief, she threw her arms round him, but he shrugged her off.

'Are Fanny and Bep alright?' she dared ask.

'Oh yes, yes, they're fine. But Fanny's front windows were blown in by the blast. Fortunately, they had already gone to bed.' Max explained how he helped Fanny clear the mess and board the window before setting off to the centre. The butcher's and baker's shops had sustained the worst of the blast, but fortunately no-one had been killed. Only Jaap, the delivery boy, had been knocked off his bike and badly grazed his hands and knees. 'He shouldn't have been out after curfew. It could have been much worse. Now tell me about the pilot.'

'No lasting damage as far as I can see. Just a swollen ankle made worse by the long walk home through the woods. He seems quite comfortable in the shed.'

'Did anyone see him?'

'No. Mr Visser was walking by at the time with his dog, but I'm not sure he noticed anything.'

Max frowned. 'Mm. I suppose he's harmless. He's always walking up and down with that dog chatting to people.'

Sara wondered whether to tell Max that she'd invited Mr Visser in tomorrow. 'He's lonely. I can't believe he's involved in anything. And what about Nigel? Isn't he more of a threat?'

'I've already made enquiries. We should be able to move him out within a few days. It'll take a bit of organising. In the meantime, it goes without saying that he must stay hidden. Now I'm going to bed.'

It was another hour before Sara could bring herself to join him.

Chapter 10

'Can Liesbeth stay tonight?' asked Sofie, wiping her milk moustache away with the back of her hand.

'Again? She's already slept here twice this week. Is everything alright with her?'

Sofie had promised Liesbeth she wouldn't say anything to her mother, but her frequent stays were bound to raise questions. 'Her mum's not been very well and lies on her bed all day. Liesbeth finds it a bit depressing.'

Sofie's mother stopped scrubbing the floor. 'Shouldn't she be looking after her?'

'She's not really ill, just feeling a bit tired. There's nothing for Liesbeth to do so she may as well come here.' Sofie fetched her coat from the peg in the hallway, eager to leave in case she said too much.

Liesbeth was waiting at the end of the road and Sofie quickened her pace when she spied her. 'What's up?' she said, peering into Liesbeth's drawn face. She had been crying.

'Mum wasn't there again last night. Dad says he doesn't know what's going on but it's driving me mad.' Liesbeth blew her nose into a screwed up hanky.

'Are you sure?'

'Mum begged me not to tell him, but it's so hard for me keeping her secrets. Can I stay over tonight?' Her eyes welled up again and Sofie hugged her.

'Course you can. But Mum's a bit suspicious. I told her your mum's not well and just wants peace and quiet.'

'And did she believe you?'

'Not sure. But don't worry. It's so much more fun when you're around.'

Sofie linked arms and they fell into step, chatting about their plans for the weekend. They talked excitedly about a new Fred Astaire musical they'd heard was playing at the cinema in Kampenveld and decided to go to the Saturday morning matinee. They were both mad about films and whenever an American one was showing they made sure they'd watch it at least four times till they could sing the songs off by heart.

Liesbeth's visits had become more and more frequent to the point that Sofie kept the camp bed up permanently in her room. Liesbeth would go home only to pick up clean clothes, freshly laundered by Tinny, the help. Even Sofie thought it a bit odd that Tinny seemed to be there so much, but Liesbeth brushed it off with the comment that her father felt guilty that her mother wasn't around to do the housework. She supposed he could afford it, given his job on the town council.

'At least he's got someone to talk to at home,' said Liesbeth, a hint of bitterness in her voice.

'But it can't be the same though. What on earth do they have in common?' asked Sofie, who was fiddling with the knob on the radio to find some dance music. Glenn Miller's orchestra crackled into life and the two girls jumped up and began dancing in their stockinged feet. Swinging their hips from side to side, they twirled each other round until they collapsed laughing in a heap on Sofie's bed. Glenn Miller's *In the Mood* came on straight after and they were up again, giggling and skipping to the rhythm.

Sofie was first to wake up the next morning and rolled onto her side so she could shake Liesbeth. 'Wake up! It's nearly 9 o'clock. The film starts at 10.'

Both girls sprang up and pulled on the clothes they'd left strewn over the floor before they'd gone to bed exhausted.

'Milk, bread and *stroop*?' called Sofie to Liesbeth on her way down the stairs. Her mother was sorting the laundry which lay in heaps beside the kitchen sink. 'I was wondering when you two were thinking of getting up. You seemed to enjoy yourselves last night.'

'Overslept. Do you think we'll get to Kampenveld by 10?' Sofie sloshed the milk from the jug into two cups, spilling a little on the draining board. No time to clear it up, she hurriedly sawed at the loaf of bread her mother had left on a board on the table.

'Only if you cycle. Has Liesbeth got her bike here?'

'No, but we can easily pick it up on the way,' said Liesbeth, who appeared at the table and helped herself to breakfast.

'Mum, can I have 25 cents please?' Sofie said through a mouthful of bread and sticky syrup.

Her mother sighed as she rummaged through the pot of loose change on the windowsill. 'And what about you, Liesbeth?' She held out two coins.

'Oh, thank you. I'll pay you back.'

'No need,' said Sofie's mother with a smile. She felt sorry for the girl, who must be worried about her ailing mother.

In the end they were running so late that they took Sofie's bike, Liesbeth sitting side-saddle on the back. It was more fun that way anyway. Out of the village, Sofie rode along the narrow roads alongside the water-filled ditches. It was a beautiful crisp morning and the only sound was the hum of the bike's tyres on the road and their chatter. The fields were dotted with black and white cows and occasionally one would lift her head from grazing and keep chewing as they raced past.

Soon they could see the outline of Kampenveld, its church tower poking up amongst the red-roofed houses. Sofie slowed and when they reached the bridge over the canal they both got off so she could push the bike to the little car park behind the church. The church clock showed it was five to ten.

They never normally had a problem getting into a matinee but were eager not to miss the beginning, so they sprinted across the empty square and down *Prinsenstraat* towards the cinema.

'Wait a minute,' said Liesbeth, placing a hand on Sofie's arm. 'Something's up.'

There was a crowd of people in front of the cinema, all talking loudly and staring at something. It can't have been the poster for the film. Liesbeth told Sofie to wait whilst she went to investigate. It didn't take her long to come back. Her face had gone pale.

'What?' said Sofie, impatiently.

Liesbeth gripped her friend's arm. 'It says: "No Jews Allowed"'.

PART 2

THE PLAN

Chapter 11

Henk Hauer drew on the tiny stub of his cigarette and surveyed the dense thicket. The others waited anxiously.

'Well, do you think it would work?' asked Max, who was growing impatient. Henk cleared his throat and began pacing the length of the thicket, whilst prodding the undergrowth as if he were measuring up in his own mind. He turned to the others, a serious expression on his face. 'Yes, it's possible, but we'll need a lot of hands.'

'We'd like you to oversee the operation,' said Dick Foppen, who had drawn up the plans.

Still Henk looked thoughtful.

'We can pay you a small sum, nothing much, you understand, but you can undertake the work after hours,' Dick confirmed.

'It's risky,' Henk narrowed his eyes as he sucked on the last of the cigarette before grinding it with his foot.

'We can let you have the lodge at the Tongeren crossroads.' Dick wasn't sure quite how he'd swing this one.

Henk lived in a tiny cramped cottage on the edge of the wood. The Tongeren house would be a big improvement.

'It has a sizeable outhouse and garden where we can store materials safely,' Dick continued.

'And it's big enough to provide temporary shelter whilst building work is underway,' added Max, who wanted the negotiations to be concluded.

Henk shifted his weight as he pondered the proposition. He was quick with his hands, but it always took him a while to mull things over. At school, he'd been teased because he wasn't quick-witted like the rest of the class. His teacher had low expectations of his abilities, so when he failed his final exams, there seemed to be little point retaking them. His father found him a job helping the forester, who soon realised that there was a lot more to Henk than first impressions suggested. The skinny, sullen 15-year-old never said much, but he was a solid worker and soon was entrusted with sawing wood destined for floorboards in houses in the village. He wasn't the only trainee apprentice, but it became clear that he was the forester's favourite. By the time the forester retired, it was obvious that his replacement would be Henk, who after twenty years knew the woods like the back of his hand. He also had excellent connections, which could prove extremely useful in the coming weeks and months. Henk knew he could be trusted not to reveal any details. Such a slip could cost them their lives.

Henk ambled over to take another look at the drawings anchored on the ground with large stones on all four corners. He slowly rolled another cigarette, all the while examining the layout of the four huts, two above and two below ground. The largest would serve as a kind of reception centre, but would have enough space to house up to eight people until they could be moved to one of the others.

'Will there be enough accommodation?' he eventually said. 'I heard on the radio people are streaming into Apeldoorn and my concern is that the huts will soon be overcrowded. I think we should be planning for a much bigger camp.' He jerked his head at the drawings, whilst looking directly at Dick.

'I don't disagree, but we have to start somewhere. We still have a lot of safe houses in Driebergen and some people are already building huts for the purpose in their own gardens. But you're right, we could soon reach full capacity and the dangers of being found out will increase. How long do you think it'll take to build these four?'

'I'll need up to six helpers, strong young men whom I can rely on.' Henk nodded his head as he made calculations. 'Two to three weeks. Less, if you don't mind people coming in before the work is finished.'

'And the newcomers can help as well,' said Dick. He removed the stones holding the edges of the plans in place. Taking a length of string from his pocket, he rolled them up.

'When do you want me to start?' said Henk, whose mind was now buzzing with the possibilities.

'As soon as we have enough helpers. We should recruit from our own families and close friends and use the skills that they have. Ideally, I'd like you to start immediately, though I know you are busy.'

'We're managing an area close to the main road to Apeldoorn. It's good spruce and pine wood which will be excellent. The Germans have requisitioned the wood, but I know how to keep some back. We'll need transport of course. Vans will do as we can chop the wood on site and then bring it over here. It won't be easy as we can only bring the vehicles as far as the crossroads, then the wood will need to be carried half a mile to the camp. Tools we can keep here. Best to bury them in the ground, just in case.'

Dick smiled broadly and held out his hand. 'We'll be doing them a great service and you will get credit for this. I'll make sure of it.'

Henk shook the outstretched hand in his own rough, calloused one and for the first time that morning smiled. His father would have been proud.

Chapter 12

Life at the Foppens was tolerable, exciting and boring, sometimes all at the same time. But most of the time it was boring as Sofie and her parents passed the day doing a few chores or playing cards round the big kitchen table. Sometimes, if Mr Foppen thought it safe, they were allowed out into the garden, but the sound of any person passing the front door which was right on the street, would send them rushing upstairs into the wardrobe with the false back and up a rickety ladder into the attic.

They shared the huge loft space with another family, refugees from Scheveningen, who missed the sea badly. Being cooped up with little to occupy them was a change that none of the Schiffer family could have anticipated. Mr Schiffer had been a fisherman all his life and was used to the daily rhythm of getting up before dawn to fetch the catch in his fishing boat with his two cousins and then selling it to wholesalers on the quayside by mid morning. His whole life was outdoors. These days, he stood for most of the day at the window high up where he could not be seen, watching the to-ings and fro-ings of the people in the street below. His wife sat hunched over her sewing, occasionally looking up to scold their six-year-old son, Frans, who would run from one to the other, looking for entertainment. When this failed, he'd retreat to his mattress where he'd lie, sucking his thumb for comfort, while fingering the scrap of blanket he'd brought.

Sofie couldn't bring herself to play with little Frans, even though she knew she should. She missed her bedroom with its wooden desk and view down the street and the piles of books in towers on the floor. Her father had never got round to making the bookshelf he'd promised. She also missed being around Liesbeth whenever she felt like it and relived their short few weeks together when they had become like sisters. Sofie and her parents had been forced to leave so quickly that she'd only managed to bring a couple of school-books her mother had insisted upon. She'd long since read them and depended on deliveries of escapist novels from Liesbeth, who came when she could after dark and after curfew, creeping through back gardens and over the roofs of the terraced houses before rapping on the attic window.

Liesbeth came one evening, just before the church clock struck eight.

'What have you brought?' asked Sofie excitedly, pulling her friend into the cramped attic space.

'News from Oscar,' said Liesbeth, regaining her balance.

'For me?' Sofie dared to breathe. She hadn't had contact with him since their sudden departure two weeks ago. Liesbeth was now her only contact with the outside world.

'Who else?' teased Liesbeth.

'Get on and tell me,' said Sofie, losing patience.

The others were staring at the pair, a welcome distraction from their own thoughts.

Sofie pulled Liesbeth onto her mattress which she'd pushed against the wall. It was covered with her flowery quilt and dark blue cushions from home. It gave them a little privacy. The others, growing bored, turned back in on themselves.

'He's working in the forest on a top secret project. He won't even tell me about it,' whispered Liesbeth with a grimace.

'In the forest? But he hates it there. Are you sure you don't know?' Sofie hated that Liesbeth might have a secret with Oscar.

'He won't tell me but wants you to come and meet him and his father tonight.'

'How? That's just stupid. I'm stuck in here. There's no way mum and dad would let me out.'

'That's why I'm here. To help you.' Liesbeth's voice squeaked with excitement.

'Sh! They'll hear you,' said Sofie, shooting a glance at her parents, who were themselves talking quietly at the other end of the attic. Liesbeth leant forward and outlined the plan in Sofie's ear.

It was the first time since she'd been incarcerated that she allowed herself to be excited.

***

The two families had agreed they would all go to bed at the same time. That way there could be no arguments. Sofie hated the early curfew and would lie for hours wide awake listening to the others as their breathing fell into the steady rhythm of sleep. Only then would she switch on her torch and read under the bedclothes, losing herself in stories of ancient kingdoms and lovelorn princesses, but tonight she lay tensely, waiting for the church clock to strike eleven. Soundlessly, she crept to the window and opened it very slowly, her hand on the hinge to stop it from creaking. Liesbeth was waiting on the other side and helped her climb through. A small cry from the sleeping Frans almost caused her to drop the window catch, but she managed to stop it from slamming shut in time. Outside, the air smelled fresh and she lifted her face to let the cool breeze wash over her.

'Come on, we haven't got all night,' called Liesbeth, who was waiting by the edge of the roof, ready to jump over to the next one. Sofie sucked in her breath and felt her hands grow damp. It wasn't a big gap but she could see all the way down to the street. Concentrating on a roof tile half a metre away, she jumped, catching Liesbeth's hand.

'This way.' Liesbeth darted lightly towards a window, slid it open and disappeared. Sofie hesitated and let out a little laugh when she saw Liesbeth's head bob up above the sill.

'It's fine,' said Liesbeth in a loud whisper. The de Jong's are quite used to me doing this.'

Sofie clambered through into a darkened bedroom. Liesbeth grabbed her hand and led her softly out onto the landing and down the stairs. She gave a little knock on the living room door and popped her head round to say hello. Sofie could hear a cheerful reply and the two girls continued their journey, out through the back door, through the squeaky gate adjoining the neighbour's garden and onto the next till they came out onto the street where Oscar lived.

'Shh...' Liesbeth pulled Sofie back. They held their breath at the sound of footsteps moving quickly along the pavement. Someone out after curfew. Probably like themselves, trying to get somewhere unnoticed. They waited till they were sure there were no other sounds to give them away, shot a glance at each other, then darted across the street to Oscar's house.

It was the first time Sofie had properly met Oscar's father. Oscar had painted such a horrible picture of him that her stomach clenched when he opened the door. He didn't smile, which made her feel worse, and there was no one else around. Not even Oscar.

Liesbeth broke the ice. 'This is Sofie,' she said and squeezed Sofie's hand.

Sofie's heart was still thumping from their clandestine route across the rooftops. Liesbeth seemed unperturbed, probably because she'd done this on many occasions. Sofie had a sneaking admiration for her friend, mixed with envy that she had the nerve to do it. Unlike Oscar, she thought. Why couldn't he have come?

Oscar's father looked hard at Sofie before speaking, making her feel uncomfortable. He ushered them in with an impatient wave.

The house was exactly as she remembered it, the pile of messy shoes behind the front door, the coats piled one on top of the other in the narrow cloakroom. She breathed in the faint smell of old furniture and spices. It must have been weeks since Oscar had invited her round for coffee, arranged when he knew his father would be out.

'They're looking after you well?' It was more a statement than a question.

'It's OK but I'd rather be at home. It was better before they put the Schiffers with us. We're not going to have any more in with us, are we?'

'No, no. Quite the opposite. You're going to have the opportunity for a fresh start. Come and sit down and I'll tell you more.'

Sofie wished he wouldn't look so serious. Why didn't Oscar turn up? And where was Oscar's mother? She was a nice, kind person. If Liesbeth hadn't been beside her, she would have fled. She sat on the edge of a kitchen chair and waited.

'The Foppens can't let you all stay with them any more. They're too busy setting up an alternative place which will be much safer. But it's not quite ready, so there's not enough space for your parents and you. We'd like you to be one of the first ones to move to the... village.'

Sofie didn't like they way he paused before he said 'village'. It felt like cold water pouring down her spine. 'What about my parents?'

'We've found them a house in Zwolle.'

Sofie swallowed. Zwolle could have been in another country. 'Why aren't I going with them?' She put her hands under her legs to stop them from shaking.

Oscar's father cleared his throat. 'Because there's only room for two. Your parents asked me to take care of you and agreed it would be safer for you to go to the village.'

'Where is it?' Her voice caught in her throat, but she already guessed the answer.

'In Berkenhout woods. No, you won't have heard of it. It's been kept a secret and it's important that you don't speak to anyone about it. A few houses are ready now and four families have moved in. There are still a few places left. You will be moving in with the Janssens. They are very kind people.'

Sofie pushed her chair back roughly and stood behind it, gripping the top tightly. 'So you're going to make me live with total strangers. Did no one think to ask me first before arranging it? What if I don't want to go? Liesbeth, you knew about this didn't you? Why didn't you tell me?'

Liesbeth played with her hands. 'It wasn't up to me...' she said, feebly.

'But you knew this was the plan and you didn't dare tell me. In case I refused to go? Well, you're right. I'll take a risk and stay. I'm going back home. Oh, and you can tell Oscar if he can't be bothered to say it to my face he can stuff it.' She was determined not to cry in front of them and made for the door before Oscar's father could say anything more. Head down, she hurried down the path and straight into Oscar.

'Whoa! What's the hurry?' he said, holding her by the arms.

She shrugged him free, her eyes wild. 'Leave me. I'm going home.'

'I'm coming with you. I want to know why you're so upset.' He fell into step alongside her. It was too risky to have a conversation out in the street so they crept along the unlit street in silence till they came to the Foppen's side gate. Sofie mouthed to Oscar to be quiet. She didn't want the Foppens to find that they'd been out.

The roof wasn't so easy to reach from ground level. They used the apple tree to reach the first floor balcony and Sofie was relieved to have Oscar to hoist her up. He kept hold of her hand as he clambered up onto the flat roof as if he did it all the time. Arriving outside the attic window, she let him pull her to him in a hug for a few moments without speaking. It felt so good and her earlier anger evaporated.

'I've missed you,' he whispered, stroking her back.

'Me too,' said Sofie, inhaling the smell of fresh air on his neck. 'It doesn't seem fair that I'm being packed off away from everyone I care about,' she murmured.

'It might not be for very long and I'll come and see you lots. Promise.'

She looked up at him distrustfully. This was the first time he'd met her at the Foppens - why would he risk his life to come to see her when she was hidden away in the woods?

'I'm working down there, helping build the huts, so it'll be easy.'

'Is that what you've been doing?'

'Mm, it's why I haven't been over to see you. I wanted to, but my father pushed me into it. Then when I heard that they still had free places, I put your name forward. I suppose you're annoyed with me now?'

Sofie allowed herself a smile. 'I wish you'd asked me first. I feel as if everyone knows about my future except me. It's no fun being cooped up in there.' She jerked her head towards the attic window.

'You won't have that living in Berkenhout. The village is already quite big and in time they want to put up to eighty people there.'

Sofie thought about this for a moment. 'All Jews?'

'Some, but not all. I've heard there'll be people who refuse to work for the Germans.'

'What about you? Would you come and live there?'

Oscar thrust his hands in his pockets and blew out his cheeks. 'It's not really an issue for me. Maybe if this war goes on long enough. But anything can happen.' He glanced at his watch. 'I've got to get back. Early start tomorrow. I'm working on a new underground hut.' Pursing his lips into a smile, he gave her a quick hug and disappeared back down the way they had come.

Sofie watched him go before clambering back into the dark attic space. Her mind was in turmoil as she tried to take in what Oscar had said and what it would mean for her, her family and her relationship, such as it was, with him. Part of her was excited at the prospect of this new start, but she'd have to share with a family she'd never met and maybe she'd hate the new regime. Would she know anyone? Would she ever finish her schooling?

Unable to sleep, she listened to the church clock as it struck each of the hours till eventually she lost count.

Chapter 13

Sofie was one of the first inhabitants of the village and the last to leave almost two years later. Of course, she had no idea she'd stay that long. No one had. Everyone thought it would be for a few weeks, months, maybe a year at most. Instead, the camp expanded from the initial four huts to twelve, divided into four sections with another smaller area annexed to it. In order to minimise the risk of being discovered, Dick Foppen devised a rule that no one was allowed to move from quarter to quarter during the day. Only after dark were they allowed to socialise with one another.

Space was no problem. With the help of Henk, they could have kept building new huts. But Dick Foppen knew there was an optimum size for the village, beyond which it would have become impossible for those on the outside to keep it running smoothly. He'd been surprised at the offers of help, some from unlikely sources. His aunt, Else, who had previously lived a solitary life with her two cats, was one of his strongest supporters and was instrumental in organising the provision of daily staples to the camp. Although there was no shortage of food in this part of the Netherlands, they had to be careful in who they dealt with, as they needed large quantities of produce, which could only be obtained on the black market. Else became friendly with all the shopkeepers, who themselves took huge risks. The baker devised a system of siphoning off food from deliveries destined for the Germans. The greengrocer offered space in his warehouse to store food and entrusted Else with a key, so she could come and go whenever the need arose.

Else was surprised at the offers of help from young people, many passionate to act against the restrictions to their freedom and ultimately to their futures. Everyone dreaded the banging on the door late at night and the grip of panic as families hurried to hide their sons who had refused to respond to the call-up to go and work for the Germans. Even moving about during the day became difficult. The sight of a young person on the street raised the question – were they doing a worthwhile job that meant they couldn't go to Germany?

Else was glad to give young people a purpose and offered to put one or two up in her own house. One of these was Liesbeth. She badly missed her mother but found it impossible to live at home. It was as if her father had blanked her mother out of his life and refused to talk about her. Accepting her mother had moved away to Belgium was bad enough, but Liesbeth couldn't excuse her father's behaviour. Not after the time she'd come home and heard murmuring from upstairs behind his closed bedroom door. How could he? And now the only friend she could confide in had been taken away from her too. To begin with, she stayed occasionally with Tante Else, as she and others called her, on the pretext that she could be more useful sorting out provisions into boxes each evening ready for the early morning delivery. Before long, Tante Else said she was welcome to stay whenever she liked and set aside a tiny attic room which Liesbeth filled with belongings from home.

Each morning, Liesbeth and several helpers hoisted the

laundry baskets filled with provisions on the bottom and linen on the top into the back of the vans parked in the yard to the side of the house. If they left early enough, they rarely encountered any German soldiers and the possibility of being stopped and searched was minimal. Taking the main road out of Kampenveld, they drove into the woods until the road ran out. Helpers from the camp would be waiting and carry or pull the goods in makeshift carts deep into the woods and away from any prying eyes.

Often, Liesbeth would slip a letter for Sofie into one of the baskets. She couldn't imagine what it must be like stuck in camp with a load of strangers, although Sofie wasted no time complaining in her letters back. It was obvious Sofie wanted nothing to do with the organisation of the village. She hated her hut even more than the Foppen's attic space. Even the fact that she was living in one of the superior huts above ground didn't impress her.

'How can they expect us to live like this? It's barbaric!' she complained to Liesbeth in one of her frequent letters. To top it all, Mr Foppen decreed that letters could only be sent to and from camp once a week, saying that too much communication might arouse suspicion.

'Such rot! Who's going to be remotely interested in what I have to say?' wrote Sofie. 'Please keep writing to me! And come and visit too. I'm sure you can find a way. If you don't, I think I'll go insane.'

Liesbeth folded the letter and tucked it into the envelope Sofie had decorated with drawings of leaves and flowers. She felt guilty that she'd pushed her friend into accepting a place at the village.

The day after they'd met with Oscar's father, Liesbeth had gone over to visit her at the Foppen's. Slipping in through the back door, she found Sofie in the kitchen doing the washing up. Briefly glancing over her shoulder, she seemed to stiffen, then carried on scrubbing an already spotless pan. Liesbeth wasn't sure what to say or do, so she stood in the doorway and waited. The pan dropped into the rack with a clatter and Sofie turned to face her.

'What have you come to say?'

Liesbeth took a step forward, but refrained from giving her the hug she wanted to. 'That I'm sorry. And I hope you'll forgive me for it.'

To her astonishment, Sofie began laughing and for a moment Liesbeth thought things almost seemed normal between them again. Until Sofie started up again, as she always did, letting the words fly out of her mouth without thought. 'You're right of course. So is Oscar. So are all of you. It's easy for you...'

'Is that what you think?' Liesbeth snapped back. 'You only ever think of you, poor you. We thought we were doing you a favour getting you out of this place to somewhere you could actually have a life. And you think I've got it easy.' Her heart was thumping and she desperately wanted to flounce out but was scared that if she did, that would be it between her and Sofie.

'So what will you do?'

The question surprised Liesbeth. 'Me? I dunno. Carry on as before, I suppose.'

'Have you heard from your mum?' asked Sofie.

They sat down at opposite sides of the kitchen table. 'I haven't told you, have I? She wrote me this letter from Ghent where she's now living with this man she met. He's got a big house there and she wants me to go and live with them.'

'That's fantastic. You're going to go, aren't you?'

Fantastic? Her mother running off with a man eight years her junior without a thought for her daughter. 'I don't know. I'm not sure...'

'What's there to be sure about? It's got to be better than sticking around with your mooching old dad, surely?'

Liesbeth let out a sigh and examined her hands. 'Hardly mooching. He's been given a new lease of life now that he's...'

'What?'

Liesbeth looked her straight in the eye. 'He's taken up with Tinny.' She let out a despairing sigh.

'No! It can't be true! But she's, she's...'

'I know. The help. But I suppose she's not married, so that's something. Though she's a lot younger than dad.' Liesbeth turned her face away so Sofie couldn't see the tears pricking at her eyes.

Sofie took both her hands in hers. 'Go to Ghent. Get away. You can and you should.'

'But I've never even met him,' she protested.

'So what? It'll get you away from all this. Just think how great it'd be to live in Ghent.'

'Maybe.' Liesbeth didn't feel like arguing.

Sofie seemed to have forgotten their differences and was doing what she liked best, arranging other people's lives. 'When this shitty war is over, I'll come and live in Ghent too. There's a university, isn't there? We can both go and study there and won't need to worry about where we live because there'll be your mum's boyfriend's house.' She said all this staring into space, her cheeks turning pink, as if oblivious to Liesbeth sitting opposite her. As far as she was concerned it was all decided and the small detail of having to live in a camp in the middle of the woods now didn't seem to bother her. Normally, Liesbeth would have argued her corner, but today she let Sofie dream on.

At least they were friends again. For now, that was all that mattered.

Chapter 14

Max worked his way into the position of leader of the Berkenhout group, partly because no one else wanted it, but mainly through Dick Foppen's insistence that he was the best person for the job. Dick had been particularly pleased at the way Max had arranged for Nigel to be passed between reliable contacts across the border into Belgium and all the way up to the coast, where he was taken by fishing boat across to England. At first, Sara had been reluctant about the plan, but became secretly impressed by Max's organisational abilities.

Tuesdays were the days when they would gather at Max's house for the weekly briefing so he could instruct them on the week's jobs. With the first huts occupied and more becoming ready by the day, Berkenhout was starting to become a community, but its isolation meant that there were daily problems to address. Max was good at drumming up support and soon had a band of a dozen helpers who had skills to offer or felt compelled to help. He'd wanted Sara to be a part of it, but she refused, saying she'd provide the coffee for his meetings but wouldn't sit down and join them. No one thought anything of it. Plenty of families had an active member involved in the underground, whilst their partners gave their silent support.

They trickled in one by one, each taking a seat round the large kitchen table. Max welcomed everyone by name, before calling over to Sara to bring the coffee so that they could start. He hated interruptions.

'Else, have you spoken to Piet about petrol? The vans are running low and I don't want to ask the chaps at the garage to give us any more for free. It only leads to questions.'

Else confirmed that she had it all in hand. Piet was able to get hold of extra fake coupons and they'd use them gradually over the next month.

'Oscar, can you spare two extra evenings? Henk's pleased with your work and he needs more hands to help with the new huts over at *Nieuwe Soerel.*'

'But we haven't finished the ones at Berkenhout. And *Nieuwe Soerel*'s another half an hour walk from there. I won't be much use if I don't get there till after five.' Oscar was annoyed his father always picked on him. There were plenty of other young men who'd come forward who weren't at school. He didn't dare say that, of course, especially in the room full of people.

Max suspected why Oscar had agreed to take on the work, but the pressure was on to get as many huts built before the winter. If they had snow like last year, essential work would have to be suspended. 'We must all cooperate if this village is to be a success,' he said, staring hard at Oscar.

Else ignored this exchange and began voicing her concerns about morale in the village. 'We're up to twenty-five people now and families are forced to take in newcomers. Space is cramped and some of them are saying they'd rather leave and face the dangers. I fear that it will only take a few people to spread dissatisfaction with conditions and we can't have that.'

Oscar fidgeted in his seat, aware that one of the people she was referring to was Sofie. He suspected she was finding it extremely hard to adapt to her new life and would not have been shy in expressing her feelings.

'Mm, yes, I thought this might happen. Which is why we need to get on with expanding the village and allocating space in a sensible fashion,' said Max.

The conversation was interrupted by a double rap on the door announcing the arrival of Dick. Immediately taking charge, he interpreted Else's concerns as a need for a more stringent regime from within.

'We need to draw up rules if we're to avoid a revolt,' he said, pulling a notebook and pencil out of his coat pocket and began taking notes. 'No one to leave Berkenhout at any time, unless for a medical emergency and pre-arranged with the committee,' he said, without looking up.

'No speaking in a normal voice or singing when outside the huts. No stoves or fires to be lit during daylight hours,' said Max, determined not to lose control as leader of the meeting.

'I'd like to make a suggestion, but it's not a rule,' said Else, who had been listening in silence.

'Hang on, we haven't dealt with chores in the camp yet,' said Max. 'The young ones are underutilised and we need to make sure they pull their weight.'

'But they won't co-operate unless we motivate them. I can think of at least one young person who's in need of emotional support,' said Else with a crinkly smile. 'Here's my plan. Every Sunday, a small group will visit Berkenhout for coffee. We'll bring freshly baked cakes and news from the village and beyond. They can air their grievances and we'll do our best to solve them. What does everyone think?'

'I'll help,' said Sara, who had been listening from the shadows of the kitchen. 'I can bake the cakes.'

'And I'll take them over,' added Oscar.

'We can both take them over,' said Sara with a smile. 'And Jan can come too. He can show us the way.'

'I know the way too, you know,' retorted Oscar.

Sara stood behind her son and put her hands on his shoulders.

'That's just what we want,' said Else. 'I'll ask Liesbeth if she'd like to come too. The young ones will be pleased to see some people of their own age.'

'Good, good. Then the matter is settled. We'll continue to meet weekly and report back of any difficulties…' said Dick.

'And make sure that the rules are being observed,' Max cut in.

'Quite. It wouldn't do to have to exclude people from the camp as soon as they've arrived,' said Dick, with a chuckle.

They carried on laying plans for the running of Berkenhout and appointed a leader whom they thought they could trust. Otto Maarten was the local bank manager and one of the first to move to Berkenhout. He'd come to Dick and asked to be admitted after receiving news that his older sister had been deported to

Ravensbrück. Initially buoyed by rumours that it wasn't as bad as some of the concentration camps over the border, he'd begun to fear for his family. Ensconced in the village, he wanted to help others going through similar traumas.

They talked on and on, bickering over who should undertake which role and new rules kept being added to the list. Oscar grew bored and stopped listening. He sat thinking about seeing Sofie again and how he might spend time alone with her. Sundays were probably the best days. Perhaps they could slip away whilst everyone was caught up in gossiping and drinking coffee. He knew the woods better now, so they'd be safe as long as they kept well away from the path. He just hoped she wasn't still angry with him.

Chapter 15

Sofie had lain awake for hours, waiting for the grey light of dawn. It was like this most nights. She'd fall asleep at nine o'clock, because there was nothing else to do, before waking far too early. At first she'd thrash about on her straw mattress trying to fall back into sleep, but recently she'd just lie, thinking about the life she'd left behind. She thought of Liesbeth being able to move about freely, making her own decisions on what she wanted to do each day. Sofie conveniently forgot how hard Liesbeth had it at home. All she could think of was that Liesbeth was out there and she was stuck in here.

Since they introduced the rules, life was even more intolerable. All this rot about not talking outside the huts during the day. Sometimes she felt like stepping outside and shouting as loud as she could, so that the birds in the treetops would fly off in fright. But of course she didn't and obeyed the rules, even though she was seething inside.

Shifting her position on the spiky mattress, she sighed deeply. The mattress rustled, but she noticed another unfamiliar sound. Someone sobbing very quietly. Straining her eyes to see if it was one of the two boys, but their shapes remained quite still. Gradually, a pale light seeped through the window crack as she made out something small huddled next to the stove. Slipping from her bed, she lowered herself next to the little person who didn't notice her.

'Hello. I'm Sofie,' she whispered.

The girl was about her own age but smaller, with short, jet

black hair and huge dark eyes. Quickly, the girl wiped away her tears but was unable to hide her sobbing breath.

'What's your name?' asked Sofie, as quietly as before.

'Laura.'

'I didn't hear you come. Did you arrive last night?'

The girl began to cry again.

'Come with me.' Sofie coaxed and held a hand out which the girl took.

The woodland was just beginning to wake up. The tops of the trees were alive with fluttering birds striking up their morning song. Two red squirrels shot across the path, their bushy tails following wave-like behind them, then one chased the other up a tall fir tree. Sofie tugged the girl's sleeve to point them out. For a moment, Laura seemed to forget her woes, her face breaking into a smile.

'Where do you come from?' Sofie ventured in a whisper.

'Ghent,' Laura said in a small voice.

'That's where I want to go and study when all this is over,' said Sofie, flicking her hand towards the huts. 'Are you by yourself?'

'Yes.' Laura spoke in a voice so quiet Sofie could barely hear.

It wasn't unusual to wake up and find that new people had joined the camp. They would be brought under cover of darkness, which meant walking the last mile from the track at the dead of night. She could well understand that Laura was scared.

'It's not so bad here,' Sofie heard herself saying. 'I'm on my own too,' she said, hoping she sounded encouraging, but recognising the painful loneliness the girl would be experiencing. In the gloom,

Sofie became aware of Laura's big dark eyes fixed on hers.

'I don't know where my mum and dad have gone. Everybody in our street was told to leave and my parents made me go in the van without them,' said Laura, her voice cracking. 'I just can't stop thinking of the tears running down Mum's face and the way she was still trying to smile at me as Dad pulled her away so they could shut the doors.' She fished around in her pocket and pulled out a scrap of paper. 'They're going to some place I've never heard of in Friesland. I can't even pronounce it.' Sofie pointed out the address which read 'Abbega'.

'At least they'll be safe there, far away from danger. The Germans wouldn't dream of going to a place called that.' She smiled, but Laura kept staring at the ground. She gave Laura back her precious address which she folded carefully and returned to her pocket.

'I was staying in a safe house with my parents before I came here, with Mr Foppen, who set up the camp. We had to move out and there were only two beds in the place my parents were going to. So they made me come here. That was three weeks ago.'

'Have you heard from them?'

'Only a message through tante Else to say they'd arrived safely. They don't encourage letter writing, but I'm sure they'd make an exception for you as you've come so far.'

'Does your aunt live here too?'

Sofie laughed. 'She's not my aunt. Everyone calls her tante Else and she makes sure we get enough to eat and drink. You'll meet her soon enough. Come on, let's get breakfast.'

Sofie's camp mother was up and preparing porridge on the little stove. Breakfast was the best meal of the day, as long as you got up early before the curfew on lighting fires. The smell of frying bacon filled the air. In a little metal saucepan milk was heating up for coffee.

Corrie reminded Sofie of her own mother, but a slightly younger, less stressed version. She was always cheerful and seemed to enjoy life in the woodland village. But then she had her husband and twin boys with her.

'Laura, come and sit at the table. I've laid you a place.' Corrie's apple cheeks glowed when she smiled. Sofie held Laura's hand and led her to the bench. The twins were oblivious, playing a game of catch round and round the table.

'Boys, run outside and find papa over by the woodpile. But no shouting.'

She ladled a scoop of steaming porridge into two bowls and swirled dark *stroop* over the top.

'Sofie, will you help with the laundry today? Laura can watch for now.'

Every other time Corrie had asked, Sofie had refused and spent most of the day sitting round the back of the hut where she couldn't be seen. She realised how childish and stupid she must have seemed and found herself blushing.

'Isn't it a day off today? Tante Else is coming, isn't she?'

'If we do a little every day, it won't seem such a big chore,' said Corrie, wiping off some spilt porridge from the rough wooden table. 'Tante Else won't be here till 11 o'clock, so there's plenty of time.'

Sofie glanced over at Laura who was staring at her porridge.

'Eat a little bit. It'll make you feel better,' coaxed Corrie.

Laura began crying softly and whispered: 'I don't like porridge.'

Corrie whisked away her bowl and without a word replaced it with another containing cooked apple and cinnamon. 'There. You like *appelmoes*, don't you?'

Laura picked up the spoon and dipped it in so the tip was covered. She tested it on the end of her tongue, then full of concentration, scooped up more in bigger mouthfuls.

'Our new addition to the family,' beamed Kees from the doorway. He washed his hands in a bowl of soapy water and sat opposite Laura so he could get a good look at her.

Sofie remembered, with a twinge of guilt, how welcoming Corrie and Kees Janssen had been when she arrived. They'd all been in the same situation, newly evacuated from their comfortable homes and transported into the middle of a wood over a mile from the nearest village. The Janssens must have hated it too, but did their best to hide it. And now they were welcoming Laura, knowing how tough it must have been to come so far completely on her own. Sofie glanced quickly at her. She mustn't let her see how homesick she also still felt.

Sofie became protective towards Laura, sensing her need to latch onto her as if her life depended on it. Neither had siblings, so understood what it was like to be with only their own thoughts for company. Often, they'd sit silently together, but it wasn't in any way awkward. Little by little, they'd spill out details of their lives and were surprised at how similar they were. Like Sofie, Laura had left behind her best friend, who'd been evacuated to a farmhouse in the middle of nowhere, miles away from the nearest town.

'I hope you'll meet my best friend, Liesbeth, today. You'll like her,' said Sofie one Sunday, scrubbing the porridge pan while sitting on a log. 'She's really lucky as she gets to ride her bike here. I bet you she'll come on it today.' She let the brush fall into the pan with a clatter. 'You know what? I really miss the sound of the wind rushing in my ears and peddling so hard that my thighs ache.' She let out a long sigh. 'I locked my bike in the shed. I couldn't bear it if the Germans stole it.'

'I haven't ridden mine for over a year. It had a basket on the front and I'd push flowers through the wickerwork,' said Laura, her eyes unfocused. 'I think I'm too big for it now.'

Sofie looked at her pensively. 'I know! You can have my old one. Dad never got round to getting rid of it. I'm sure it'd fit you. What do you think?'

For the first time since she arrived, Laura's face broke into a big gappy smile.

Chapter 16

Tante Else, Liesbeth, Oscar, Jan, Sara and Mrs Foppen arrived at eleven with baskets of delicious food none had seen for a while, and news from outside. They couldn't risk being overheard, so instead of sitting outside in the morning sunshine, everyone crammed into the reception hut which was a little larger than the rest.

Tante Else put down her basket and took out a packet of coffee and a cake wrapped in a tea towel. The smell of cinnamon filled the room. She must have baked it that morning. Everyone crowded round to see and soon the hut was filled with chatter and laughter.

'It's real coffee,' cried Corrie, taking a deep sniff as she spooned it out into the pan. Tante Else smiled, but wouldn't let on where she'd obtained such a rare commodity. None had tasted real coffee for months. Everyone had grown sick of the *ersatz* stuff made from roasted chicory that didn't taste at all like coffee, just burnt. The smell of coffee filled the air and its effect was as intoxicating as alcohol.

Sofie squeezed herself between Liesbeth and Oscar. Liesbeth's hair was now long enough to be tied back in a ribbon. Oscar's cheeks were ruddy and his hands calloused. Sofie felt shy before him.

'How are you?' he said, his eyes looking bluer against his tanned skin.

'Bored really. I never thought I'd say it but I miss school and Mevrouw Klein's stupid maths tests.' *And you?* she didn't say.

'I can bring you some text books if you like,' said Oscar with a mischievous look.

'On second thoughts, I'd rather be here,' she said, returning his gaze.

Tante Else brought over a tray of coffee. 'So you're settling in now, are you, Sofie?'

Sofie didn't want them to know how much things had improved since Laura'd arrived. 'I don't like being miles away from civilisation. And not being able to send letters when I want. Can't you change that?'

Tante Else picked up a stool so she could sit opposite her. 'I wish I could, but I don't make the rules. Once the village is properly established, I'm sure things will be different. Do you think you can wait?'

'I haven't any choice, have I? I didn't want to come here but...'

'The alternative would have been far worse. You do realise that, don't you?'

Sofie was aware of three pairs of eyes on her, all showing concern. 'Like what?' she said, a note of defiance in her voice.

Liesbeth exchanged glances with tante Else who gave her a tiny nod. 'They're forcing Jews to wear a big yellow star when they go out. Everyone and anyone can be stopped and searched and if they don't have ID on them, they'll be arrested. Every day we're hearing about people disappearing,' said Liesbeth.

'My uncle was arrested in Amsterdam last month. He only just avoided being sent to Vught. Father's been so angry about this. It's why he wants this village to be a success,' said Oscar quietly.

'This is why it's best you're here for the time being. I hope you understand now why we have these rules, which might seem petty, but are for everyone's safety,' said tante Else, whose gaze landed on Sofie.

It was too much to bear. Sofie looked away, irritated that tante Else thought it necessary to lecture them in front of all these visitors who could come and go as they pleased. It just made everything worse.

Laura was standing beside tante Else, her eyes big and dark. She was holding a plate of the sweet-smelling cake Corrie had asked to hand round.

'Come and sit down Laura and let's try some of that cake,' said tante Else, brightly.

Sofie wriggled free and pretended to go and help Corrie. She couldn't look at Oscar conversing with Laura who was now in her place. With her back to them, all she could hear was happy chatter and laughter. Now that she wasn't sitting amongst them.

***

After the committee had gone, leaving fresh bread, cake and apples, Sofie went back to her hut to lie down. Her earlier good mood had evaporated and she didn't feel like conversing with Laura. She'd so been looking forward to the new Sunday visits and chatting with Liesbeth, like old times. And she'd been daydreaming for days about being close to Oscar. But he didn't even attempt to take her hand.

The distance between them was getting bigger by the day. It scared her to think that if the war carried on they'd eventually forget her and stop coming to visit.

Under her pillow she kept a small felt bag. She let the weight of it sit in her hand before rolling out the smooth pebble that reflected pink or blue depending on the light. Her father had given it to her one summer holiday when the three of them had been walking along the stony shoreline as they bent into the bracing wind. The pebble had stood out from the rest of the unremarkable grey stones and they'd laughed that maybe it hadn't belonged there and been dropped by someone. It didn't matter. Sofie slipped the treasure into her pocket as a reminder of the best holiday ever. The last holiday they were to have together as a family.

Sticking her finger in the bag, she hooked out a small black and white picture and felt a familiar tug in her chest. But before she could look more closely at the figure staring solemnly into the camera, a noise at the door made her push both objects back in the bag and slip it back under her pillow.

'Are you OK?' said Laura, hesitating in the doorway.

Sofie swung her legs over the side of the bed into a sitting position. 'I just get these headaches, but I'm better now,' she said, rubbing her temples. 'Come and sit next to me and tell me what you think about Oscar.'

Laura's face lit up. 'He's really nice, isn't he? You're so lucky having him for your friend. All the boys I know are dead boring and never have anything to say to girls. But Oscar's different.'

'You think so? In what way?'

'He listens to what you have to say and there are none of those awkward silences you normally get with boys.' She paused to think. 'And he's really nice looking too.'

'He's got a girlfriend, actually.' Sofie watched Laura's face.

'Oh, does he? But that doesn't mean he can't have other girl friends, can it?'

'No, I expect not,' sighed Sofie. 'Don't you want to know who his girlfriend is?'

Laura frowned. 'Should I know her?'

'You do. You're talking to her.'

Laura's hand flew to her mouth. 'I'm so sorry, talking about Oscar like that. I had no idea. You must think I'm after him, but I'm not.'

Sofie laughed. 'I know that. And besides, why should you know?'

'I guessed from the way he was talking about you, but then just now I thought you meant...'

'What did he say? About me?'

'That he was hoping to see you without all the others being there because there was never an opportunity to be with you.'

'Did he really say that?'

'Why did you go off like that? You could have joined in.'

'I was so looking forward to seeing him. But when he turned up with everyone, there was no chance to be just with him and talk like we used to. It's like he's becoming a stranger and I can't do anything about it.'

'Do you write to him?'

'A bit, but he hardly ever writes back,' Sofie sighed.

'Why don't you ask him to come and visit you without the others? After all, he comes into the woods most days to work.'

'You know it's not allowed to have visitors unless it's agreed with the leaders and I don't want to have some organised visit. I just want to see him on my terms.'

'Then why don't you organise it with him?'

'Didn't you hear what I said? They won't allow it.'

'But if you don't tell them? I'll cover for you.' Laura looked at her boldly. 'We'll arrange to go and fetch water together from the pump on the Tongeren road. You know how long it takes to carry those milk churns, so no one will notice if we've gone longer than normal. What do you think?'

'I think that's the best idea I've heard in ages,' said Sofie, leaning over and giving Laura a warm hug.

PART 3

FALLEN PILOT

Chapter 17

Whether it was because he'd just turned eleven, or that his parents trusted him more since the English pilot incident, Jan had a lot more freedom these days. He was still too young to help with the building of huts, but because he knew the woods so well, he'd take his brother to his workplace, before scarpering off to meet his friends.

They had a new den now, or rather series of dens, scattered throughout various parts of the wood where few people went. Jan was particularly pleased he'd created a den that even Henk Hauer didn't know anything about. It was in a dip on the edge of the wood right next to the farmer's turnip field. They'd seen his workers pulling the turnips and waited in the den till they'd finished before sending Lex out, because he was the smallest and fastest. His job was to fill the hemp bag Jan had brought from home. Jan decreed it much safer that only one of them dug for turnips, just in case the farmer came back. When Lex objected, Jan said he wouldn't be allowed to come with them the next day.

'He's only little,' objected Nico, after Lex was sent stumbling and sobbing over the ruts to the place Jan had indicated.

'Then he shouldn't be in our gang. He's useful and willing and … over there, Lex! No, stupid, there!'

Jan was tough but fair. When the bag looked full enough, he called Lex back and pulled out four large turnips and handed them to him. 'For your family,' he said, magnanimously.

Lex beamed and stuffed the turnips in his pockets, so he was forced to walk bandy-legged. Jan and Nico fell about laughing and Lex laughed along with them.

'There's loads of turnips. Shall we store them here?' asked Nico.

'Don't be stupid. What if the farmer finds out? We'll be meat,' said Jan, scornfully, tying up the bag with a piece of twine. 'We'll sell these on the black market and make ourselves a bit of money.'

'We can't do that,' retorted Nico. 'They'll know we've stolen them.'

'When you sell on the black market, you never divulge your sources. So we'll be safe. Besides, I'll take them to tante Else. She always needs food for the village. Leave it to me.'

***

It started with turnips and soon Jan was trading in carrots and cabbages too. It was simple. All he did was keep his ears open, especially when the Berkenhout group met on Tuesday evenings. He didn't want to make it obvious, so listened from the top of the stairs, whilst his father, Foppen and Else discussed the availability of goods. At first, he thought of involving Oscar, as he was one of the group, but realised that dividing up the spoils between two and, when he felt like it, three, was as far as he was prepared to go.

So it was one Saturday morning, when he decided to investigate a new source of produce that he came across something odd, right next to the main path leading in the direction of Berkenhout. He was whistling to himself and minding his own business, when something large and white caught his eye. From afar, it looked as if there'd been a sudden drop of snow over the tall beech trees. But he knew it couldn't be – the leaves on the beech trees were still in full leaf. He jumped off the path and edged forward through some scraggy undergrowth, looking hard for any signs of life. It wasn't till he was a few metres away that he saw it was something like a large white sheet snagged between the branches. But why would a sheet be hanging in the trees? He noticed that there were ropes attached to it and gradually it dawned on him what he was seeing and that there must be someone nearby.

'Hello? Is anyone there?' he called, excitement growing at the memory of the English pilot. He thought he saw the flash of a boot disappearing into the undergrowth, but might have been mistaken. 'I'm Dutch,' he called.

He was right. A scuffle and a voice from a little way away. 'I'm American,' said a voice.

'I can help you,' said Jan, moving forward in the direction of where he saw the boot.

'God save the President.' The man who appeared was wearing a green uniform with a name stitched on in white letters. He walked towards Jan and held out his hand. 'Donald C. McDonald,' he said, watching Jan peer at the name on his uniform. 'But you can call me Don. Pleased to meet you. See that, there? That saved my life,' he jerked his thumb towards the parachute dangling from the tree.

'You can't leave it there. The Germans will find it and if they find it they'll find you,' gabbled Jan, breathless at the prospect of helping another pilot.

The man, who had a short spiky haircut, didn't seem too bothered, and laughed, his teeth gleaming. Jan tried to stop himself from staring but had never seen anyone with such perfect teeth before.

Donald C. McDonald leant nonchalantly against a tree and pulled out a packet of cigarettes with the picture of a camel on the front. He tapped one into the palm of his hand and lit it one-handed. Drawing deeply on it, he then held the packet out. 'You want one?' he said, exhaling a plume of smoke.

No one had ever offered Jan a cigarette before and he wasn't sure whether to accept. Perhaps the American thought he was older than eleven, or perhaps American boys of his age smoked. Jan didn't want to appear childish, but knew that his father would beat him if he found out he'd been smoking.

'You can have the whole pack, if you want. I've got more,' said the man, patting his breast pocket.

'I...,' began Jan, then took the pack and stared at it as if it might jump up and bite him.

'Haven't you seen one of those before?' said the man, who kept pulling on his cigarette and exhaling through pursed lips.

'Of course I have. But we don't have ones like this here. With the picture of a camel.'

'Then all the more reason to have it. Light one?' He flicked open the lighter, ready to fire it up.

Jan tapped out a cigarette, like he'd seen the man do, put it between his lips and waited while the man clicked the lighter three times until the flame flared. The end of the cigarette glowed briefly red, as Jan tried to get it to light, but it went out.

'Here, let me do it for you,' said the man, taking the cigarette and deftly lit it, before handing it back.

Jan pretended to take a puff and was grateful that the man didn't try to give him a lesson on how to smoke. Standing, the two of them, cigarettes in hand, made him feel quite grown-up. He quietly slipped the packet into his trouser pocket.

'Where are you from?' he asked.

'Ohio. The US of A. There's probably half a dozen of us, all bailed out when our plane caught fire. Can your people help me?'

'There's a place in the woods I'll take you. You'll be safe there.'

'Sure? Can't take any risks. I've heard the place is crawling with Jerries.'

'Not where we're going. But we need to get rid of that thing and get off the track. They come down in their trucks, but no further.'

Together they set about untangling the parachute, but on the ground it looked even bigger and whiter.

'We have to hide it,' said the man, dragging it towards a clump of trees, but it remained stubbornly visible.

'I know. We'll bury it,' said Jan, but the man looked at him as if he were mad.

'Better to burn it, surely?' He began folding it into a tight bundle, but Jan was uneasy about the idea.

'What if they see the smoke? Or smell it?'

The pilot stopped. 'OK. Can you get hold of something to dig a hole with?'

Jan thought hard. If he ran back home to fetch a spade, he might run into someone he knew and it would take him at least half an hour before he was back again. Or he could head down to the camp and ask to borrow a spade. But he'd have to tell them about the pilot and they might say he couldn't stay there.

The man sat down and lit another cigarette. He didn't offer Jan one this time, perhaps because he'd already given him a complete packet.

'Can you wait here till I get back?' said Jan. Plan A, rushing home and back, was probably less risky.

'Sure. I'll stick right here. But bring me back something to eat and drink, will you? I could murder a Pepsi-Cola.'

'A…what?'

'Don't you guys have Pepsi-Cola here? Oh well, anything fizzy will do.'

Again, Jan didn't want to appear ignorant, so he nodded and said he'd be back as quick as he could. He set off on a jog back home, avoiding the main path. He thought about dropping in on Nico, but decided he'd keep this one to himself. Nico could wait.

***

Jan's mind was whirring as he sped back after fetching the supplies. He couldn't believe his luck finding a second pilot, and an American too. When Nigel had left, he'd felt sad, as if he'd lost a friend. It wouldn't be like that with Donald, the man with the funny double name, he was sure. Still, excitement drove him on as he imagined a role for himself, picking up servicemen and bringing them to safety. Surely his father would be pleased with his efforts? Lost in thought, he arrived back at the spot and swung the heavy bag onto the ground.

'Donald…Don…are you there?'

He scoured the clearing, but there were no signs of Donald, or of the parachute. Jan rubbed the top of his head, back-tracked a little way from where he'd come, although he knew he couldn't be mistaken.

In the distance he heard a familiar low rumble, quickly grabbed the bag and made himself scarce. Peering out from the bushes, he saw a pair of headlights bounce along as the army vehicle roared along the road towards him. There were two soldiers in the truck and they looked not much older than Oscar as they laughed and joked above the noise of the engine. Jan knew they'd get to the point that the road ran out, do an about-turn and roar back again. They never continued off-track further into the woods and Jan guessed they were too scared of being ambushed. Yet they kept up this daily façade of bravado, stopping and searching anyone they came across, before driving off in a plume of dust.

Jan waited till he heard the vehicle on its return journey, then jumped up to relieve the cramp in his legs. He supposed he'd better go back home, but the mystery of the missing pilot still puzzled him. Another quick look round confirmed he was definitely not hiding and Jan began trudging back the way he came.

He failed to spot the truck up ahead, well hidden off the side of the road. It wasn't till they stepped out onto the path, blocking his way that he realised he had nowhere to go but to confront them. Immediately, his mind flew to the bag on his back, but worse, what if they searched his pockets and found the packet of American cigarettes? His heart felt as if it was about to jump out of his chest.

'*Halt! Heil Hitler!*' said one of the Germans and both soldiers held up their hands in salute.

Jan pretended to look surprised and fiddled with his bag. The soldiers muttered something among themselves that Jan didn't understand. They didn't look particularly aggressive, perhaps because they were so young, but still Jan didn't dare say anything.

Then one of them spoke in heavily accented Dutch, which gave him further courage. 'What are you doing out in the woods by yourself? Where are you going?'

'I was visiting a friend who lives in a cottage over there,' Jan said, jerking his head vaguely in the direction of the thickest part of the wood.

'Show me the bag,' said the German, looking grim.

Jan took his time opening the bag for inspection so he could work out the next part of his story.

'A spade? What's that for? Digging a grave?' The Germans both laughed.

'He lent me the spade because my father's broke and he needs to dig the vegetables,' lied Jan.

'What's this? Bread, cheese, cake? Did he give you that because he thought you'd get hungry, then?' A smirk curled round the young man's lips.

'Um, no I brought it for him, but he said he had enough.' That lie sounded a bit thin, but Jan couldn't think of anything else to say.

The Dutch-speaking German spat on the ground and looked bored. He began walking back to his truck when he spun round and took another look at Jan.

'Pockets. Turn them out.'

Jan's heart flapped like a dying fish and his hands became damp.

'I haven't got anything in them.' He could feel his face turn red.

'Turn them out!' The German's cold blue eyes bore into him.

Slowly, Jan pulled his left pocket inside out, empty, then the other, the one with the cigarette packet. He handed it over, eyes down.

The Dutch-speaking German's face broke into a triumphant grin. 'So. Cigarettes, hm? American cigarettes. You're going to tell me that your friend gave you those, aren't you?'

'I... found them. Back there. They were lying on the ground and I picked them up. I was going to give them to my father. He smokes.' Jan hoped this would be enough.

'Then let's go and see where you found them, shall we?' The soldier tucked the packet into an inside pocket and patted it.

Jan was relieved that they weren't suggesting bundling him into their vehicle and taking him away for questioning. He almost skipped back down the path, but then it dawned on him that the American pilot might have returned. He began walking more slowly, whistling as loudly as he could.

'Shut up and march!' The other soldier prodded Jan in the

back.

Please don't let him come back!

'It was there. That's where they were, lying on the ground.'
Jan pointed to a likely spot, not exactly where he'd met Donald, but
close enough. The two Germans began poking around in the dead
leaves as if they might find some more packs of Camel. At least they
weren't thrashing around in the thicket where Donald could be
hiding.

'Are you sure you weren't given these by an American?'

'Of course not. I never met any Americans.'

The two Germans spoke rapidly to one another and kept
looking in the direction of Berkenhout. Little do they know, thought
Jan, his face expressionless.

The Dutch-German narrowed his eyes at Jan and spat on the
ground again. 'I don't want to see you on this path again. Next time,
you'll be dealt with.' With that, the two soldiers marched off back
down to their truck.

Jan waited until he could hear the truck was almost out of
earshot before he set off home again. At least he wouldn't have to
explain the cigarettes to his father, who would have been bound to
find them. The thought made him scared all over again.

Chapter 18

Gradually, Sofie's mood improved as she and Laura became firm friends. It wouldn't do to complain knowing Laura's situation was so much worse than her own. Sofie stopped feeling sorry for herself and was soon offering to help with the daily chores, including cooking, which she discovered she loved. It was also a time when they could sit round the table and chat freely whilst preparing the next meal. Corrie showed the two girls how to chop vegetables quickly and efficiently, without any waste. Soon they moved onto mixing pancake batter and watched as Corrie expertly tipped a ladle of the creamy mix into a pan, already sizzling with bacon.

'Can I do the next one?' asked Sofie, fascinated at how easy it looked.

'Of course,' said Corrie, after she slid the first one onto a plate. Sofie's first attempt was a bit raggedy and the three of them laughed as the so-called pancake ended up more like a failed omelette in the middle of the pan. Determined to get the next one right, she screwed up her face in concentration as she swirled the batter into the hot pan for the second time. She watched the bubbling mass intently and when the edges turned brown and crispy she eased the spatula underneath and executed a neat flip. Whether it was luck or a skill she had just discovered didn't matter. Her success spurred her on to want to cook the remaining pancakes for lunch.

Soon Corrie had Sofie trying out more complicated dishes, all the while helped by Laura who was happy in her supporting role.

'Shall we bake a cake for a change?' Corrie asked her one day.

'How can we do that? We don't have an oven,' said Sofie, checking the brown beans she'd been boiling to see if they were tender.

'I thought we'd try and bake one in the black pan. What do you think?' said Corrie, smiling.

They decided on a basic cake mix with small pieces of chopped apple flavoured with cinnamon. Like the pancake experiment, the first attempt resulted in something that resembled a flat biscuit, but it still tasted delicious.

'If we put more egg in the mixture, won't that help it become more fluffy?' asked Sofie.

It was the answer and after thirty minutes Sofie turned out a perfect, fragrant-smelling cake which the Janssen boys, Laura, Corrie, Kees and Sofie devoured in one sitting.

'Did you bake just one?' teased Kees, wiping the crumbs from his mouth. 'You can bake us one like that every day.'

It was all she needed to spur her on to create her own recipes, which she scribbled in the black diary she kept under her pillow. Despite the lack of additional ingredients, she became inventive with what she had. Her favourite was a plain cake which she drizzled with a sweet *ersatz* coffee syrup, making it so moist, you had to use a fork to scoop it up.

'Try this and tell me what you think.' Sofie cut a small slice of the warm cake for Corrie's approval.

'It's coffee isn't it? It really tastes like the real thing,' said Corrie, but not before she'd finished the whole slice.

'I thought it might work, even though it's just the *ersatz* stuff. It's amazing what you can disguise in something like a cake.'

'I think this is good enough to give to tante Else on Sunday,' said Corrie.

'But this isn't a patch on her cakes. And what if it doesn't turn out right?' Secretly, she was pleased, wanting to impress tante Else who'd been so kind and patient with her.

'Well, if it doesn't, we won't tell her,' said Corrie.

'Can I practise it again before Sunday, then?'

'No, better not. We're running low on flour and I don't want to bother Piet for more.' It was the first time Sofie had seen Corrie look anxious and it unsettled her.

'I thought there was a plentiful supply of stuff like flour.'

'It's fine, but we depend on others to bring it to us and I don't want to inconvenience them for more.'

'I won't make any more cakes, then.' The old Sofie looked at Corrie defiantly.

'Make the cake for Sunday. Then if she's impressed, we can perhaps ask for an increase in ingredients.'

Sofie was placated, but was left wondering how she could adapt her recipes if supplies ran short.

***

Laura was playing with the twins in the reception hut, which doubled as a place for the children during the day. Sofie watched from the doorway as Laura cut out square shapes of paper for a memory game, then gave them each one to colour in.

'Sofie, Sofie, come and help,' cried Pim, making a space on the bench for her.

'I was wondering where you'd got to,' said Laura, raising her head for a moment. Sofie was about to answer when the boys began to squabble as soon as Laura turned their attention away from them.

'Do you think you can finish these by yourselves quietly for a few minutes? I'm just going to have a word with Sofie.'

The twins nodded their heads in unison, before bursting into fits of giggles.

'I'll be watching you,' said Laura, with a mock-stern look in her eyes.

'It's all sorted. Mr Maarten has agreed we can fetch water from the Tongeren pump tomorrow. If we get there at four, then Oscar will be coming to work not long after. How does that sound?'

'Laura, you're a genius,' said Sofie, grabbing her hands and swinging her round.

'Oh, and one more thing,' said Laura, catching her breath. 'Mr Maarten wants to set up proper classes for the children. I said we'd help with teaching. What do you think?'

Sofie burst out laughing. 'Me, teach? You should have seen me in class. I was always the quiet one…'

'You, quiet?' Laura's dark hair swung in front of her face as she shook her head in disbelief.

Sofie wasn't listening any more and she stood staring into the middle distance. It seemed such a long time ago, although it was only a few months. 'You're the best in the class,' Oscar had told her that time and she hadn't believed him. But she hadn't had a chance to prove it in the end of term exams, which never happened.

'When was the last time you were at school?' she asked Laura, who was staring at her.

'Ages, but my mother taught me at home. I learnt more from her in three months than I did in three years at school,' she said with a sigh.

'My mother never had time to teach me anything. Even when we were at the Foppens,' said Sofie, bitterly. Did her mother ever really wonder how she was coping here, or did she assume that because she was 'safe' she was happy? She realised with a dull pang that she hadn't received a letter from her parents in weeks, but gazing into Laura's expectant face she realised she was happier than she'd been for a long time.

Chapter 19

Within a month, the village had doubled in size. Two families had arrived from Rotterdam and Delft, along with several young men who refused to go to work in Germany and an elderly Polish man. Sofie was pleased that they weren't forced to take in more people into their already crowded hut, but was curious to find out more about the new arrivals. She vaguely recognised one of them, a young sullen-looking man called Wouter, who had been a postman in Kampenveld.

One early morning before curfew, he was sitting on a log on the edge of the village, smoking a cigarette. Sofie went and sat next to him and introduced herself. He nodded, but didn't seem willing to start a conversation.

'It's not that bad when you've been here for a while,' she ventured.

'What do you know?' He looked pityingly at her, then chucked his cigarette stub down and ground it with his heel.

'You can't leave that there. We have to account for all our rubbish.' Sofie wouldn't have said anything if he hadn't responded to her so rudely. She was surprised to see him pick it up and tuck it into his trouser pocket.

'Look, I know what you're thinking. I hated it when I first came but it does get better, honest.' She had no idea why she was talking to him like this. He meant nothing to her and she could just as well walk away. But there was something mournful about his grey eyes making him look older than he probably was.

'Why are you here?' she whispered.

His expression suggested he thought she was crazy for asking. 'I had no choice, did I? They just think they can make you go and work in their stinking factories for them. Tim went. Now his family won't have anything to do with him. He wrote to me, begging me to come. What, to keep him company? I feel bad I didn't write back. He was my best friend. But he went and worked for the *moffen*. How can anyone want to do that?'

Sofie didn't know what to say.

'And now I've got nothing. How could I carry on my job? They'd have found me straightaway and deported me. I hid first. Can you believe, at Tim's old house? His dad was so angry with him for going so easily, no conscience or anything. He dug this sort of room right under the summerhouse in the garden. I once had to stay there forty-eight hours straight with only a bottle of water and some dry biscuits for company. It wasn't damp, just dark, dark and boring. Sometimes Francine came and pretended to be digging up vegetables in the garden. She'd keep up this conversation like she was talking to herself. That kept me going.'

Wouter tapped another cigarette out of the squashed packet and held it out expectantly. Sofie shook her head, waiting for him to continue.

'But it got too dangerous for me to stay there. Too many raids. Three nights in a row.' He shivered. 'He told me about this place. I didn't want to come but he said, do it for me, do it for Tim. I thought about Francine. How would I see her? So that last evening, only two days ago, I asked her to marry me. And she accepted.'

For just a moment, his face broke into a smile and Sofie noticed his eyes weren't grey at all, but blue. He kept on pulling at the cigarette and exhaling as if he were sighing.

'And now I can't see her at all. So what was the point?' This time he looked at Sofie, expecting an answer.

'It won't be forever, this. We heard on the radio yesterday that the Allies are on their way. Americans, British…'

Wouter snorted. 'Do you believe all that? After the way that the Germans just came in and trampled all over us, took away our best people, treated us like dogs?'

Again, Sofie was lost for words. Everyone seemed to have a different opinion, but these days she just wanted to believe the positives.

'I'm sorry, I didn't mean to upset you,' said Wouter, suddenly. 'I just feel as if I've lost everything that's of any importance to me.'

'You've got Francine. Maybe she can join the visiting committee who come on Sundays.' Sofie told him of the weekly visits that everyone looked forward to and that several, like herself, had friends who came too.

Wouter shook his head vigorously. 'I don't want any sitting around with a load of people I don't know when I'd rather be with Francine on our own. But you wouldn't understand that, would you?'

Sofie felt herself boil with rage. 'What do you know? I've sat in that room next to my…friend, wanting to have a conversation on our own. It's the best you can ask for if you want to stay here.'

Her eyes started to prick, but she was determined to retain her composure. Fortunately, Corrie called her in to start preparing breakfast and was so busy weighing out ingredients that she didn't seem to notice how quiet Sofie had become. Bending over the batter she was mixing a little too vigorously, Sofie tried to block out thoughts of Oscar. It all seemed so hopeless.

***

The day they'd gone to the Tongeren pump had started out in such high spirits. She and Laura were like children let out of class early.

'Are you sure you'll be able to carry the water in those cans?' Mr Maarten had turned up just as they were setting off.

'We'll carry one full one between us with another half full one for balance,' Laura had said.

'Hmm. See how you go this time, but I'd rather the men did it.'

They'd rushed off before he could find an objection, swinging the cans as they went. The instructions were clear: only use the pump if the blue rag was hanging from the pine tree. If the dog was tied up outside the house, they'd know it wasn't safe to proceed. The old man who lived by himself was happy enough to help, but hadn't dared tell anyone for fear of being betrayed. He'd arranged these signals after a German soldier had come snooping one morning and hung about for hours, watching the house. The story went that no one had come to use the pump that day, but he'd had palpitations from the anxiety of being found out.

Laura and Sofie had been told to fill the cans and return as quickly as they could. They'd timed it so they would arrive just before 4.30pm when Laura had been sure Oscar would arrive. It was perfectly still in the woods and the blue rag hung limply from the tree. They waited.

'Did he actually say he'd be coming?' said Sofie, squinting down the long path for any signs of life. Laura shrugged, saying she might have got the day wrong. Shaking her head in irritation, Sofie stooped to pick up one of the cans. 'Come on. Let's fill this thing and get back.' She applied her full weight to the handle of the pump, forcing it up and down. Most of the water gushed around the outside of the milkcan, but she didn't care. Laura giggled and joined in, turning it into a game.

'Shh!' Sofie suddenly broke off and turned her ear to the direction of the path leading away from them. The rumble of army vehicles in the distance was unmistakeable.

'Quick, run!' whispered Sofie.

The two girls picked up the milk cans, one empty, the other only half full and rushed into the woods back towards Berkenhout. Behind them the sound receded. For now, they were safe.

Arriving back, they found Mr Maarten was waiting for them.

'We'd only just got to the pump when we heard the sound of army vehicles,' explained Sofie breathlessly.

'No one saw us, honestly,' said Laura anxiously.

Mr Maarten narrowed his eyes, then gave a thin smile. 'Hmm. Good thing too, but I suspected it would be a wasted journey.'

Sofie bit her lip. She knew they wouldn't be given a second

chance.

***

A few days later, Sofie received a letter from Oscar. It started off by saying how much he missed her and that he hoped the news coming over *Radio Oranje* about the Allies was true. She would soon be out and they would be able to go back to normal life again. The next paragraph gave Sofie a jolt to her stomach as he told her his father wanted him to go to Hilversum for a few weeks to work in an office job, but he didn't tell her what it was. He would come with the Sunday committee and tell her more then. Overwhelmingly, she felt a sense of abandonment as if her main contact to the outside world had been cut off.

When he came on the Sunday, Sofie had convinced herself he wouldn't. She managed to grab a few words with him outside before they all went in for their weekly pep talk from tante Else.

Oscar tried to kiss her but she turned her head away. 'What's the matter?' said Oscar, frowning.

'Can't you guess?' said Sofie.

'Look, it's not my fault I have to go. My father insisted.'

'And what your father says you have to do,' said Sofie, sarcastically, but he didn't reply to her remark. 'Anyway, that's not why I'm annoyed. Laura and I went down to the pump just to meet you and you never turned up. Then we had to run all the way back because we heard the sound of German trucks coming towards us.'

'Look, I'm sorry. I really meant to come but it was too risky. Kampenveld was overrun with German vehicles that day. Four raids, just in our street. I couldn't just wander off into the woods. They would've spotted me in a flash.'

Sofie's shoulders slumped as she whispered 'sorry'. She let Oscar put his arm round her and squeeze her towards him.

'I won't be gone long, honest. But look, I have something for you.' He fumbled in his coat pocket and brought out a dusty book.

'It's in English,' Sofie said softly, looking puzzled while taking it from him and reading the title *Great Expectations* by Charles Dickens.

'I found it in the bookcase. It's my mother's but I don't think she'll miss it. She never reads anything these days.'

'I can't accept this.' She was about to give it back when she saw the look in his eyes. 'I'm not sure my English is good enough to understand this, but I'll give it a go.' She turned over the pages whilst he watched her eagerly.

'If there's anything you don't understand, put it in a letter to me and I'll translate if for you.'

'It could be a very long letter.' They both laughed and Sofie let him hug her.

After he'd gone, she wished she hadn't been so hard on him, especially after he'd given her the gift. But it somehow made things more final between them.

***

It scared her that things could have changed so rapidly in the few weeks she'd been away from home. Oscar had told her, laughing, how they were now forced to have identity cards on them showing their face half in profile so the left ear was showing. They also had to supply a print of their left forefinger. The Germans, and there were far more of them patrolling the streets, could now stop anyone for no reason, demanding to see their ID. Although Oscar didn't say it directly, he implied that his 'top secret' work in Hilversum had something to do with forging ID cards for Jews. There was a shortage of volunteers, he'd been told. He hoped it would only be for a short time.

The rumours reached the camp that life outside was changing. Was it true that German vans had been patrolling Kampenveld and had taken the Vos family, who had two young children, one no older than six months? Could they really have been taken to Vught, the concentration camp in Brabant where conditions were said to be terrible? No one was able to say for sure. The thought was so terrible they chose to ignore it.

Chapter 20

Jan was fed up. His father had been unnecessarily harsh after finding out about the episode with the two Germans in the woods. Angrily, he thought his father would have made a good SS-er, the way he wheedled the information out of him.

He hadn't expected his father home so early when he arrived back that day. If only he hadn't left the bag with the spade sticking out leaning against the fence. He'd meant to take it round to the back, but Nico had turned up and began yakking on about some turnips he'd heard about and that they should get down to the field before they'd all gone. By the time Jan had got rid of him, his father had come marching down the path and shouted at him from the door to come and explain what the bag and spade were all about. Flustered, he decided to tell the truth for once, the look in his father's eye was so fierce. He hadn't meant to say anything about the cigarettes, but somehow it just slipped out.

'So, tell me, why didn't they believe your story about visiting a friend in the woods?' glared his father.

'Er, they made me empty my pockets and...'

'And what?'

'They found the cigarettes. American ones.' He fished around in his mind wondering whether to say he'd been given them or found them. He'd already confessed to finding the pilot and had told him about how they'd hidden the parachute. He'd been hoping he could skate over the episode of the cigarettes.

'You little fool. Did you steal them?'

'No! Of course I didn't. It's just, he gave me the packet and I liked the picture on the front. I thought you might like them.' Jan looked up sheepishly.

'Mm. Alright, but you should be aware that those *moffen* will stop at nothing. But searching a child, it's…unforgiveable.'

With his father off on a different tack, Jan inwardly breathed a sigh of relief. But no, he was off again with that look in his eye.

'So, what happened after they found the cigarettes?'

'One of them took them off me and put them in his pocket.'

His father made a grunting sound, suggesting it didn't surprise him.

'And they let you go after that?'

Thinking about it afterwards, Jan knew he'd made a mistake by not replying immediately. It meant that anything else he said his father would question.

'I hoped you didn't take them to where you'd found the pilot? Did you?'

What else could he have said? His father would never have believed him if he'd said he'd come straight home.

'But I knew he'd already gone, though of course I didn't tell them that. I pretended I'd just picked them up off the ground and they believed me. Well, sort of.'

'They either did or they didn't. Well?' That glare again.

'They didn't have anything more on me so I suppose they had to let me go.'

'Mm. Look, Jan, you're not to go prowling around in the

woods any more. If you get picked up again, there'll be no second chance, not even at your age. You stay well away and you can tell your friends to do the same.' The glare had been replaced with something else, worry even.

'But it's boring!'

'Stop that. Boring or not, I'm not having a son of mine running around loose in the woods and potentially betraying all our good work.'

So that's what it is, thought Jan. He's not worried about me, only that the stuff he's doing will get found out.

'Alright, father. I won't,' he decided to say, crossing his fingers behind his back.

***

Later, he cycled over to Nico's house and saw Lex's bike lying on the path. 'Damn!' he breathed to himself as he parked his bike against the fence. He found the two of them out the back playing ball.

'Jan! Come and join in, we need a goalie,' said Lex, all red in the face.

Jan shook his head. He was in no mood for ball games, which seemed silly, childish even, now.

'You carry on. I'll watch.'

Nico came over, peeling off his gloves. 'It's boring if you don't join in,' he said.

Boring. Not as boring as not going down to the woods.

'Na. Didn't come to play games.' Jan began kicking at the loose stones on the path.

'What then?' snapped Nico.

'Those turnips you were talking about. Let's do it tomorrow.'

Lex bounded up like an enthusiastic puppy. 'Can I come? I can carry loads in my mum's shopping bag. Please?'

'Can I trust you not to say anything to anyone?' Jan narrowed his eyes at Lex.

'I promise, I promise. I never said anything to anyone about the turnips last time. Well, only Mum, 'cos you let me have those ones for her.'

Why hadn't Jan thought of that? Now he wished he hadn't discussed the turnip plan with Lex there.

'No, Lex, not this time. Haven't you heard about the Germans patrolling the woods? I think we'll drop the whole idea.'

'Come on, Jan. I told you we can't miss out on this opportunity. Who knows when I'll get another tip-off like that?' said Nico, clearly annoyed that Jan was scuppering his idea.

'There'll be others. There always are. But I don't think now's the time. Come on, don't look at me like that.'

Nico was furious. 'I know why you won't do it. Because it's not your idea. Everything we do has to be your idea and you can't bear it if someone else comes up with a good scheme.'

Jan needed to have this out with Nico but not with Lex listening in. He put his hand round Nico's shoulder and lowered his voice. 'Believe me, now's not a good time. I saw the *moffen* with my own eyes and they're just waiting to pounce.'

'I'm going home. This is boring,' said Lex, who'd been bouncing the ball impatiently.

'Why don't you both go?' said Nico, going back into the house and slamming the door.

Jan smiled at Lex. 'We'll do it another time, promise. Let's go. I don't think we're wanted round here.'

'It's me, isn't it?' Lex said boldly.

But Jan's mind was already miles away, planning how to win Nico back over.

'You just think I'm stupid and that I'm going to muck things up, don't you? Like over that pilot.' Lex picked up his bike but didn't seem in any hurry to cycle off home.

Jan's mind swung back to present as he heard the word 'pilot'. Did he know?

'I never told anyone about him. I can keep my word. You can trust me.'

Jan found Lex's whining voice annoying, but was relieved he was talking about Nigel, not Donald C. McDonald.

'Look, Lex, things aren't like they used be to anymore. I wish they were. I also wish we could just go and hang out in our den again, and maybe we will.'

'I don't care about the dens any more. I want to do all this new stuff, you know, you, me and Nico.'

Jan needed to shake him off. Needed to think about what to do next.

'Don't you worry. I've got something in mind, but can't say anything just now. So no going and saying anything to Nico.'

Lex beamed at him, nodded vigorously and cycled off in the direction of home.

PART 4

EVACUATION

Chapter 21

One evening, Otto Maarten called everyone to the reception hut for a meeting. This wasn't like the Sunday morning get-togethers when everyone was in high spirits. His serious demeanour let them know that he had bad news to impart.

Sofie arrived early with Laura and they sat together on the long bench at the front. What with the new arrivals, who seemed to come in daily, the benches were soon full and latecomers had to stand at the back. People were murmuring amongst themselves and when it became apparent that nothing much was happening, the chatter became louder. Wouter, the postman from Kampenveld, had been one of the last to arrive at Berkenhout. He'd kept himself to himself since Sofie had spoken to him about leaving his fiancée and she wondered if he would ever settle. They hadn't spoken since.

Otto, a quiet man, who seemed uncomfortable speaking in public, cleared his throat several times. A couple of men at the back made loud shushing noises until all were silent.

'Thank you. And thank you for all coming here this evening. Some of you may have heard the rumours that the Germans are close to finding out about our village. We don't know whether the rumours are true but we have to assume that they may be right. Young Jan Mulder was recently accosted by two SS-ers when he was walking home through the woods. They discovered he had a packet of American cigarettes on him. He said he'd found them lying on the ground. They let him go, but every day since then there have been

German patrols. You may have heard the trucks in the distance.' Otto began to turn over some sheets of paper he had as if he was looking for something he'd missed.

'But there's no road up to the village, so we'll be alright, won't we?' called out Kees Janssen.

'In theory, but we've decided we can't take any chances. Until the threat lessens, we're going to have to clear the village and move back into safe houses.'

A gasp went up and several people began to murmur amongst themselves.

'Shut up and let him finish.' Wouter spoke, with a fierce look on his face. Everybody fell quiet again.

'Thank you. I promise it won't be for long, just until we get to the bottom of the rumours,' said Otto. 'Nobody needs to worry unduly. The committee has arranged housing for everyone, but unfortunately some of us will be split up for a while.' He started to read names from a list, but people started speaking amongst themselves. Wouter stepped forward, said something to Otto and took the list from him. His deep voice soon stopped the chatter. One by one they learned where they'd be going. Some were to stay with people they all knew in Kampenveld who had been helping with the organisation of the village. Others would be staying in the woods several kilometres away, where a large army tent had been requisitioned by the organisers.

Sofie listened for her name to be read out, her heart beating fast. She sat holding Laura's hand, neither daring to look at each other.

'Janssens, Kees, Corrie, Pim and Wim. Army Tent.'

Sofie caught Corrie's eye and gave her a sympathetic look. She didn't yet know where she'd be going, but hoped it wouldn't be the tent, as much as she wanted to stay with the Janssens.

'Mulder, Sofie. Kampenveld. Wechsler, Laura, Kampenveld.'

Sofie squeezed Laura's hand. She wouldn't be sent off alone and she was going back to Kampenveld. The dread she'd been feeling was mixed with excitement that she was going home, although she knew it wasn't home at all.

The evacuation happened quickly. No sooner had Wouter finished reading the list, then they were each ordered to fetch a bag with a small number of possessions before lining up ready to be sent off walking in groups of four and five through the beech wood and towards the track where they'd been told the cars would be waiting. There was barely time to say goodbye, as Sofie and Laura clung first to Corrie and then Kees, who were with the first group with Wouter.

'Wherever you go, make sure you keep practising your spice cake,' Corrie said, hugging Sofie warmly.

'I will. And you must think up some new recipes we can try out together when we get back home.' It didn't seem like goodbye, but Sofie was sad to be parted from the Janssens who had become so much of a family to her. At least she'd be going with Laura, although it wasn't clear whether they'd be housed together.

The night air was cold with a partial moon throwing shadows through the tall bare trees as the group, led by Wouter, walked along in silence. Sofie and Laura fell into step next to each other, resisting the temptation to discuss where they were going. They were told they would find out on arrival in Kampenveld, where Dick Foppen and his wife were to meet them.

Sofie remembered the last time she'd come this way in the opposite direction on her journey to Berkenhout. She'd reacted rudely to the kind volunteers who had taken her to the village, deliberately dragging her feet and complaining every few metres. The thought made the heat rise in her cheeks. What must Corrie and Kees have thought of this stroppy young girl with the wild hair who refused to participate in village life, but patiently put themselves out to make her welcome? She shook the thought away, ashamed at the person she'd been.

She recognised the man standing beside the van parked a little way up from where the track began. It was Henk Hauer, whom she'd been told was the head woodman responsible for the building of the huts. He nodded briefly at Wouter, ground his cigarette stub beneath his foot and opened the door of his van without a word.

It was a squash for the six of them in the van. Laura was wedged in at the back on a make-shift bench between Sofie and Wouter, their bags shoved under their feet. Every time the van went over a bump, and there were many, they were jolted against the hard metal sides, but no one dared to complain. How Henk was able to drive down the track without headlights was a miracle.

Up ahead they could see the dark shape of the house at the Tongeren crossroads. Sofie felt Laura grip her arm. Even that seemed a long time ago, especially now that Oscar was living in Hilversum. Sofie reminded herself to write to him as soon as she knew where she was going. Who knows, maybe she wouldn't be going back to Berkenhout and could go and help Oscar in his work.

Anything for a normal life again.

Laura must have fallen asleep as she was leaning heavily against Sofie's arm, giving her pins and needles. Sofie shut her eyes and tried to block out the persistent growl of the engine reverberating in her head, but she couldn't sleep.

Kampenveld. She recognised the distinct shape of the church tower in the square which was in darkness. Henk stopped the engine and issued instructions whilst they were still inside the car. They were to hurry across the square to the side door of the church and knock four times. No one was to talk. Silently, Wouter shook Henk's hand, clapped him on the shoulder before gesturing to the others to follow him. Sofie hardly recognised him from the despairing man she'd met only weeks before.

Behind them, they heard Henk drive off. He couldn't risk hanging around. The square was empty. Their shoes clattered on the cobblestones however lightly they walked. It would only take a German to appear from the shadows and it would be over. Sofie held on tightly to Laura's hand, spurred on by the thought.

Tonight, they were lucky. There were no patrols and the streets remained eerily quiet.

Dick and his wife were waiting inside the church for them. He hurried them in and closed the door, before turning on a small light which threw flickering shadows across the cold flagstones. Only then did they all hug each other in relief that the first part of their journey was over. Sofie saw how Wouter and Laura clung to each other just that little bit longer.

Whispering, Dick told that it wouldn't be for long and that

they hoped to move everyone back to Berkenhout within two weeks. Wouter was to stay with the Foppens, who had erected a summerhouse in the garden for the purpose. Sofie felt sorry for the young Jewish couple, who would be staying in the Foppen's attic. At least they had each other. Sofie and Laura were going to stay with Tante Else. Sofie's heart soared at the news, knowing that it meant being back together with Liesbeth.

'Remember, this is not going to be the same as before. The raids are far more frequent now, so you will have to remain indoors at all times. It's a risk none of us can take,' warned Dick.

Sofie didn't care. The prospect of staying at tante Else's with Liesbeth seemed like a holiday. She couldn't wait to see her again.

Chapter 22

The knocking on the door was insistent. Instinctively, Sofie leapt up, but was confused by her surroundings which she hadn't seen in daylight. Sunshine seeped round the edges of the makeshift floral curtains someone must have pulled tightly shut, but hadn't managed a total blackout. There were two mattresses side by side on the wooden floor. Laura still lay on hers, rubbing her eyes.

Hesitantly, Sofie opened the door a crack, then flung it wide when she saw Liesbeth on the other side.

'Shh, go back in,' laughed Liesbeth, pushing past her and closing the door. 'I had no idea. When did you get here?'

'Really late. It was weird because they took us straight here without seeing tante Else or you. Didn't anyone say we were coming?'

'No, you know what it's like. Everyone's so guarded. I've only just found out so I came straight out to see you.' Liesbeth beamed. 'Come on into the kitchen. Tante Else is making breakfast for everyone.'

'Is it safe?' Laura asked, rolling onto her side and stretching.

'As safe as anyone knows. You can just sit there and starve if you prefer,' said Liesbeth, flinging the door open and stepping back out towards the winter sunshine.

The summerhouse was hidden away under some tall pine trees. It was quite invisible if you didn't know it was there. Someone, probably tante Else, had planted shrubs and climbers all the way round so that from the house it just looked liked an untidy part of the garden.

As the three of them walked into the house, Sofie experienced a feeling of intense happiness, a little like the first day of a holiday when you've got it all before you. She knew it wasn't right to feel this way, but she couldn't help letting the worries of the past few weeks melt away. For now, the sun was shining and filled her with a warmth she'd forgotten existed.

Tante Else was busy preparing breakfast and had laid half a dozen places at the kitchen table. Sofie couldn't see anyone else. She was intrigued to see who else was staying, but didn't dare ask.

'I'm sorry I wasn't there to meet you last night, but we had to make sure everyone was placed safely,' said tante Else, pouring coffee into mugs. 'We tried to keep the families together, but even the army tent wasn't big enough in the end, so I brought a couple more back here. I suspect they're still sleeping. It must have been after two by the time we got home.'

'You must be exhausted yourself,' said Sofie, looking for signs of tiredness in tante Else's ruddy face.

'*Ach,* you get used to it,' she said, brushing off Sofie's comment. 'Now, sit down and eat your breakfast. There'll be plenty of work to do after, I can assure you.' She spoke kindly, but Liesbeth pulled a mock serious face in Sofie and Laura's direction, making them both laugh.

'I hope you two can cook because we have a lot of food to prepare to take down to the army tent,' said tante Else.

After a quick breakfast of eggs and warm bread with butter,

the three of them were put to work chopping up potatoes, onions and carrots for soup. Once they had filled three large saucepans and put them onto the stove to simmer, Else allowed them to take a break for coffee.

'It's a shame I haven't got you here all the time. I could do with the extra help,' she said, sinking onto a chair and releasing a sigh. She began telling them about the increasing strain on the system. Worry was etched on her face. 'There are meant to be another forty Jews arriving next week from Rotterdam. I can't see how we can find them places to go, especially now. And the more people there are in the village the harder it'll be to evacuate if it comes to it.'

'Why do they all have to come here? Surely this isn't the only place that is safe,' asked Sofie.

'Safe? Nowhere's safe anymore, dear,' said Else, sadly. 'But you're right, this isn't the only place. The trouble is that Berkenhout's the only one of its kind. Everywhere else, people are doing the best they can and putting them up in their houses, cellars, attics. I fear too many believe our hidden village to be the solution.'

They were interrupted by the two late arrivals creaking down the stairs. Sofie knew the two young men by sight. They hadn't been long in the camp.

'Jaap, Willem, come and join us. Did you sleep alright?' Else welcomed them into their midst and found two more cups for coffee.

'Like a log. It's so nice to sleep on a proper bed for a change,' said Jaap, who looked to be the younger of the two. They were obviously brothers with their spiky fair hair and freckles.

'Though he woke me up as usual with his snoring,' said Willem with a grimace.

'Excuse me. I was woken up by your snoring,' Jaap came back at him, but he said it with good humour.

'Hello Laura. I didn't know you'd be here,' said Willem, who'd been looking at her all the while. Laura blushed.

'Enough chit-chat. We need to get on with today's work. You didn't think this was a holiday, did you?' said Else with a smile. 'Laura, Sofie, go and see to the soup and make sure there's enough water in the pot. Liesbeth, clear these things away.' She looked Jaap and Willem up and down. 'You can help move the boxes ready to go onto the vans.'

They were all busy with their chores when there was a knock at the door. Not the kind of hard rap they'd all grown to dread, but even so, they all froze. Else gestured to them to be quiet and waved the new arrivals up the stairs. Wiping her hands on her apron, she went to open it and found Jan on the other side carrying a lumpy bag.

'Come in quickly. Did anyone see you?' Else shooed him in and closed the door. 'What have you here? Potatoes?'

Jan grabbed the bag from her before she could look inside. 'You'll never guess. Apples!' He proudly pulled out two shiny yellow-green apples and presented her with them. She smiled and ruffled his hair. They never discussed where he got hold of his produce.

'You can come down now. It's only Jan,' Else called up. 'He's brought some apples. We can make them into puree.'

Jan stared at the five of them trooping back into the kitchen. 'Sofie?' he said.

'Surprise, isn't it? It was for us too. We didn't know we were evacuating till late last night. Didn't your dad tell you?'

'No. He doesn't tell me anything these days. Just tells me to stay out of the woods.' Jan pulled a face, looking down at his canvas bag.

'I'll bet that's hard. You spend most of your free time down there, don't you?' said Sofie.

'Mm.' Jan was uncharacteristically quiet on the subject. 'Look, I have to go. I only came to drop these off.'

Else took a few coins from a jar she kept on the shelf above the cooker and pressed them into his hand. 'Now be careful. You don't have to take any risks on our behalf, you know.'

'It's fine and I can get loads more any time you want.' Jan flipped one of the coins before pocketing them.

'He'll go far, that boy,' laughed Willem, after Jan had left.

'Not if he doesn't stop getting into trouble,' said Else, tipping the bag of apples out onto the table and counting them. 'You know it's because of him that you're all here. He was the one who found the American pilot.'

'Well, I think he was really brave to help him. I wouldn't be surprised if there are loads of airmen and others, you know, in the woods just waiting to be caught by the Germans,' said Sofie. 'Anyway, it's no different to helping Jews evacuate.'

'Except Jan is an eleven-year-old boy who's decided he can do it on his own. It'll only take one slip for the Germans to find the village which we've all worked so hard to keep secret,' said Else. 'And why they may well be raiding right now as we speak. Now, we've work to do. Willem, Jaap, let's get those boxes ready.'

Chapter 23

Sofie's holiday feeling wore off quickly and she found herself wondering why she'd been so keen to get away from Berkenhout. She missed the Janssens, especially Corrie, and the predictable rhythm of the day. Only a week before they evacuated, Mr Maarten arranged for the reception hut to double as a schoolroom in the mornings, so that Sofie and Laura could spend time with the young ones. Laura helped teach reading and writing. Sofie used the maths book Oscar had sent via Jan to devise sums which she wrote out on sheets of paper, presenting them like a game. The five children under seven loved their lessons and competed to be the first to finish and get top marks. Sofie had no idea where the children were now and was certain they'd be missing their daily routine.

It was the uncertainty she hated most. No one knew when they might return. There was the constant fear that they'd be found, more so than when they were in the woods. Sometimes three, four times a day there'd be an alert, usually from an informant who would run down the street knocking on doors and shouting '*Razzia!*' Ten minutes later there would be the sound of hobnailed boots marching down the road followed by the banging on doors with the butts of rifles. Every time it happened, the episode of the two German soldiers forcing entry into her house flashed through her like a cold wind. She prayed her parents were safe.

They were yet to receive one of these unwelcome visits, but Else made sure they were drilled in what to do. She got the two boys to rig up a bell system between the house and the summerhouse. The bell was hidden behind a wooden panel by the back door. As soon as there was disturbance out in the road, whoever was nearest would ring the alarm for Sofie, Laura and the boys to get out of the house. After three raids in one night, Else decreed it best that they slept in their clothes, in case they needed a quick escape through the hedge at the back of the garden which faced onto a field.

The raid came at 6pm, just as they were finishing their soup round the kitchen table.

Liesbeth sprung up, grabbed four bowls and spoons which she shoved to the back of the cupboard under the sink. Sofie began to push chairs away from the table but froze at the sickening sound of banging on the door.

Like clockwork, the four young people slipped out quietly through the back and down the garden.

'What business do you have banging on my door like that?' shouted Else through the closed door, buying a little time. Liesbeth stood at the sink, washing two bowls and two spoons.

'Open up, immediately!' came a gruff German voice.

Taking a deep breath, she pulled back the latch and three Germans pushed passed her into the kitchen.

'What are you doing barging into my house like this?' Else shrieked.

'Where is your radio? You must hand it over. Orders,' barked the gruff one.

Else couldn't help laughing in relief. She knew she could deal with this.

'You won't find any radio in this house. We were told to hand them in weeks ago,' she said, telling a half-truth.

The three soldiers clearly didn't believe her and began their search, tossing furniture aside and pulling open drawers and cupboards. Liesbeth stood with her back to them, praying they wouldn't come over.

'Move!' shouted one of them.

Silently, Liesbeth moved aside, her eyes on the floor. Crouching down, his knees cracking, the soldier pulled at the door which stuck, then flew open, causing him to lose his balance. Liesbeth couldn't help letting out a snigger and quickly tried to disguise it with a cough.

'What's this? Crockery under the sink?' he said, regaining his balance.

'Oh, Liesbeth. Have you been hiding the dirty dishes again? I've told you before...' Else jumped in, when she saw what was unfolding. 'She's a little...' Else said to the man, raising her eyes.

Liesbeth knew she must play mute.

'Four bowls, four spoons and two in the drainer. That makes six. So where are the others?' He stood up, stretching, a sneer on his face.

Else pretended not to understand. 'That's all there is. They're part of a set, you can see.'

'Idiot! Where are the four who have been using these bowls?'

'I'm sorry, I didn't explain. My daughter put them under the sink after our last meal and thought I wouldn't notice.' Her explanation sounded less and less plausible.

Liesbeth decided to grin broadly at the man and nodded her head vigorously.

The gruff one, who had been continuing his search, called over to his colleague in German. Else understood him, but didn't let on. They'd decided to continue their search upstairs, gesticulating to Else and Liesbeth to stay where they were.

From below, they could hear the three men stomping around, banging doors and overturning furniture. It was terrifying. Else clung to Liesbeth as they waited for the worst.

'I really hope Willem secured the door properly,' she whispered, her eyes on the ceiling. She'd been told by Piet, the carpenter, that the entrance to the attic through the wardrobe was foolproof, but by the sounds of it, they were determined to find something, someone.

The search seemed to go on for ages, but probably only lasted a couple of minutes before they came stomping downstairs, grim faced.

'Nothing there,' said the gruff one, obviously disappointed. 'You should get that one seen to,' he said, jerking his head in Liesbeth's direction. Liesbeth didn't respond and neither did Else. She just nodded and went to the front door to let them out. Her earlier bravado gone, she just wanted them out before they changed their mind.

They didn't dare speak until they were sure they could no longer hear the boots as the group marched off to another unsuspecting family.

Upstairs, it was chaos. Bedding strewn across the floor,

drawers pulled out, their contents dumped on the floor. But the back of the wardrobe was still intact.

Else stood shaking her head.

* * *

They had to make sure they were better prepared. Else drew up rules and made them practise them at least once a day. Nothing could be left around that might arouse any suspicion and the boys had to keep the wardrobe door closed at all times. And Liesbeth had to remember that she must act dumb whenever there were unexpected visitors.

One evening, after about a week, Dick Foppen came to visit. They all crowded round the kitchen table, eager to hear any news. But there were no plans to move back and only talk of more relocations.

'Else, do you think you have space for another four?' said Dick, frowning.

'Four? I really don't know. My house isn't big and we've already had a raid. It's very risky.'

'You're right, I shouldn't have asked,' he said, with a sigh. 'I'll ask Max and Sara. With Oscar away, they can put up more people.'

'But Oscar only went for three weeks. He'll be back any day soon,' spoke Sofie softly.

Dick focused his eyes on Sofie. 'I don't know about that. I've heard he's doing good work. They're unlikely to let him go.'

Laura squeezed her hand under the table.

'And what about Berkenhout? We can't stay here forever,' Sofie blurted out.

'I don't want to promise anything. Until we can be sure the village won't be discovered…'

'So never then. We may as well resign ourselves to staying here,' she said, quickly looking at each person in turn before settling her gaze on Willem.

'Wouldn't it be safer for us all to go back? It won't be long before one of the so-called safe houses is raided and we'll all be in for it,' said Willem to Dick.

'I wish it were that simple. But just in the time you've been here, the numbers have increased by thirty percent. It's becoming a huge logistical operation to move you all back.'

'You mean there's not enough space, don't you?' said Sofie who was close to tears.

'Not exactly. No, no, there's always space in the woods. Henk can build a few more huts. That's not the problem. You see, it's not just the families pouring in from the north coast. Two more pilots have bailed out near Berkenhout. There's also a Russian looking for refuge and a German defector.'

'Another German defector?' Sofie almost spat. 'None of us are happy that Fritz joined us, so why on earth are you letting another in?'

'How do you know he's not a spy sent to betray us?' piped up Laura, who had been listening to the conversation with wide eyes.

'That's one of the reasons it's taking so long to get you all back. We've had to make extensive checks on the newcomers so we can be certain they have a right to be in the camp.'

'I don't see how that should affect us going back first. Why not send the reliable ones back first to prepare the living quarters, rather than create chaos by everyone arriving at once?' Willem said in a firm voice.

'That's what we've been debating and I'm glad you think it's a good idea. With the increased size, we're looking for new leaders. Would you be prepared to take on the role?' said Dick.

'Me?' said Willem, unable to stop himself from smiling. 'What about the others here? We all know each other well enough by now and can form a committee. What do you all think?'

Chapter 24

Henk examined his stash of *jenever* with a feeling of satisfaction. Plenty there for himself and plenty to use as barter should the need arise. He hoisted a couple of crates onto his shoulder and negotiated the winding steps down into his musty cellar. In addition to *jenever*, he had jars of preserved meat, vegetables and fruit and several bags of flour stacked neatly on shelves for the purpose.

A sharp rap at the door gave him a jolt and he hurriedly pushed the crates into a dark corner before sprinting up the stairs and shutting the cellar door behind him. Again the rap, this time more impatiently.

'Just a minute, I'm coming,' he called out, sure it would be Dieter. Opening up, he found Dieter with another young man in German uniform.

'Can we come in?' said Dieter in a rush, pulling the other man by the sleeve.

Henk frowned, noticing that the man was carrying a small rucksack. 'What's the panic?' he said, arms folded. The three men filled the small hallway, but Henk didn't feel inclined to invite them in. Allowing Dieter to offload his troubles was one thing. They'd come to trust each other, even becoming friends in a way. But this was overstepping the mark.

'Sorry, I should have introduced you. This is Karl. Don't worry. He arrived a couple of weeks ago and...'

'Slow down. Perhaps Karl can speak for himself. Come on,

you'd best come in,' said Henk, sighing, feeling sorry for the young man, who looked barely more than eighteen. 'Sit down,' ordered Henk.

Karl perched stiffly on the edge of the armchair, turning his cap over and over in his hands. 'I was never cut out to be a soldier, all that talk of killing the enemy. I wouldn't be able to shoot a man but that's what's expected of you. I didn't know where to turn till I met Dieter. He said you'd be able to help.'

'Did he now?' Henk liked what he was hearing less and less.

Karl let his gaze dart round the gloomy room. 'I can't go back. Is there somewhere I can stay, only till I can work out what to do next?'

'Dieter, what have you promised? You know I can't possibly hide a German here. What if your people found out? I'd be shot. No, I'm very sorry, Karl, but you'll have to find another solution.'

It was an impossible dilemma. It would have been so easy to say he'd take him in. Hide him in the small attic space above the kitchen. Hardly anyone came visiting after the first few times, except for Dieter and the occasional call from Dick or one of the group. He'd learned to keep the patrolling Germans at arms length whilst keeping them sweet with the occasional bribe.

Dieter seemed to second guess his thoughts. 'I swear I won't tell anyone. You know you can trust me,' he pleaded.

Henk shook his head. 'And what happens when they realise he's gone missing. The first thing they'll do is search anyone living in the woods.'

Dieter stood up abruptly, his face contorted with emotion. 'I thought I could rely on you. Who else can we turn to?' He made for the door, nodding at Karl, who looked desperate.

'Wait. Alright, one night, but that's all. And he can't stay in the house. I'll show you the woodshed out the back. There's not a lot of space in there to sleep, but it is warm.'

Henk went to unlock the back door, checking there was no one about and led the two young men out into the cold night and down to the tiny shed he'd built and covered with moss. Inside, a resinous scent wafted from the logs, stacked in piles. Telling them to wait, he shifted some logs about to make a space on the floor, then pushed open the little window at the back.

'I take it you won't be wanting a bed for the night?' he asked Dieter sarcastically. 'Come, Karl. You sleep there. I'll come and get you in the morning.'

'Thank you, sir. I'm very grateful.' Karl held out his right hand.

Grim-faced, Henk remained at the door and nodded.

Back inside the cottage, Henk turned on Dieter. 'You are going to have to sort this one out.' He jabbed his finger as he spoke.

'I…will. Give me a couple of days. No, wait!' Dieter lifted his hands to fend off Henk, whose face shone dark red in the low light. 'I need to get back now otherwise they'll be suspicious. It's getting late and the rest will be getting back from their patrol.'

'And how are you going to explain that you're arriving back without Karl?'

Dieter looked uncomfortable. 'I'm hoping they won't notice. There's lots of us coming and going and it's pretty crowded in camp.'

'You know I'm not happy about this. One night. That's it.'

Henk marched to the front door and let Dieter out without another word.

Despite his fury, he grabbed a half drunk bottle of *jenever* and went to check on Karl. Pushing open the shed door, he peered inside. Karl was already asleep, curled up with his head resting on his rucksack. Henk left the bottle just inside the door and left.

***

Every time he fell asleep, he was wrenched awake by thoughts of loud thumping on the door. Already nervous at the prospect of being found out for his part in the evacuation of Berkenhout, he found it impossible even to doze off. By daybreak, he was so exhausted that he fell into a deep sleep. But as soon as he woke, he was filled with dread that he was about to be found out. Karl had to go and the only solution was for Henk to get him as far away as possible. With a heavy heart, he went to fetch him.

Karl looked even more scared than when Henk had left him. The young man scrambled to his feet, clutching his bag to him. 'You won't make me go back, will you?'

'No. But we have to leave. Now.' Henk was in no mood for explanations.

Once they were rattling along the track with Karl hidden in the back, Henk began to breathe more easily. This was no different to transporting people to and from Berkenhout, he told himself. Except this was the first time he had a German defector in the back.

It was still barely light and the woods were peaceful. Just the occasional squirrel darting across the rutted track with its wavy red tail streaking out behind.

'Are you alright back there?' Henk cocked his ear, but there was silence from the back of the van. He'd piled in some empty sacks and crates which did a good job of concealing Karl.

As they emerged from the trees, they joined the road lined with green pastures and dotted with the occasional farmhouse. With a sigh, Henk let his shoulders relax. 'We're out of the woods now. I'm taking you to someone who can help you better than I can. I believe he's helped other German soldiers escape, but I want you to promise that if you change your mind or get caught you will not say a word that I helped you.'

Karl didn't answer. Henk wondered if he was asleep or had passed out under the sacking.

'Hey, you. I'm talking to you.'

'I heard. This person, he won't send me back, will he?' Karl said in a quavering voice.

'I told you, he'll help you, but I have no idea how. I don't get involved once I...I don't get involved,' he said, before letting slip too much. He didn't really believe this Karl was capable of betraying him.

They entered Kampenveld and drove up to the roadblock which was unmanned today.

'Lucky, none of your lot are out yet,' said Henk, keeping his eyes on the road ahead. They wouldn't have taken much notice of him anyway as he often passed through two or three times a day, always with a cheery wave and smile at the soldiers on duty. Every time he went to Dick's, he'd take a different route, never parking too close to his house. Today, he parked down a narrow lane with only the occasional house on either side.

'Stay here and don't move. I'm going to tell him you're here.' Looking around to make sure no one was about, Henk got out and closed the van door quietly. The lane was deserted. He quickly walked down the alley that led to the back of Dick's garden.

'Hello, Henk. What brings you here so early?' Dick frowned, as he looked up from the vegetable patch he was digging.

'Can we go inside?' Henk just wanted to get this over with and get back home.

'What's up? You look anxious,' said Dick, throwing his gloves down on the table inside the front door.

'I've brought someone. He's in the van. He mustn't be seen. I'm hoping you can find him somewhere to go.'

'Now, look here. You know I can't take any more on. Haven't you heard? I'm taking deserving people in every day and every available cellar and attic is taken.'

Dick sounded resigned, but Henk had heard him talk this way before. Eventually, he'd find a place for everyone, but Karl wasn't everyone. Karl was German.

'I appreciate your problem, but I can't have him with me. Just imagine what would happen if I got found hiding someone. That'd be the end of Berkenhout.'

'Come, come. Don't be so dramatic. Tell me who this person

is and where you found him.' Dick seemed to be calming down. Henk decided to take his chance and tell him it straight.

Dick blew out his cheeks. 'Well. This is most irregular. Most irregular. Young man, is he? Based outside Kampenveld? Sounds as if he might have been set up.'

'No, I'm absolutely sure he hasn't. Last night, he was panicking and in no mood to go back to his camp. I let him sleep in my wood shed, but I can't have him there for longer.'

'Fetch him. But make sure you're not seen.'

Henk nodded and left. As he walked back down the alley, an elderly man walking slowly with the aid of a stick shuffled towards him. When he saw Henk, he stopped in greeting. Henk nodded, but the man seemed intent on having a conversation.

'Such a lovely day, isn't it?'

'Mm, very nice.' Henk hadn't noticed the sun had come out and fidgeted from foot to foot.

'Are you visiting someone? I don't think I've seen you round these parts.' The man peered at Henk.

'Just calling on a friend.' Henk thought he'd better smile in case the man didn't believe him.

'That's nice. I don't get many visitors these days. All my friends have died.' The man tried to laugh, but ended up coughing. 'Oh well, I must be going. I hope to bump into you again.'

'Yes, me too,' lied Henk.

The man hobbled off in the direction of Dick's house. Was he an acquaintance of Dick? Henk didn't want to risk asking.

He unlocked the back door of the van and had to pull away the sacks to see Karl who was cowering in the corner.

'Come on, move. I haven't got all day,' said Henk, irritated that he'd been in such a hurry to leave that he hadn't thought that Karl was still wearing his SS uniform. 'Take your stupid hat off at least. Do you want anyone to recognise you?'

'Just a minute. I've got some clothes in my bag.' Karl rummaged in his rucksack and brought out a dark brown sweater.

'Good man. At least someone's got a brain round here,' said Henk in a moment of rare generosity. 'The house isn't far from here, but don't say anything if we meet anyone. Leave any talking to me.'

Karl nodded and scrambled out of the back of the van, his knees buckling slightly after the cramped conditions.

Halfway down the alley, Henk saw the old man shuffling back in his direction. Henk made to touch his cap, hoping that would be sufficient, but the man stopped to lean on his stick.

'Good morning again. Is this another friend?'

'My friend's son. I thought I'd walk down with him,' said Henk, knowing his answer sounded lame. He bowed his head and continued walking.

'Who's that old man I've now met twice in your alley?' asked Henk, before he'd even introduced Karl.

'Nosey old man, wanted to stop you for a chat? Does that with everyone. He's harmless, but I've warned him on more than one occasion to watch who he talks to. He never listens, though.'

'Will he talk?'

'Adriaan? No, no he wouldn't. I call on him from time to time to check how he is and sound him out, but I'm not worried. Now, this one I am worried about.' Dick waited for Henk to be introduced to Karl.

'I'm Karl, sir. I'm ever so grateful,' began Karl.

'You speak good Dutch. That helps. Where did you learn it?'

'My family lives just over the border and we used to come and visit my aunt and uncle in Nijmegen. They refused to speak German, so that's how I learnt Dutch.'

Dick listened as Karl told him about how his aunt and uncle had instilled a hatred of the Nazis leading to his decision to defect. His aunt Sigrid's best friend turned up one day at her house with a box full of jewellery and silverware. She'd been frightened that if she and her family were ever to be arrested, the Germans would look for her family heirlooms. She was, of course, right. She, her husband and two young girls disappeared one night and Sigrid never found out what happened to them. But she stashed her friend's valuables under the floorboards in the hope that one day they would return.

'How could I be one of those monsters knowing what they were up to? But I did, forced by my father who was convinced I'd get arrested if I didn't join. There wasn't really a choice. But I soon saw the way being a soldier changes people who accept orders and do stuff even though they must know it's morally wrong.' He tailed off and gazed expectantly at Dick who looked pensive.

'I only take on young men if they can show themselves to be of use. What skills do you have?'

'I'm a trained sports teacher and know a lot about doing exercises to keep fit,' he said with a hopeful look on his face.

'Can you teach anything else? I'm not sure PE is the thing on most people's minds right now.'

Karl shook his head. 'I suppose not. But I've seen how it cheers people up. Doing drills helps take your mind off things and the fitter you are, the more able you are to cope with life.'

Dick looked pensive. 'Listen. I have space in my attic where you can stay till I decide what to do with you. You'll have to put up with being in there with eight others and two are young ones who cry a lot.'

'Anything's better than fighting.' Karl said, his voice suddenly loud.

'It can only be temporary, though, till I think what to do with you. Don't worry, I won't have you sent back, but now you've defected you'll have to remain in hiding as long as this war is on. I'll show you upstairs. Can you wait a moment, Henk?'

Henk just wanted to leave, but something in Dick's voice made him nod his head. As he waited, he mulled over what it could be that Dick wanted to talk to him about. Eight people in his attic, and now nine with Karl. Was the whole Berkenhout operation about to collapse? He looked up at the sound of Dick's footsteps on the stairs.

'Those people up there.' He jerked his head in the direction of the attic. 'You've probably guessed. They're from Berkenhout. No idea how long for, but there's no way the operation can take on any newcomers.'

'How long till they can go back?'

'No one knows. It depends on what happens in the woods and if they step up the *razzias* in Kampenveld. The *moffen* think they're onto something at last and won't leave a stone unturned till they have proof. You, me and everyone involved in Berkenhout need to keep our noses clean. You do understand, don't you?'

'Of course. I'll keep a watch on the woods and report anything suspicious back to you.' Henk drew himself up, pleased to be included as one of the gang.

'That's what I was hoping you'd say. We need all the support we can muster.' Dick clapped Henk on the shoulder as he steered him towards the door. 'Now, I have to get on with dealing with this lot.' He smiled for the first time, jerking his head towards the attic.

Henk walked quickly back to his van with a spring in his step.

Chapter 25

Jan was bored. Nico had lost interest in their little enterprise and inexplicably only wanted to sit around at home reading books or tinkering with his bike. Jan suspected that his parents didn't want him wandering off into the woods either. He thought about Lex, but it wouldn't have been any fun just hanging around with him, although he was still useful whenever he needed to steal vegetables. Mostly Jan wandered around by himself, keeping a watch on what was happening. You never knew what you might see.

If only he was Oscar's age, then he could escape to Hilversum too and do some proper useful work. Oscar wasn't allowed to say anything in letters home, but Jan reckoned he had a pretty good idea. His parents refused to comment on Oscar's work so he'd been forced to crouch at the top of the stairs late at night and listen to their conversation. They'd said something about identity papers and coupons. That could only mean Oscar was involved in producing fakes or distributing them.

There'd be no point asking his father. 'You're far too young' or 'It's not safe', he'd say. And he didn't want to worry his mum. She had enough on her plate, what with father disappearing off for days without saying where he was going and Oscar away in Hilversum.

He needed to go to his den to think. He might even take Lex with him. Shame about Nico. He'd be game, he knew it.

Jan grabbed a few cookies from the jar and stuffed them into a greaseproof bag and down the pocket of his shorts. Didn't matter if they got a bit crumbly on the way. He preferred them like that.

He called out of the window to his mum, who was pulling carrots in the garden. 'Back for lunch!' he shouted and didn't wait for her reply. Why couldn't his father trust him like she did?

He sniffed the early morning air as he pulled the door behind him, full of anticipation of returning to his beloved woods.

Nico was hunched over his bike, polishing it up or something.

'Hi! What are you up to?' Jan sidled up to him.

'Can't you see, idiot? Got a puncture,' said Nico, without looking up. The tyre looked a mess from all the times it had been patched up. But no one could buy new inner tubes any more, not since the Germans requisitioned all spare parts for themselves.

'Here, let me have a go,' said Jan, who started pumping up the tyre and putting his ear close to it until he heard a hissing noise. 'There you go, just there,' he stuck his finger on where he thought the hole was. Nico pressed the patch he'd been holding onto the spot and kept it firm for a minute or two, before applying another patch.

'You need to ride it. See if it holds. I'll walk along with you,' said Jan, a plan forming in his mind.

Nico glanced from the house to his bike. 'OK, but I shouldn't be too long.' He began to wheel it onto the road before tentatively mounting it. Jan ran alongside looking at the tyre. 'It's fine, but we need to put more weight on it to see if it holds.' And he hopped on the back, with his legs swinging out to the side.

'Hey, get off,' shouted Nico, not really meaning it as they headed down the road in the direction of the path at the edge of the woods.

'Let's go and see our den. See if it's still intact,' said Jan from behind.

'I can't be gone long…'

'You don't need to be, not with the bike.'

It felt good being out in the woods again, just the two of them with no one about. Jan wished he'd brought his own bike as it was getting uncomfortable hanging on the back, but it would do.

Shafts of sunlight shot through the bare tops of the trees creating a dappled effect on the path ahead. The only sound was Nico's bike swishing along and the occasional crack as it went over last autumn's husks. Further in, the wood grew denser with tall beech trees crowding out most of the daylight. That meant they were near the crossroads where they would need to leave the bike and carry on by foot.

'Look, no dog,' said Jan, jumping off the back. He bounced on the spot to get the feeling back in his legs. He marched up to the door of the cottage and knocked. A loud barking started up from inside.

'What are you doing?' said Nico, examining his tyres for any further damage.

The door opened with a creak and the old man who lived there poked his head round. His face cracked into a wrinkly smile when he saw who it was.

'Can we leave the bike round the back, please? We're going foraging in the wood', said Jan.

'Wait,' said the old man, who was restraining his dog by the collar. He shut the door and they could hear him remonstrate with the dog, before opening it wider to let them in.

'We don't get many visitors now,' he beamed. 'Please come in. What are you doing over this way?'

'Just out for a ride. It's such a nice morning,' said Jan, adjusting his eyes to the gloomy interior which belied the perfect sunny day outside.

'I've got some lemonade somewhere. Sit down, sit,' he said, first to the boys and then the dog, who was growling and eyeing them up suspiciously. The man shuffled over to the ancient dark brown dresser and fiddled two glasses onto a tray, encrusted with something that didn't look too savoury, then poured some clear liquid from a bottle.

Nico shot Jan a look as if to say: 'What are you playing at?'

The glasses clinked against each other as he shakily placed the tray on the low table which was covered with books and old journals. Jan leaned forward and grabbed the glasses before they toppled over and, with a stare, handed one to Nico.

'Thank you, it's very refreshing,' said Jan taking a sip. The lemonade wasn't as bad as he was expecting.

The old man chuckled loudly. 'If I tell you where it came from, you wouldn't believe me,' he said, willing them to guess.

'Tante Else?' said Jan, although he thought it unlikely. Lemonade hadn't been seen in the shops for months.

'No, a visitor brought a crate,' said the man mysteriously.

'Anyone we know?' said Nico, starting to get irritated with this game.

'I don't think so,' said Jan, pausing theatrically. 'A German!'

Jan and Nico clunked down their glasses simultaneously.

The old man's face clouded over as he told them how he missed the daily comings and goings of the Berkenhout people fetching water from the pump. 'They knew when it was safe to fill up their containers because I'd make sure the rag was hanging from the tree. But then they stopped and no one told me what was going on. Not even Hauer. He seemed to disappear too. Then one morning came the bang on the door and there stood a German soldier, really no more than a boy, asking if he could use the pump. I was so taken aback him asking, that I just stood there with my mouth open and Fido barking and all. He didn't get angry, not like the others, but started up a conversation about my garden and how nice it looked.

'It was like he was waiting to be asked in, but I didn't want that. He might have turned nasty. So I said of course he could use the pump, any time he wanted. I watched as he scooped up great handfuls of water and rubbed it all over his face. He reminded me of my brother's boy, so I invited him to rest on the bench under the apple tree, which he accepted. You know, they're just like us.' He stopped a moment and scrutinised the boys' intent faces.

Continuing, he said: 'He came back the next day, very polite he was, always knocking on the door before using the pump. And I liked sitting on the bench with him, listening to him, though I was still careful not to tell him anything about me. He's from just over the border in Münchengladbach. His parents were best friends with a Dutch family, but daren't keep in contact now. They're just as likely to be hauled off by the Germans as any of us are if we betray them.

Crazy, just crazy.' He was staring into the distance and seemed to forget the two boys.

'Does he still visit?' asked Jan, curious to know if he was a threat.

'No, he got moved off down to Apeldoorn, just last week. Just before he left he came in a German truck and pulled up right outside. It gave me a shock. He normally turned up on foot. It was because he had these two crates of lemonade he wanted to give me.' His face broke into a smile. 'A thank you for listening to him and being sympathetic. Truth be told, I felt a bit embarrassed, because that's all I did, listen to him. But the boy was so homesick and no one in his regiment would have understood, he told me.'

'How did he get hold of bottles of lemonade?' asked Nico.

'I thought it best not to ask, but I think it showed his contempt of his own people and what they've been doing to us.'

Jan suddenly stood up. 'We've got to go now.'

'Oh, please come and see me again, won't you?' The old man looked crestfallen.

'We'll try, but we're not really allowed in the woods these days, though it seems really quiet,' said Jan.

'There aren't many of them now the regiment have moved on. I don't think they can have found Berkenhout, else I would have heard.'

'The camp was cleared a couple of weeks ago now and everyone's scattered across Kampenveld. Some are still in the woods where the big army tent is. We're thinking of going to visit, aren't we, Nico?' said Jan, the idea only just coming to him.

'Well, I hope the Berkenhout lot'll be back. The Germans don't really bother that much with the woods. It scares them that they might get ambushed. At least that's what my Ger..., the German soldier told me.'

He followed them outside, told them where the best blueberry bushes were and waved them off as they followed the overgrown track away from the cottage.

'He seemed a bit friendly towards that German, don't you think?' said Nico, thrashing the weeds away from the path with a large stick he'd picked up.

'He's harmless. But now we know the Germans aren't swarming around the woods, that's good news for us. Means we can start using the den again,' said Jan with a chuckle.

It turned out to be a disappointment. Full of debris and not even any signs of the logs they'd dragged in for seats.

'I reckon Hauer's done that,' said Jan, kicking away some twigs where the logs had been. 'Come on, let's go down to Berkenhout and see what's going on there.'

'I should be getting back. I haven't even told my mum I was going off,' said Nico anxiously.

'Won't take long, then we can race back on your bike. Here, want a cookie?' Jan pulled the crumpled bag out of his pocket. 'Oh, have some crumbs. Taste just as good.' He began stuffing broken bits into his mouth, then handed the bag with the remainder to Nico.

'Thanks, but no thanks,' said Nico, stomping off ahead. A little way ahead, he stopped and lifted his head with a sniff. 'What's that? I thought there was no one over at Berkenhout?'

Jan smelled it too. It was woodsmoke and came from the direction of the village. 'Over there,' he whispered, pointing at one of the underground huts. The foliage and branches that usually hid the entrance had been pulled aside and a tiny wisp of smoke was just visible escaping from the chimney. Jan waved Nico to hang back, whilst he crept forward and tried to peer through the entrance, but the gloomy interior made it impossible to see anything within.

The sound of a single click had the two boys frozen in their tracks. They squeezed themselves back through the undergrowth that formed a rough edge around the perimeter and waited.

A bearded man dressed in shabby dirty overalls emerged from the hut, a pistol in his hand. He squinted his eyes as he scanned the camp, but stayed in front of the hut.

Jan's heart was thumping so loudly he was scared the man would hear it. He desperately wanted to shout out, but didn't dare. Neither did he dare tell Nico what he knew. Then Nico lost his balance, making a snapping noise as he sat back suddenly onto a load of twigs and dead leaves. Jan couldn't help himself from thumping him.

'God save the President! Show yourself or I'll shoot!' cried the pilot, pointing the gun in the direction of their bushes.

'It's me, Jan, the Dutch boy. Don't you remember?' Jan peered through the foliage, but didn't dare come out yet.

Donald laughed and dropped his gun hand to his side. 'I've been waiting ages for that food you said you'd bring me and now you spring a surprise on me.'

He tossed his gun back into the hut and pulled out a packet of cigarettes. This time he didn't offer Jan one.

'I came back but you'd gone, so what was I supposed to do?' Jan said, indignantly.

'I had to get out of there quick after I heard a truck come stormin' down the track. Those guys looked as if they meant business. I thought I'd find my way back but got confused in the woods. I couldn't find my way back to the path for ages and when I did I came out at a completely different place down by the cross-roads.'

'Oh, where the cottage is with the pump outside,' said Jan.

'Yeah, that's right. If it hadn't been for the man living there, I don't know what would've happened. He put me up for a few nights then came up with the idea that I should come down here. I was expecting to find loads of people living here, but that obviously didn't happen,' he laughed, clearly unperturbed by the turn of events.

'You can't just stay here. It's trespassing,' Jan said, making Donald laugh even louder.

'I would have asked permission, except there was no one here to do so. Fortunately, whoever was living here left some food and with my trips down to the pump, I've been doing just fine.' He examined the cigarette stub, then took a last drag before squashing it under his heel. 'Any idea where everyone's gone?' he asked carelessly.

Jan exchanged a quick glance with Nico before answering. Probably no harm in telling him. 'They stopped me when I came back looking for you. Quizzed me and made me go to the spot where I said I'd found the cigarettes. I didn't say I'd seen you, but I don't think they believed me. That's why they were all moved out of the village, 'cos they thought the Germans would come looking.'

'Old Hendrik said there were eighty of them living here. That must have been quite some manoeuvre getting them out of here. Where are they all now?'

'Scattered all over. Some are still in the woods, deeper in, where someone's put up an army tent. Others are with families in Kampenveld.'

'Any idea when they'll be coming back? Stocks are running a bit low now, y'see.' His laugh turned into a cough.

'No one tells us anything. I got the blame for all this anyway. We're not really meant to be in the woods now.' Jan turned to Nico and quickly explained what they'd been discussing, reassuring him that they'd be heading back now.

'I'll see what I can find out and come back as soon as I can,' Jan told Donald.

'Try and bring some proper food for me this time, will you? I'm getting fed up with boiled potatoes.' That coughing laugh again.

'Promise you'll still be here?' Jan furrowed his forehead.

Donald clapped him on the back, nodding vigorously.

Delighted he'd found his pilot, Jan couldn't wait to get back home. He might even tell his mother, though was apprehensive that she'd tell his father. Nico was just pleased to get out of the woods.

Chapter 26

Sara was a lot less sympathetic this time and insisted that Jan tell his father about Donald. But first they had to wait for him to come home from Kampenveld, where he must have been visiting Fanny again. At least that's where she thought he was, for whenever she asked him, he just snapped at her, so she'd taken to saying nothing.

It was six o'clock, when finally a key could be heard in the lock. Jan had been on tenterhooks, rehearsing in his mind what he intended to say.

'All well?' said Max, removing his jacket and hanging it on his peg in the middle of the coat rack. He had a bag with him, pulled out a bottle of lemonade and plonked it on the kitchen table. Jan thought his heart would jump out of his chest.

'Sara, fetch some glasses. Let's enjoy a drink together,' said Max, with a rare smile on his face.

'I haven't seen any of this for about two years, Max. Where did you get it?' said Sara, pouring the cloudy liquid into three glasses.

Max tapped the side of his nose and Sara knew better than to quiz him further. At least it was lemonade and not something stronger, though there were times when he returned that she wondered if he'd been on the bottle. 'If you like it, there's more where this came from. But don't tell anyone else, or they'll all be wanting some.' He made himself comfortable in his armchair by the stove and proceeded to ask them about their day.

'Jan has some news for you,' said Sara, folding her arms.

Jan stood in front of his father, his eyes on the floor. 'Erm...I', he began.

'He's found the pilot. The American.' Sara sighed.

'Where? Not in the woods again?' said Max, straightening up in his seat.

'Donald's, he's, the same pilot I came across, you know, when I got stopped by those soldiers and...'

'Look, I'm not going to ask what you were doing in the woods for now, but that was over two weeks ago. Where has he been all this time?'

'He got lost, then stayed with old Mr Hendrik who sent him down to Berkenhout. That's where we saw him.'

'But there's no one there.' Max furrowed his brow.

'He's been staying in one of the underground huts and I suppose waiting for someone to turn up. He's got a gun, you know.' Jan flinched, wishing he hadn't let that slip out.

'Jan! He could have killed you! I've told you about wandering off along like that. Max, what are we to do with this boy?'

'Later, dear. What did you tell him about the village?'

Jan felt uncomfortable under his father's hard stare. 'He knew all about it. That they'd all been moved out. Mr Hendrik told him. Father, we need to help him. He's got hardly anything to eat. Can't we have him here?'

'Absolutely not. It's far too much work and worry for your mother. He's better off where he is.'

Jan thought his mother shook her head ever so slightly, but she didn't say anything.

'I'll see if I can organise someone to take him supplies,' his father carried on.

'I can, father. Will you let me?' Jan pleaded. Donald was his pilot and he didn't want to let him go.

'Jan, I want you to stay away, for your own safety. We've managed to send those Germans on a false trail but it took a lot of doing. Now, some good news,' he stood up, rubbing his hands together. 'Oscar's coming home.'

'That's wonderful news!' Sara hugged Max and beckoned Jan over, but he was in no mood for celebration. Let them be pleased about Oscar and then maybe they'd stop going on at him.

***

Oscar was back with a bag full of food and clothing coupons which he kept locked away in a drawer in his room. Not that the clothing coupons were much use, with hardly anything to buy in the shops. Still, they had some value and could even be used as barter should things get worse. But when his father wanted to take the whole lot off him saying they could be distributed by the network, Oscar refused. They ended up rowing, with Jan listening from his crouching place at the top of the stairs, but Oscar got his way. No longer the timid schoolboy who never stood up to his father, Oscar had become a different person in Jan's eyes.

Later, after his father had left the house, Jan went and knocked on Oscar's door. Before, Jan would have leapt on the bed and jumped up and down, but he wanted Oscar to think that he was more grown up than that. He found Oscar sitting at his old desk, scribbling away in a notebook, which he quickly closed when he saw Jan at the door.

'Why did you come home then?'

'Oh, just for a short holiday. Thought I'd come and see you lot while I can.' Oscar stretched back in this chair and surveyed Jan. 'You've grown. And you're more skinny.'

Jan immediately pulled himself up taller. 'I'm eleven now. You know, it's dead boring with you away from home now. Father's hardly around either, so it's just me and Mum. Not that I mind, but they don't let me go off with Nico and Lex like they used to.' He sat on the edge of the bed and tested it out for bounce.

'I'm not really surprised. There are a lot more Germans on the streets now and probably in the woods too.'

'Don't you have to hide?'

'Probably,' he yawned. 'I'll stick myself up in the attic if anyone comes knocking.'

Jan wished he could be that relaxed.

'Now tell me about your latest pilot. We should get him over here, don't you think?'

Jan's face broke into a smile. 'I want him too, but father won't let us. I don't see why not. It worked fine with Nigel...'

'Maybe he didn't like it that mother got so friendly with him,' Oscar laughed.

'Wasn't that because he was English?' Jan didn't want to admit he hadn't noticed, but then why would he? He'd just been pleased his mother had taken his side. Then he remembered the letter she'd received about a month after Nigel had gone. How grateful he'd been for their kindness and a promise to come back and visit after the war. Maybe she had seemed a lot more cheerful than normal, but Jan imagined that to be perfectly normal. He thought back to his father's reaction when he'd asked if Donald could be hidden. Now it seemed to make sense.

'I tell you what. Why don't you offer to help Donald? Father's more likely to listen to you than me. You might even be able to persuade him it's a good idea to get him over here,' said Jan, eagerly.

'Why tell father?' Oscar was gazing out of the window, miles away, then turned to Jan and smiled.

Why tell him, indeed.

Chapter 27

Since returning home, Jan noticed Oscar's new-found confidence. Jan now had an ally, so if they were found out Jan wouldn't have to take all the blame. He didn't need Nico or Lex now. He and Oscar were in this together. Jan hesitated before telling Oscar about his plan to rescue even more pilots, just in case he changed his mind. Best get Donald sorted first.

Donald hadn't seemed surprised at all when Jan turned up with Oscar. They'd each brought two large bags of provisions, enough to last him several days until the next part of the plan, to bring him back home with them.

Which is where it all went wrong. Oscar fell into an argument with Donald when he told him he'd be safer coming back home with them.

'You can stay in our attic for the time being. We've already had one pilot and our father arranged for his safe exit back to England,' said Oscar, after the introductions had been made.

'Count me out. I'd rather stay here. The Germans don't come this far in. I reckon it's a lot safer here than hiding back in those woods. You're the only people I've seen since I got here. Why put myself at greater risk?' His eyes flicked from one to the other as if wanting reassurance.

'Don't you want to go home to America?' said Oscar with an exasperated sigh.

'No chance of that. I never heard of any airmen who made it

home in one piece. As long as the war's on, I'm staying here.' He fished around in the bags, pulling out the packages. 'Any cigarettes?'

'No. No one smokes at home,' said Oscar curtly. He was fed up with the arrogance of this man. 'You can't stay here. It's for the Jews.'

'But they're not here, are they?' said Donald, pretending to look around for them. 'Look, can you get hold of some cigarettes next time you come?' Donald opened up a greaseproof package and took a sniff, then returned it into the bag.

'Didn't you hear what I said? We don't smoke in our house. Come on Jan.'

Jan didn't want them to go just yet. Besides, he thought he heard something, but couldn't be sure.

'Can you make us some tea first, as we've come all this way? We've brought some. Here.' He extracted a twist of paper and held it out to Donald who gave a funny snort.

'Jan, what are you doing?' said Oscar from the opening of the hut.

'You heard what Donald said. He hasn't had any visitors. We're visitors so we should stay awhile.'

'That's my boy!' joked Donald, slapping Jan on the back. 'Great idea. I just need to find something to boil some water in.' He picked up the milk can and shook it. The sloshing sound told them it was almost empty. 'Sorry guys. Out of water. You wouldn't like to accompany me down to the pump?'

'I thought you didn't want to go back into the woods.' Oscar kicked at an imaginary stone, a look of disdain on his face.

'You're right, but now you're here…' He pulled on his jacket and, pushing past Oscar, strode out of the hut, the milk can swinging from side to side. Jan skipped alongside. Oscar reluctantly followed.

They only made it to the edge of the path when the huge roar of an engine rent the air. The van must have been hidden in the bushes and seemed to rear up out of nowhere. Thinking they were about to be mown down, Jan jumped into the undergrowth, but the van skidded to an abrupt halt alongside them and two German soldiers sprung out, shouting: '*Halt! Hände hoch!*'

This time, there was no pretending what they were doing. Donald's uniform and the milk can gave them away. Jan immediately recognised them and desperately hoped they wouldn't remember him. Too late.

'*Ach so!* The little Dutch boy. With his American pilot this time. And who is this?' The soldier poked Oscar with the butt of his rifle.

Oscar wasn't having any and tried to grab the rifle, shouting: 'Leave off. I've done nothing.' Jan was impressed at his bravado and hoped he'd say something to make them go away. But Oscar's action riled the soldier who grabbed his arm, thrusting his face right up close. 'Don't fool around with me. Unless you want to get shot,' he said, spitting out the words. Oscar jerked his head so he wouldn't have to look into the glowering face, but desisted from saying anything back.

The Dutch-German soldier turned his attention to Jan, who had been looking around for an escape. But he had the sense to realise that even if he did manage to outrun them, they could gun him down in a flash. He was particularly nervous about the other soldier whose cold blue eyes seemed to bore into his head and read his thoughts.

'So, you will now show us where your pilot has been hiding?' the Dutch-German one commanded. He was staring at the milk can.

Jan needed to think fast. He knew he mustn't lead them back to Berkenhout. He looked at Donald who was watching, uncomprehending. 'He's asking where you've been hiding,' Jan made sure his eyes didn't flick back in the direction they'd come.

'Tell him I got lost and I've been sleeping rough.' He rubbed his bristly chin as if to make the point.

'And you two have been helping him,' the Dutch soldier replied to Jan, with satisfaction.

Jan and Oscar stayed silent. There'd been no time to corroborate their stories and both knew they were in danger of slipping up. However, their silence just made the two start shouting in German again.

'I'm going to tell them the truth,' said Donald at last.

'What? You can't. You'll wreck it for all of us,' Jan implored.

'It's over. Don't you see?' His voice rose in agitation.

Jan was furious to see Donald give up so easily. Where was the bravado he'd so admired when he first came across Donald and been offered those cigarettes? Maybe that's what he wanted.

'What is he saying?' said the Dutch-German to Jan.

'He wanted me to ask you if you have any cigarettes,' said Jan, in desperation. 'Do you?'

The soldier barked a short laugh and spat on the floor, before fishing in his pocket for a packet. 'Here. Take one.' He shook the packet in front of Donald's face. Donald tentatively took one and waited for the soldier to light it.

'Thank you. I needed that.' Donald sucked on the cigarette whilst the others watched him.

'Now any other requests before we go?' the Dutch-German smirked.

Oscar gave Jan a warning look.

The other soldier walked back to the van and opened the back doors. Jan couldn't see what he was doing but he seemed to be shifting stuff around. There was a click and when he turned round, Jan saw the rifle pointing straight at them.

Chapter 28

The van shook and shuddered as it jumped over the ruts in the track. In the back it was pitch black, stifling hot and horribly cramped. Surely they must be out of the woods by now? Perhaps they'd taken a wrong turn and got lost, but the bragging tone of the two voices from the front suggested they knew exactly where they were heading.

The three of them were pressed close together, but didn't dare breathe a word, even when the scrawny one shouted out commands every so often. Oscar must be able to understand him. He'd done German at school, but he knew better than to answer.

The van made a sudden jolt, before settling into a smooth rhythm after it took a right turn. The main road. Jan searched the map he'd laid out in his mind and worked out that they must now be heading south. South? Where on earth could that lead to?

If only there was a window they could open. It wasn't so much the darkness, but the feeling that they'd breathed in all the air and there was none left. A minute sliver of light was visible in the partition. Jan traced his finger along it to see if he could force it open a fraction more. It didn't budge. He placed his nose right up to it to suck in air from the front cabin. A thump on the partition sent him flying back with a shock.

Laughter from the front. Oscar grabbed Jan's arm roughly. Jan heard Donald sigh and began worrying again that there'd be no air left for the rest of them.

Eventually, the thick atmosphere sent Jan into a half sleep where he was back in the woods climbing into the cabin of a large army tank. There was no one about but he knew he'd have to get this beast out of here before the Germans turned up. Faced with a panel of knobs and buttons, he began pressing them randomly until the machine roared into life and slowly rolled down the track. Spurred on by screaming voices behind him, he somehow found an accelerator pedal and took off, but couldn't see a thing in front of him. All he had to do was steer a path through the trees, but if he couldn't see them? His heart banged like a drum as the tank rolled along, swerving with a life of its own. Where was everyone? He tried to remember if Oscar and Sofie had climbed aboard but was unable to shout out. A sharp pain in his right arm coincided with a bang as the tank hit something big. Jan's eyes flew open and the momentary relief at being back in the present was replaced with a feeling of dread that the van had come to a sharp halt.

The door of the van sprang open, bringing with it fresh air. The soldiers were shouting at them and Oscar nodded to Jan to get out. He almost fell onto the dark road outside some tall official-looking buildings. Oscar asked the soldiers a question which they ignored, instead they gestured to the trio to climb the steps, through an oak door and into a high-ceilinged hall with people milling around.

'American. Here,' barked a German official, taking Donald off to a side room. Jan wanted to follow him, scared of what might happen next, but at least Oscar was still by his side. The German gesticulated towards a queue of people waiting to be questioned at the main desk. Hearing Dutch spoken by the man behind the desk, the tight feeling in his stomach began to ease. They were in this together. Surely it wouldn't be that bad?

But the man behind the desk didn't look anyone in the eye whose turn it was. The queue was made up mainly of young men, with a few boys, but none as young as Jan.

It took ages to snake their way to the front of the queue. Each person was required to show their ID, while the desk man droned his way through a two-page questionnaire. When he was satisfied, each person was handed over to a smirking SS-er, who accompanied him to a closed door, which he took his time unlocking, before handing him over to another person on the other side. Each time the door opened, Jan tried to peer through it to see where it went, but he wasn't tall enough to see over the heads of those waiting in line.

'Is this a prison?' he whispered to Oscar, who stood, white-faced, next to him.

'It's a police station but there are cells through that door,' said Oscar.

'They're going to lock us up?'

'Looks like it.'

Jan wished Oscar could be a bit more encouraging.

It was their turn next and they went up to the desk together.

'Name,' said the man behind the desk without looking up.

'Oscar Mulder and Jan Mulder,' said Oscar.

'One at a time.'

'We're brothers. He's only eleven,' said Oscar.

Jan pushed close against him.

The man lifted his gaze for a brief moment, before going back to his form. After a short pause, he pulled out another from a pile and wrote Jan's name in capitals across the top, followed by a line and a squiggle Jan couldn't read.

Jan decided to let Oscar answer the questions. When he'd finished, they were both led by the smirking SS-er to the door leading to the cells. Again a feeling of panic rose from Jan's abdomen at the prospect of being separated from his brother. They were marched along an echo-y corridor lined with closed doors. Jan had to break into a trot to keep up. At the end was a metal door that needed four keys to open it.

Jan and Oscar didn't need telling. They walked through and the door swung back behind them with a decisive clang.

PART 5

RETURN TO BERKENHOUT

Chapter 29

Sofie didn't want to go back. She'd grown used to living with her friends at tante Else's house. She would never have admitted it, but the threat of raids was no longer scary; they were exciting. How could life back at Berkenhout compare? And it meant being separated from Liesbeth again. She couldn't bear the thought that they'd no longer have evenings together, playing board games, chatting, falling into fits of laughter about nothing and forgetting about the war. Laura was sweet, but always carried a sadness around with her. Even at their most silly, when the three of them sat around poking fun at the boys they knew, Laura was usually the most restrained.

Not for the first time, tante Else came down to the summerhouse and told them to keep the noise down.

'Girls! Do you want the Germans to come and round you up?' Her tone of voice made Sofie and Liesbeth descend into another fit of the giggles.

'Shh! Tante Else has something to tell us.' Laura sat on the edge of her mattress, her dark eyes wide.

'Thank you, Laura. At least someone is sensible around here,' tante Else said, with a wink.

Sofie was uncontrollable. It didn't matter what anyone said. Everything was funny to her, and, when she descended into another bout of laughter, Liesbeth joined in.

Tante Else waited until Sofie and Liesbeth were able to control themselves. 'I don't want to spoil your fun, but the day has now come for you to relocate to Berkenhout.'

All mirth forgotten, Sofie's heart lurched. She shot a glance at Liesbeth whose cheeks still glowed pink. Laura's expression hadn't changed, though she now gripped the edge of the mattress.

'We're all hoping it won't be for long this time. The Allies are making progress. We heard it on the radio,' whispered tante Else, even though there was no chance of the enemy listening in.

A smile lit Laura's face. 'Maybe I'll get to see my parents soon.'

'Me too,' said Sofie, half-heartedly, then wished Laura hadn't brought up the subject of parents with Liesbeth there. She was the only one who was unlikely to see her mother any time soon. Not because of the war, but because of her mother's decision to leave. Liesbeth rarely heard from her mother. When she did, her letters were always full of news about how wonderful life was in Ghent. Somehow it was easier that Sofie didn't have any news.

The girls hugged one another, joined in sympathy for each other's plight.

'Come on. I'll help you pack,' said tante Else. For now, a mother substitute to them all.

***

Laura found Wouter standing in the doorway of his hut, a puzzled look on his face.

'I'm sure I didn't leave it in such a mess. I think someone's been here,' he frowned.

'Look, is that yours?' Laura pointed to a crumpled pack of cigarettes just visible under the bed.

'It certainly is not. I don't smoke ones like that.' Wouter retrieved it and straightened it out so the picture of the camel was visible. 'Turkish and Domestic Blend Cigarettes,' he read in a faltering English accent. 'American. It must have been that pilot. The one who got us evacuated.' He scrunched up the packet and hurled it to the floor.

Laura flinched. She'd never seen Wouter so angry.

'The cheek of it. It's like he was waiting for us to clear off so he could come and have the place to himself.'

'I'm sure that's not true,' Laura stuttered. 'You can't know for certain it was him. Maybe there are other Americans lost in the woods. Anyway, he's not here now.'

'Don't you see how serious it is? He's not here now, so something's happened.'

'You don't mean, the Germans…?'

'Quite. Waiting till we're all…safely…back. Then ready to ambush. Laura, I'm going to call a meeting.'

'Stop. We don't want to panic everyone just as we're all settling back.' She held onto his sleeve. Turning to her, the fierce look on his face softened.

'Maybe you're right. I'll speak to Willem and Otto. See what they think.' He took her hands in his and kissed them. 'You're good for me.'

Blushing, she smiled up at him through her lashes. 'I'm so

pleased to be back,' she whispered.

***

Together with Willem and Otto, Wouter instigated new rules to ensure their safety. Every evening, night watchmen were appointed to guard the exit to the village. They were under strict instructions not to fall asleep, though policing this wasn't easy. Even Wouter, whose idea it was, found it difficult to stay awake all night when there was nothing to occupy him but the rustling of the wind through the trees and the occasional hoot of an owl.

There were many more people now living in the camp, Jewish refugees from North Holland, several young men on the run from the Germans, a skilled carpenter from Russia and Karl, the German defector. Despite assurances from Dick Foppen that he'd thoroughly vetted Karl, suspicions ran deep that he'd been sent to betray them. For the first two weeks after they'd returned, Dick turned up daily, visiting everyone individually to convince them that Karl was not a threat. Wouter took the most persuading.

'He's fine. His aunt and uncle are Dutch and Karl speaks it perfectly, although with an accent. He loves Holland and used to spend summers with them,' Foppen told Wouter.

'Yet he signed up to the Hitler Jugend?' Wouter sneered.

Dick sighed. 'Yes he did. Like thousands of other young impressionable men. He told me he didn't really have much choice. He was called up, just like all of his friends. But he hated the idea that the Nazis thought he fitted their description of an Aryan, just because he's blonde with blue eyes.'

'So why did it take him so long to defect?'

'He managed to get himself transferred to Holland with the intention of escaping to his relatives. But it didn't work out. They didn't want anything to do with him, calling him a Nazi traitor. He didn't know where to turn. That's when he came to me.'

'And you said he could come to Berkenhout?'

'Yes. I've always wanted us to welcome anyone in difficult situations, regardless of nationality or belief. Well, perhaps not entirely.' He let out a short laugh. 'Not Nazi sympathisers and certainly not Nazis. And Karl fits that description. Do you understand now?'

'Maybe. But I don't want him guarding the village. We have to be careful.'

'You're right. We can't be too careful. I'm pleased you've taken your responsibilities so seriously. I knew I could rely on you.'

Wouter let a smile slip out. It was the first time anyone had praised him in a long time.

Chapter 30

As a youngster, Karl had represented his school in gymnastics. It was natural that he'd train to be a PE teacher, allowing him to indulge his love of exercise. Every morning, just as it was getting light, he was outside, running through his routine. He rigged up some equipment using logs with ropes he slung from sturdy branches, which supported his weight.

Sofie liked to sit watching him, enjoying the daily performance which he executed with precision and in silence. When he'd finished, his muscles gleamed with the exertion.

'Would you like to have a go?' he called over one day. It was the first time he'd said anything to her and she couldn't help giggling. 'I can show you some easy moves.'

'OK, show me,' said Sofie, pleased he'd asked. She'd been the best in the class at sprinting and missed the weekly sports sessions at school.

Karl stood behind her, ready to lift her onto the rope which hung just above her head. She wanted to show him she could do it herself and jumped up, deftly catching hold of the rope, then swung against the tree to steady herself, before climbing up. She caught sight of his upturned face and decided to try one of his moves, but she lost her grip and slid down the rope, her hands on fire. He was there to catch her, but she wriggled free, her face hot with embarrassment.

'You could be really good with a little practice. I fell lots of times at first, but it's the sign of a trier. Are you alright?' he added.

'Of course I'm alright. I just slipped. I think I'll go back to watching.'

'If you want. I'll show you a couple of moves.'

He took the rope and nimbly scaled it, making sure his left foot was anchored at all times. Sofie couldn't stop herself admiring his skill and the way his body twisted this way and that as he tumbled through the air. Then he was on his way down and landed softly at her feet with an encouraging smile on his face.

'How did you become so good?'

Wiping his face and hands with a cloth he'd tucked into the waistband of his trousers, he said, 'Practice and practice.'

'Yes, but you must have had a good teacher.'

'It's true, Herr Fischer was exceptional but the most important thing was that he believed in me. He entered me into competitions from when I was eight and was always there to support me. Mind you, I wasn't the only one. Our school had a really strong gymnastics team and we all encouraged each other. Did you do gymnastics at school?'

'No, it was only a small school. There wasn't the space. But I'd have loved to.' Sofie stared at the rope which swung gently from side to side.

'I can teach you.' Karl busied himself tidying up the logs and tying up the rope so it was out of temptation's way. 'We'll start tomorrow morning before everyone gets up,' he said with a wink.

'I'd like that,' said Sofie with a little shiver of excitement. She decided to keep her rendez-vous quiet from Laura.

***

Next morning, Sofie was awake before dawn, worrying what to wear for her first lesson. Perhaps the reason she'd slid down the rope because of her long skirt which had wrapped itself around it. She crept out of bed and pulled on her blouse. She only had the one skirt. It would have to do. So she experimented with rolling the waistband over and over until she was happy with the length. She didn't want to have it too short.

Tiptoeing to the doorway of the hut, she peered out at the grey light and was surprised to see Karl already limbering up, doing press ups. He didn't notice her and she stood watching, impressed by the ease he kept doing them without seeming to take breath. When he finished, she walked over in bare feet and clapped her hands quietly.

Karl jumped up and his face broke into a smile when he saw her. 'I'm glad you came.'

'Why wouldn't I?' Sofie pushed her springy hair back over one ear.

With a little shock, she realised how much she liked his accent when he spoke Dutch and pushed away the thought that it was because he was German.

It was still not quite light, but already there was a rustling from the birds in the trees. After he showed her some simple moves, none involving the rope, she noted with disappointment, the sky took on a rosy hue and suddenly a ray of sunshine broke through the branches.

'We must finish for today,' said Karl after a while, turning his face towards the glow.

'But we've only just started,' protested Sofie.

'You've been working hard. We've been out here for nearly an hour. Unless you'd like to put on a show already,' he joked.

'Of course not,' she said, reddening a little. 'I wouldn't want to anyway.'

'You're good enough. With a little practice you'll be really good.'

'You say all the right things, but I'm not sure I believe you,' said Sofie, embarrassed to accept the compliment.

'Same time tomorrow, then?'

Sofie nodded vigorously and left him to carry on with his own routine.

Every morning, she woke early with a sense of anticipation and every morning Karl was already outside. She wasn't sure he was even waiting for her because he always seemed surprised to see her. Then at the end of one of their sessions, perhaps a week or so after they'd started, he told her that they would be joined by several others the following day. Sofie's face must have fallen.

'I spoke to Wouter who thinks it's a good idea to give people regular exercise. I've seen how much you are benefiting from our classes and I'm keen for others to take exercise as well,' he said.

'But I thought...' Sofie hesitated, realising her words would sound pathetic. 'Of course, it's a good idea. Who are you thinking of asking?' she asked, more brightly.

'We're putting up a notice in the reception hut today. I'm

going to offer daily classes to whoever wants to come. But any more than six and I'll have to think about doing more than one.'

Sofie swallowed hard, but managed a smile. 'It's a great idea. I'll spread the word too,' she said.

***

The classes were extremely popular and Karl was forced to have a rota depending on people's ability and age. The children were of course most keen and their parents were glad there was an outlet for their natural boisterousness and energy.

PE soon became part of the daily routine, but had to take place very early to minimise daytime noise. Sofie began to lose interest when Karl's classes filled up. She missed their one-to-one sessions but didn't feel she could ask any special favours. Instead, she threw herself into preparing lessons for the children. There were fifteen since the move back, ranging from five to sixteen. She opted to teach maths and history, her two favourite subjects at school. Despite the lack of books and a blackboard to write on, she got by, writing out exercises every evening in each of the children's books, after she'd marked their homework.

'What are you going to do after the war?' asked Laura one afternoon, when they were packing up after class. She didn't have class preparation as she was teaching the very youngest children.

Sofie looked up from her writing and looked pensive. 'You know, I haven't given it a thought recently. All the time we were staying with Tante Else I had this dream that the war would end and

Mum and Dad would come home and everything would go back to normal. Now… I don't know. What about you?'

Laura closed the book she'd been reading. 'When I first came here, all I could think of was returning to Ghent. It was everything I'd ever known and couldn't imagine being happy anywhere else. And I really hated it here.'

Sofie laughed. 'Don't I remember! I was shocked when you told me you were fifteen. I thought you were about ten.'

'Thanks. Anyway, I realised how boring my life actually was in Ghent, just me, Mum and Dad and my grandmother whom we went to visit once a week. It was safe, but boring. That was before, of course.'

'I know what you mean. I feel a bit that way too. I suppose it's being an only child. But I was already quite restless and although I kicked up a fuss about Berkenhout I was secretly pleased to get away. Does that sound bad?' Sofie didn't really expect Laura to answer and continued, 'I'm not sure I miss Oscar any more. When I heard he was home, I expected him to come straight to see me. But when he didn't, I realised I didn't actually mind. I suppose he feels the same way as I do,' she sighed.

'Is it Karl?' Laura narrowed her eyes.

'Course not,' said Sofie quickly and her heart gave a little jump. 'What makes you say that?' she couldn't help herself saying.

'Do you think I didn't notice you go off in the early mornings?' Laura smiled.

'He was only practising a few gymnastic moves with me and now he's giving classes.'

'And you're not going any more. Why not?'

Sofie wished she'd shut up about Karl. 'I lost interest.'

'Because you're not the only one?' teased Laura.

'OK, yes, because I'm not the only one. But all that means is that I don't want to do gymnastics with five others.'

'Mm.'

'Anyway. What about you and Wouter?'

Laura gave a little snort. 'Don't be ridiculous. He's got a fiancée.'

'So?'

'It wouldn't be right.'

'But it's war-time. We've got to live a little.'

'OK, if I make a play for Wouter, then why don't you go after Karl?' Laura challenged. 'Is it because he's German? I don't think I could.'

'I knew that'd be your reaction! Not all Germans are bad, you know.'

Laura didn't seem to hear her. 'I'd always be thinking he'd be looking down on me and ready to betray me. I'm sorry, but I can't help it. I've seen what they've done to my aunt and uncle who were such sweet people and would never have hurt anyone.' She wiped her eyes with her sleeve. 'They're the reason I'm here and there's never a day that goes by when I don't think about them.' She went over to her bed and pulled out a linen bag from under her pillow, shaking out the contents into her hand. 'Here look, that's me with them.' She gazed down at the little black and white photograph in which three faces smiled up at her. 'I last saw them in Utrecht when they invited me to stay for the holidays. I used to go every summer.'

It was the first time Laura had spoken about her family. Sofie kept quiet and let her carry on.

'My uncle ran a printing business, really successful it was too. Then one day out of the blue, his office was raided and he and two others he employed were just marched out and driven off to Brabant, Vught. Tante Cor only knew that because he managed to get a message out with someone who was let out because he wasn't a Jew. She managed to telephone my mother, her sister, who said she must come to us at once. And that's the last time we heard from her. She never made it to Ghent and we think she must have been picked up at the train station and sent to Ravensbrück.'

An involuntary shiver ran down Sofie's spine when she heard the name Ravensbrück.

'Do you think she'll come back?' Laura's dark eyes seemed larger than normal.

Sofie had heard terrible rumours about the camp. Women stripped of everything they owned and made to wear a thin dress with no shoes, even on the coldest days. No comforts and no medicines for the weakest. Can it be true that no one had ever been let out? Surely the rumours weren't true?

'You have to keep hoping. It's all you can do. Maybe she wasn't picked up but managed to find a safe house,' said Sofie, tactfully, but Laura looked unconvinced. 'I saw you received a letter. Was it from your parents?'

Laura's face brightened. 'Yes, they're now in England. They said they wished I could join them and are trying to arrange a safe passage for me soon. But I can't go, can I?' She looked scared again. Sofie tried to put herself in Laura's shoes. Her parents were in hiding just forty miles away. It wouldn't have occurred to her to try to go to them. But England... the name alone sounded full of promise. A million miles away from here. And not under the boot.

'No, you can't chance it. But after the war, why not? Maybe I'll come with you too.'

The seed of this idea would sustain Sofie over the coming months and years. Right now, freedom seemed an impossible dream.

Chapter 31

The door burst open and Max stood there with a look of triumph on his face. 'You can stop crying now. They're home.'

Oscar and Jan trailed in behind him, looking sheepish. Sara sprung up from her chair and rushed forward, shouting, 'I can't believe it! Come, tell me what happened.' Tears still streaming down her face, she fussed over her sons, pulling off their grubby jackets and shooing them into seats beside the stove, then filling the kettle from the tap to make tea.

'Where's Donald? Did they let him go?' Jan said miserably. Sara gave him a squeeze, knowing how disappointed he must be feeling after such an exciting experience. Why did Max always have to put such a dampener on his son's enthusiasm?

Max shot Jan a strange look and proceeded to tell Sara what had happened. 'The message came through that these two clowns had been picked up and taken to Apeldoorn, which we all know is where prisoners are processed before being sent onto one of the camps.'

Sara gasped as she took in the seriousness of the situation.

'If it hadn't been for Dirk,' Max cleared his throat, 'then I suspect these two would not be sitting here now.'

'Who's Dirk?' said Sara, trying to piece together Max's story. 'Is he one of the underground?'

Max banged his fist on the table, making the cups rattle in their saucers. 'How many times do I have to tell you? Do not use that word in this house!'

'Come on, Max. Do you think I'm going to betray you?'

Max sniffed deeply and continued as if their exchange hadn't taken place. 'So the question remains, what were you two doing in the woods when I had said so explicitly that you weren't allowed to go.' He glared from one to the other.

'We couldn't just leave Donald there by himself. He'd starve,' said Jan in a small voice.

'Father, I take responsibility. I agreed to go with Jan. It was a risk but one we had to take,' added Oscar calmly. 'You must understand this. Look at the work you do.'

'What I do is my business. You're both too young to be playing games like that.'

'It wasn't a game!' Jan burst out.

'Shh, darling. You're safe now. That's all that matters,' Sara hugged him to her but he struggled free. 'Now tell me about Donald. He's that American pilot, isn't he?'

Jan's face brightened. 'He'd been in those woods for weeks. I thought he'd want to come home, like Nigel did, but he was really stubborn and refused. All we did was walk with him to the pump at Tongeren. They must have been hiding on purpose 'cos they just sprang out at us and made us go with them in the van. They took him off and we haven't seen him since. Will he be alright?'

'I don't know, sweetheart. We can only hope they decide to let him go,' sighed Sara.

'But he's got nowhere to go! He should have come with us and now the Germans have got him. I only wanted to help him.' Jan began to sob.

'Stupid, stupid.' Max pursed his lips tight and shook his head.

'We had no choice. I'd like to see you get out of that situation.' Oscar spat back. 'Aren't you pleased we're home now? No, you just think we're idiots. Well, how would you like it if we just sat around and did nothing? We're doing our bit just as much as you think you're doing yours.'

Sara flinched at the contempt in his voice.

Max made no reply and left the house, slamming the door behind him.

'See? He knows he's in the wrong,' raged Oscar. 'Mum, I can't stand it any longer. I'm going back to Hilversum.'

Sara knew better than to try to stop him. It frightened her how similar in temperament he was to his father. The senseless raging against perceived injustices were all too familiar. She could only hope that by keeping his distance from his father, Oscar would learn to calm down.

***

He left for Hilversum the following week, one day after his seventeenth birthday. It was a relief that Max was out that day, on 'business', as he said so frequently. Sara had learnt not to question him after the first few times he blew up at her. Why he was so secretive about his underground work escaped her, but she had her suspicions it was not the only thing that kept him away.

Oscar came home from time to time, but always checked his

father wasn't around. 'Mother, I don't know why you put up with him. He's a bully,' he said, on one of his visits home.

'It's really not that bad and he's away so often, I can just get on with things,' she said, as she swept the kitchen floor. There was always so much to do and she wanted to keep on top of it, so at least her husband couldn't criticise her for the state of the household. She leant on her broom for a moment and frowned. 'I'm worried about your safety, Oscar. I think it best you don't visit us for now.'

Oscar heaved a sigh. 'I'm fine, mother. It's not nearly as bad as you think and I'm careful, especially after my stint in the police station.' He gave a wry smile and went over to hug her. 'I'm staying in one of those big houses outside the centre with four other boys my age. Tante Lotte, er... Mevrouw Diepeveen, isn't like a landlady at all. Every night she cooks for us and we sit together, while she tells stories about her ex-husbands. It's hilarious, especially when she gets a bit tipsy. She always has a bottle of brandy on the table next to her. Don't worry, mother, she never offers us any. It's good entertainment, all the same.'

'She sounds... fun,' said Sara, searching for an appropriate word. She couldn't remember the last time she'd had any fun. 'Go on, tell me more.'

'We all share an attic room you wouldn't know is there, so it's really quite safe. It's above the main attic. You get to it through a secret door in the back of a wardrobe. You should see it. It's plenty big enough for the four of us.' He paused for a moment. 'But I could come back if you want,' he said with a wink.

Hearing him say it, made Sara regret she'd voiced her concern.

Of course she was pleased he was well looked after, but she would much prefer to have him close by. Since he'd left home, she could see how fast he was growing up and it wasn't just his appearance. She was sure he'd grown another centimetre or two and the soft down on his cheeks had been replaced by a light stubble. It was also the way he talked so much more confidently. If only this dreadful war would stop. She so wanted him to make the most of himself, become a teacher, accountant or something.

'But will you be alright? I want you to write and tell me if things get too bad and I'll come straight back.' He didn't need to say what he was referring to.

'Now what good would that do? You'd only be coming straight back into a hornet's nest. No, you stay put in Hilversum and keep safe.'

They both looked up at the sound of Jan crashing through the back door and kicking his shoes off into the corner. 'Hello, I didn't know you were coming home,' he said, pushing past his mother to the sink to pour himself a glass of water.

'It's just a flying visit. I'm just about to go. How's school?'

Jan made a face and turned back to the sink to fill up his glass again. 'Mum, is there anything to eat? I can't stop long. Tante Else wants me to deliver some stuff.'

'You still going over to Berkenhout? How's Sofie?' said Oscar.

Jan drained his glass and started munching the bread and butter sandwich his mother handed him. 'Fine, I think. I don't see her much. I usually drop the stuff off in a special spot outside the village and head straight back. Just in case I get followed. It's stupid, 'cos I'm very careful and go different ways and always look about me.' Jan shot a look at his mother as he said this.

'Do you think you could deliver a letter for me? Mum, where's the writing paper?' Oscar went over to the bureau, but it was locked.

'Wait, let me open if for you.' Sara removed the ribbon which hung round her neck, selected the smallest key and turned the lock.

'Since when do you do that?' asked Oscar, taking a sheet and pencil.

'Since the raids.'

'Here? You've had raids?'

'Fortunately, we haven't had any. But Mr Visser's been visited twice already. Poor man, I'm surprised his heart can stand it.'

Oscar wasn't listening. Head bent over his letter, he wrote rapidly filling one side of the paper before folding it over. 'Here, make sure she gets this, won't you,' said Oscar, once he'd sealed it into an envelope and scribbled 'Sofie' on the front. Jan grabbed it and jammed it into his pocket, making Oscar wince. 'Do you mind...' he began, but Jan had already pulled on his shoes and was out of the house.

'There's no stopping him,' said Sara, going over to shut the door properly. 'Especially with his father not being around so much. But at least he's doing good things,' she sighed. 'Now let me get you a cup of tea before you go. I don't know when I'll next see you, do I?'

'Letter for you Sofie,' said Karl, who'd picked up the latest delivery and was sorting out the provisions into piles for each hut. The letter was tucked down the side of the box. He watched her face change as she read her name on the envelope. 'From your sweetheart?' he joked.

She didn't answer, just gave him a little smile. She tucked it into her skirt pocket for later. 'Let me help you with those.' She worked alongside him in silence for a while. He seemed to respect that and didn't press her about the letter.

Oscar. It was weeks since she'd heard from him. Of course she'd heard about the terrible incident with him, Jan and that pilot, but she found out after the event from Mr Foppen, so she knew he was safe. Even then, he hadn't been in touch so she'd tried to forget about him. This was the first letter.

She glanced at Karl's profile and then back down at the potatoes and carrots she was sorting.

'Do you miss your family?'

'I try not to think about them too much,' said Karl, with a sigh. 'I know they'd be really angry if they knew I deserted. In fact, I try not to think at all about what'll happen afterwards. I can't go back to Germany. At first, all I could think of was going to get a job at the sports department at university, but I don't know now. Sometimes I think I'll be here for ever. Sofie? Will you marry me?' he blurted out. 'Not now, of course, I mean after the war. We don't have to stay in Holland. Let's go to England, no America.' He grabbed her dirty hands and gazed earnestly at her.

This wasn't how it was meant to be. She was fond of Karl and, if she admitted it to herself, even a bit infatuated by his attentions, but marry him? It was the first time he'd really shown that he was interested in her in that way.

'You don't really mean it, Karl. Don't look like that. I might want to, but not for a while yet.'

'I'm sorry, I shouldn't have rushed you. I didn't just say it on the spur of the moment. I've been thinking a lot about you for some time,' he said, searching her eyes. Before she could answer, he leant in to kiss her, whilst still holding her hands. When she didn't resist, he pulled her closer.

Sofie didn't want to think about marriage, after the war or anything like that. This wasn't a kiss like the innocent pecks she and Oscar used to exchange. She let it continue and started to lose herself in its softness and warmth. Then she remembered the letter in her pocket and stiffened.

'Are you alright?' Karl let her move away.

'I'm sorry. I can't right now. Look, it's all so sudden.'

'Is it? Our early morning lessons together. Didn't they mean anything?'

'But you stopped them. I thought you weren't interested in me.' Sofie felt the colour flood her cheeks.

Shaking his head, Karl answered her with another kiss and this time she didn't resist.

That night, her whole body still tingling, she remembered

Oscar's letter with a sharp pang of guilt. After everyone was asleep, she crept out of the hut and sat on the log where she and Karl first practised their exercises. The moon shone enough light for her to read the single page. She saw from the writing he'd scribbled it off in a hurry, which made her feel slightly better.

Lieve Sofie,

I've been visiting mother today and Jan said he'd get this letter to you. I hope he remembers! I meant to write before, but after the arrest I wanted to get away. Father and I rowed again and I just couldn't stand it any more. So I've moved to Hilversum where I'm living in a wonderful house. I can't say much more, but let's just say it's safe enough. I still think of you lots, but the circumstances have changed so much and so have I. I know I said I'd wait for you, but this damned war just keeps dragging on. I suppose you know what I'm trying to say and it isn't easy. I'll understand if you don't want to reply to this letter, and perhaps it's best you don't. We don't want it falling into the wrong hands, even with 'trusty' Jan delivering it! Maybe I'll think differently at the end of all this. I hope so. I really think you and I had something special.

Love and wishes, Oscar

No kisses, just signed Oscar. Sofie screwed the letter in her hand and held it there tightly. Why did he have to go and write now? She smoothed out the sheet and scanned over it again, looking for meaning in the words. But she wasn't sure what she was looking for. She told herself if he'd been more direct, she would have been much happier.

Tomorrow she would reply. Tell him she didn't mind, that their lives were so different now, how could either expect any more? Then he'd be let off the hook.

That night she dreamed of Oscar for the first time since she'd been at Berkenhout. At least that's who it seemed to be after she'd woken fitfully when it was still dark. In her dream Oscar had the right build, curly blonde hair and his new rugged look she hadn't quite got used to. But when he spoke she heard Karl. 'Come away with me to Leiden,' he cajoled. 'My car's just outside the village. We'll be there in no time and you can forget all of this.' Sofie let him take her by the hand, but instead of leaving they started kissing. It felt so right but why was she crying so? She woke with a jolt and found her cheeks damp with tears.

Chapter 33

Early next morning, she lay in bed, listening to Karl take his class outside. She waited till it went quiet before getting up.

'Aren't you well?' asked Corrie, who was stirring batter for pancakes.

Sofie realised her face must look awful after her bout of crying. 'I'm fine. Just didn't sleep too well.' She tried to rub her swollen eyes back to normal. 'Here, I'll cook those,' she said more brightly.

The morning routine soothed her. The hiss of the batter as it hit the hot pan; the way it bubbled after a few seconds until the pancake lifted slightly, allowing her to slide her spatula underneath and flip it over. Corrie stood ready with a plate. Within a few minutes, it was piled high with golden pancakes.

'Boys! Come and sit down!' she called to the twins who were arguing over a puzzle they'd started on the dirt floor. There were tiny bits everywhere. Corrie didn't seem to mind the mess. Sofie knew better than to override her authority.

Wim and Pim continued their argument at the table and hardly seemed to notice the pancakes which they shovelled in and gulped down.

'You went and lost the most important piece,' whined one.

'Wasn't me. It was you who tipped them out. I tried to stop them rolling under the bunk but…'

'Boys! Enough now. What do you say to Sofie?'

They turned to her in surprise. 'Sorry, miss,' they chorused, bursting out into laughter. This happened all the time since Sofie became their teacher. All the children called her 'miss' in class.

She playfully rapped the spatula on the table. 'If you spend more time eating and less arguing you won't be late for class. Now that wouldn't be such a good idea, would it?' She winked at Wim who'd opened his mouth to object. Instead he looked down at his plate and mumbled, 'We're nearly finished. Oh, and thank you for the pancakes. They're *heel lekker.*'

'That's better,' said Corrie, ruffling first Wim's, then Pim's hair.

Sofie was about to dip the pan in the bucket they kept for washing up, when Corrie put a hand out to stop her. 'Shall we keep some warm for Kees?'

Sofie stopped. 'Sorry, I didn't realise he'd be back for breakfast.'

Kees left early each morning with a group of workers whose help was needed on a new development of huts to the south of Berkenhout. The idea was they wouldn't be inhabited permanently but would provide emergency shelter if they needed to evacuate the village at short notice. Kees, the most senior of the party, often didn't return for several days, as he was needed to supervise the work. They had to ensure nothing was left behind that might give the impression of anything untoward. Several times he'd arrived home unexpectedly to find that Corrie hadn't left any food ready.

'He's never been away for more than three nights, so he'll be back today. Boys, help clear away your plates and get yourselves ready for school.' If Corrie had been feeling anxious, she didn't let it show in front of Sofie and the children.

'I'll take them over to class,' said Sofie with a smile.

The morning routine was important in creating a sense of normality for the children. Each day, the main hut became the schoolroom where Laura and Sofie arranged stools round small wooden tables which Petr, the Russian, had carved from chunks of wood delivered by Henk. Petr had his own little workshop in one of the above-ground huts as he had to have light to work by. It was filled with commissions he'd been given from people in the village with many half-finished items lying around. Mr Foppen kept an eye on his work in progress, ensuring that he completed items, like beds, chairs and tables, before concentrating on wood ornaments and toys shaped into animals, birds, trikes and jigsaws, all painted in bright colours. It made Sofie and Laura's job easier as there was such a scarcity of educational material for the children.

Sofie settled the twins down at their allocated table and gave them one of the school jigsaws. Under her watchful eye they behaved better than at home.

'Meet me after class. I have something to tell you,' whispered Sofie to Laura who was unpacking exercise books from a wooden crate.

'Something good I hope,' Laura smiled without looking up.

The other children arrived silently, as they had been instructed to, but as soon as the door was pulled to, their chatter filled the classroom as if a pressure valve had been released. It always made Sofie smile to see the children relax and be themselves. It also made her job much easier, although some of the more boisterous ones found it difficult to pay attention when they were asked.

Sofie and Laura planned each school day together the night before, dividing the lessons into half-hour sessions. The older children always wrote a story on any subject they wanted but it had to be well structured, show an understanding of grammar and use of vocabulary. Not one ever wrote about the war or living in the village. Their stories were always about their real homes, friends and pets they left behind, as well as interests, like skating between villages on frozen canals in winter.

'Is this normal?' Sofie had asked tante Else, on one of her weekly visits to keep an eye on the curriculum. 'It's like they are in denial.' She asked knowing that tante Else would be reassuring. She had that kind of creased face that spoke of a life of fun and laughter. Sofie wondered what her life had been like before the war.

'You're doing the right thing allowing them to express themselves through stories of their own choice. It'll come out if it needs to,' said tante Else.

As the children settled down to their stories, Sofie let her mind wander back to Karl. He'd seemed so impetuous last night that it was hard to see that he'd been planning to ask her. Then she remembered how Laura had joked about the two of them. Sofie had dismissed her comments. She found it easier to talk about Laura and Wouter who everyone knew were seeing one another. It was funny how Laura seemed to notice something going on between Sofie and Karl, even when nothing had happened as such. Sofie hadn't wanted to talk about her feelings in case it had been one-sided on her part.

Until now, she thought, inwardly smiling.

Sofie gathered up the exercise books at the end of the lesson, stacking them neatly for marking later. Laura was finishing working with the smaller ones who needed more guidance.

Shouts and the sound of something scraping along the ground made everyone jump. It was so unusual to hear any noise during the day that even the children were aware something was wrong. The smaller ones began to cry and the older children began talking in raised voices.

Sofie and Laura glanced at one another. They instinctively knew they had to maintain calm. Sofie's heart thumped painfully in her chest as she remembered the time they had to abandon the village; it seemed like yesterday.

'I'll go and see what it is,' whispered Sofie. 'You stay here with the children. I'll be as quick as I can.' Turning to the children she said, 'There's nothing to worry about. Miss Wechsler will look after you.'

From the door, Sofie saw a huddle of men beneath the tall fir tree in the centre of the square. The clamour of their voices rang out. She had to suppress a desire to call out to be quiet as she hurried over. Over Wouter's shoulder she saw Kees lying on a makeshift stretcher. He was awake but moaning softly as the men tried to move him into a more comfortable position. Sofie shot a glance back at the schoolroom, before hurrying over to her hut. It was empty. She found Corrie round the back pegging washing onto the line Kees had rigged up between two hazel trees. Her face brightened when she caught sight of Sofie.

'You're back early.'

'Corrie, you must come quickly. It's Kees.'

Corrie dropped the blouse she'd been holding and ran crying to the square. '*Kees, Kees,* where are you?

The men parted to let her through. She dropped to her knees and clasped his hands in hers. '*Wat is er gebeurd*?' What happened?

Wouter rested a hand on her shoulder. 'He was on the roof, fixing the turf when he lost his footing. He slid down landing awkwardly onto a pile of logs. We don't know, but it might be his back. We've sent Petr down to Kampenveld to get transport.'

Corrie was weeping openly as Wouter told her; all the while she kept hold of Kees' hand. Kees had stopped moaning but his face was very pale and his body limp.

'Will the doctor come here?' Corrie's voice came out in sobs.

'We'll try to get him to come but he'll probably want Kees to go back with him for treatment.'

Corrie's crying became a wail as she laid her cheek on Kees' chest. Wouter tried to prise her away, gently whispering, 'You must be careful. He's in a lot of pain.'

Corrie pushed him aside, still sobbing. 'Do you think I don't know my own husband? Leave me.'

Wouter appealed to Sofie with a look. She crouched next to Corrie. Kees' face was now twisted with pain. His back seemed to arch. Then she remembered the first aid Oscar had shown her one day as part of his training as a scout.

'It would be better to lie him on his side,' she called up to Wouter. The others were standing around muttering to themselves.

Corrie let them gently move Kees. His body seemed to relax. Opening his eyes, he fixed them on Corrie's. 'Will I be alright?' he asked in a barely audible mumble.

'The doctor will help you. He's on his way,' said Sofie encouragingly, though inwardly she was shaking. What if he were badly injured? What if he died?

A small commotion behind them alerted her to the children who were being led by Laura out of the schoolroom. Laura tried to shield them from the scene beneath the tree, but the twins ran over shouting, 'Papa! Papa! What's the matter?'

Sofie grabbed each boy by the hand to stop them from throwing themselves at their father.

'Come back to the hut with me. Your father's had a little accident. I'm sure he'll be fine.'

They were easily distracted and Sofie got them searching for the missing jigsaw pieces. She really wanted to go and comfort Corrie but didn't want the children to be upset. Corrie had always been so strong and cheerful. Seeing her crumble made Sofie shiver. She'd come to rely on Corrie to create a sense of normality when everything around them was anything but. Crouching down, she helped the boys with their game until one of them complained they were hungry.

'We're going to have a picnic on the floor today. Bread and cheese and apples,' she said brightly.

'Where's mama? We always have a *warme maaltijd* when we get back from school,' whined Pim.

'It'll be fun to have a picnic instead of something hot,' Sofie said firmly and laid a blue and white chequered tablecloth over the rough floor and handed a plate to each boy. It wasn't much of a picnic. The bread was from yesterday and hard to cut. The heel of cheese was barely enough for one. Sofie shaved wafer-thin slivers onto three chunks of bread. Once they had food in their hands, the boys didn't notice it wasn't much and began munching happily.

Sofie could no longer make out movement outside. Her gaze kept darting to the entrance as she expected Corrie to come back in. Settling the boys down with a cup of milk, she said she was popping out for a moment.

Kees had been moved into the schoolroom to lay on a makeshift bed. Corrie, calmer now, sat alone beside him, holding his hand.

'How is he?' asked Sofie softly.

'It only hurts him when he tries to move. I don't see how he'll manage the journey along those bumpy roads.' Corrie glanced anxiously at Kees, whose eyes were closed. They sat together in silence till the doctor arrived. He was an elderly man, who'd been persuaded to work again, with wispy white hair that stood out from his head.

'Dokter Voss,' said Corrie, lifting her head in greeting. He nodded and began examining the patient. Opening his battered black bag, he laid out the flap containing rows of little brown glass bottles and pill jars. He listened to Kees' chest, took his pulse and prodded him whilst murmuring in a low voice. Kees, now awake, grunted, but didn't yell out in pain.

The doctor carefully packed his instruments away and shook

some tablets out of one on the bottles. Corrie and Sofie looked at him expectantly.

'I think he's just badly bruised but we must get him to hospital to be X-rayed. We'll move him after the tablets take effect.'

Corrie squeezed Sofie's hand. 'I'll go with him. Will you stay with the boys?'

Dokter Voss jerked his head up when she said this. 'Oh no, you can't come. There's no room in the van and it isn't wise to put yourself in danger.'

Corrie widened her eyes in fear. 'What about Kees? I can't let him go without me.'

The doctor's stern features softened as he patted her hand. 'Don't worry. He'll be in safe hands, I promise.'

Kees opened his eyes again and forced a small smile at Corrie. 'Stay here,' he whispered.

She didn't make a fuss when at last Petr arrived back with the van which he'd managed to back up close to the village. Wouter instructed the other helpers to rake over the deep tracks after they'd gone.

Corrie and Sofie sat on a wooden bench until they could no longer hear the rumble of the van.

'Kees and I have rarely been apart for more than a few days,' said Corrie, staring in the direction of the van. 'I always knew that with him around everything would be fine. And it was, till now. I don't know how I'm going to cope.' Fishing a hanky from her skirt pocket, she blew her nose.

'You'll get through this. You're strong. And you must be

strong for the boys,' said Sofie, pulling her cardigan tightly round her against the chill air.

Chapter 34

Waking early, as she always did these days, Sofie listened for the murmurings of the forest as it unfolded, but there was only silence. The early morning light had a strange pale quality, bright but not sunlight. Quietly, she slipped on her cardigan against the piercing cold and felt her way to the hut opening. She tried to push aside the fir branches that concealed the entrance. It was as if something was leaning against them. She leant a little harder and the branches gave way, causing her to stumble. The world had turned white overnight.

No one else was up yet. She could tell by the smooth untrampled snow that lay thick like icing sugar. Breathing deeply, she tested its depth, her bare feet sinking into its softness. The only sound came from her creaking footsteps and her breath which she blew out in long white plumes.

A soft thud and something struck her shoulder, making her swing round. She brushed off a shower of snow and looked up, but the white fingers stretching out from the fir trees were still all intact. A small sound made her twist towards it, then another snowball caught her square in the back.

'Hey, stop it!' She swivelled on the spot, laughing, but still couldn't see who or what was assaulting her. Then Karl popped out from behind a tree holding a fir frond in front of his face. He pranced towards her, lifting his feet high through the drift, then grabbed her round the waist lifting her up in a twirl. Losing his balance, they collapsed onto the soft snow into a warm embrace. It didn't last long as the snow melted on their necks chilling their skin, making her squeal. By now, Sofie's feet were icy cold and she'd lost all feeling in them. Karl rubbed them but his hands were cold too. Sofie didn't care. She would have stayed with him all day like that.

'Look at the mess we've made,' she giggled.

Thwack! Two snowballs came hurtling through the air as Laura and Wouter came wading towards them, scooping up more snow and throwing it at Karl and Sofie before they could respond. Their shrieks brought the children out of their huts, eager to join in the fun. Wouter kept trying to bring everyone to order, but as soon as another snowball splattered against him, he couldn't resist turning on the perpetrator with one of his own. Eventually, the whole village turned out to watch the spectacle, calling out in support of those about to launch another missile on an unsuspecting victim. They all knew they should keep their voices down, but no one tried to stop it. It was the best fun anyone had had in all the time they'd been in the village.

Dripping, Sofie picked her way to her hut which felt like a furnace after the cold morning air. Corrie was preparing breakfast.

'You should have come,' gasped Sofie, collapsing on a stool and lifting her feet towards the warmth of the *kachel*.

'It's enough to see you all enjoy yourselves.'

Corrie's mood was so different since she'd assumed the role of head of household. She carried out her chores exactly as before but Sofie noticed a sadness in her eyes. Corrie would still be cheerful around the boys but was never as spontaneous as when Kees had been there, cracking jokes and often squeezing an arm round her waist.

Laura burst into the hut not long after Sofie, followed by a wet snowball that landed on top of the *kachel*, causing it to hiss and splutter. 'I'm really sorry.' She grabbed a cloth and tried to dab the worst of it away. Corrie watched with a weary smile. 'Sofie, can you fetch the boys and make sure they don't bring the winter in with them?'

By midday, it started to snow again. The first few flakes grew thicker and thicker till they became a white curtain. Soon the yard was covered again, all signs of the earlier snow-fight erased. The village had never looked so beautiful. Heavy grey skies dumping huge quantities of snow had been replaced by a crystal clear blueness. The sun sparkled on the snow which became crunchy underfoot. At night, the temperature dropped sharply. By day, the sun lacked any strength to melt the snow.

The villagers faced a dilemma. The fresh snowfall would cover any obvious tracks that would give them away, but if they didn't start clearing soon, they ran the risk of being totally cut off.

The snow kept falling thickly throughout the day and the following night. The forest fell silent and seemed to retreat into itself. After their earlier exhilaration at the novelty of fresh snow, the villagers became more subdued, surveying the snowy scene from the shelter of their huts. The younger men were sent off to uncover log piles, but the wood was damp filling the huts with smoke when they tried to light it.

Supplies of food began to run short. There was still plenty of flour, carrots and potatoes, but all the milk had been drunk and the eggs had disappeared into pancakes and omelettes. For the first time, the Berkenhout inhabitants realised just how dependent they were on help from the outside.

Four days after the initial snowfall, Wouter held an emergency meeting for the committee. They all trooped miserably into the reception hut and huddled round the *kachel* which gave off a weak glow.

'We have to make plans in case the bad weather continues,' he began. They all looked up as a cold wind blew through the door with the arrival of a latecomer.

'Petr, Willem. You both know the woods well. Do you think you can get over to Henk Hauer's cottage without leaving tracks? You'll need to sweep away traces with every step you take.'

Petr looked solemn, Willem irritated. Willem lit the stub of a cigarette and opened the *kachel* door to flick the match into the embers which briefly flared. Petr spoke. 'It'll take far too long to do that. I suggest you come part way with us to cover our tracks. Then once we get as far as the road we'll zig zag through the trees so we're harder to follow.'

Willem's face brightened. 'I'll second that. We'll go after dark. The Germans won't be patrolling then and with any luck we'll get light from the moon.'

'We'll be fine even if it's cloudy with all this snow. The only problem will be finding the path,' said Petr, stroking his chin.

'That's why I want two of you to go. And Petr, you know these woods well. It shouldn't be a problem for you.'

'Only around these parts. Henk showed me where to gather

wood for my work, but I never stray very far.' Wouter sighed and looked at the rest of the group who remained silent. No one relished the idea of venturing out in such bitter weather.

Willem examined his stub, before patting his empty pocket. It was his last cigarette. 'This snow could be here for weeks. I'll go.' He gave a throaty laugh ending in a phlegmy coughing fit.

Joris, a quiet young man, who liked to sit smoking at the back, piped up, 'If you want a volunteer, I'll go.'

'If it's cigarettes that motivate you, that's fine,' smiled Wouter. 'Anyone else run out of cigarettes?'

Laughter rippled through the group, releasing the tension, but there were no more volunteers. Wouter decided four were better than three in case they were ambushed, so he would have to join them. He quite relished the thought of an adventure outside the village. For some time, he'd been mulling over whether he really should be in Berkenhout. The demand for spaces had been growing as Jews poured into the area from all over Holland. If he hadn't made such a fuss, he probably wouldn't have been given a place here, but he'd panicked after Tim had gone away so willingly. He now realised it wasn't right that Tim's father had looked after Wouter when his own son had made such a sacrifice. For some time, he'd been feeling guilty that Tim had been cut off from his own family, that they had made an example of Wouter by providing him with the means to hide.

Time away had enabled him to reflect on his decision; he was coming to the conclusion it wasn't the right one. He'd already had a quiet word with Dick Foppen about leaving, but Dick believed it would unsettle the villagers. And Dick was very persuasive, praising him on his leadership qualities which they could ill afford to lose. He'd see how things went with Petr and Willem and then he'd make up his mind.

Laura cooked him a last meal and had obviously made an effort. She'd fried potatoes in a little bacon fat with brown beans she'd boiled until they turned thick. 'You don't know when your next meal is, so eat as much as you can,' she said when he complained she was wasting good food. As soon as the words were out he wished he hadn't been so sharp. She didn't deserve it. Despite himself, he'd grown fond of her.

'It's not for long. We just need to establish a different supply route whilst the weather is bad,' he said in a gentler voice, putting his arms round her.

'Why must you go? Can't you leave it to the others?'

He detected a whine in her voice which strengthened his resolve. Pulling out of her embrace, he said, 'No. I must go myself. Only then will I be satisfied that the task is done correctly.' Relenting a little, he kissed her on the mouth. It was no good giving the impression he didn't care for her.

Chapter 35

Jan hadn't been into the woods for over two weeks. Not since his father had gone. His leaving shouldn't have been a surprise, after all those times Jan had crouched on the landing listening to their rows. But it was still a shock that he actually carried out what he'd been threatening to do all these months.

Sara took it stoically, but had become nervous about Jan leaving her on her own. So he thought it best to leave it a while till she'd got used to the idea.

Then the snow came. This meant no school and normally, he would have been off with Nico and Lex for hours till they became so cold and wet that they were forced to return home. Now, he had to do all the jobs his father would have done, clearing the snow, chopping the wood, mending a tile in the roof where there'd been a leak.

He was finishing breaking up the kindling for the stove while Sara peeled potatoes for their evening meal. These days, it was always the same: potatoes, carrots, brown beans and a tiny amount of bacon for flavour. He knew he should be grateful they still had plentiful supplies, but he yearned for the sweet cakes and biscuits she used to make twice a week.

Simultaneously, they looked up at the knock on the door. It didn't sound threatening, but you could never be sure. Since the snow, the Germans weren't so much in evidence on the streets and the late night raids had ceased. For that reason alone, people hoped the snow wouldn't melt any time soon.

Sara hurriedly wiped her hands on her apron and fetched the key from the nail behind the door. Someone was stamping their feet on the doormat. She opened the door to find a youngish man with unkempt sandy hair wearing a boiler suit. He cleared his throat, before speaking in English with an American accent.

'Excuse me, ma'am...'

'Donald!' shrieked Jan. 'Where have you been?'

Sara stared as Jan threw himself at Donald whose face opened up into a wide grin.

'Can Donald come in? Please say yes!' Jan was back to his old self, charging this way and that like an excited puppy.

'Is this the...?' she began.

'Donald C. McDonald,' said Donald, with the familiar white smile Jan remembered. 'Yes, I'm the American pilot your son found and so kindly helped. Which is why I've come looking to say thank you.'

'Don't stand in the door. Someone might see you.' Sara hurriedly glanced up and down the road before ushering him in.

Stepping inside, he lifted his hand as if to take off his cap, then ruffled his hair away from his face. His presence seemed to fill the small entrance hall.

'Come through, please. Can I get you some tea?' said Sara, putting the kettle on the stove before he could answer.

'I'd love that, thanks. You're English, aren't you?'

'Yes. Where are you from?'

'Ohio. The U S of A,' Jan piped up in a mock American

accent.

They all laughed, but Jan's face had turned bright red.

'I can't believe you're here, right here. Where have you been?' Jan was desperate for Donald to take notice of him, but his mother took over again.

'Please, take a seat. There's plenty of time for that.' She took her time swirling boiling water round the pot, pouring it into the sink, then measuring out three scoops of the tea she'd been keeping for an event just like this, filling the pot up again with water from the kettle which was whistling gently on the stove. Donald sat where she pointed and watched her patiently. Jan pulled cups and saucers out of the cupboard above the sink in an attempt to speed things up. But still Sara wasn't ready. She fussed finding her best wooden tray with the carved handles, which she set out with a little white lace cloth, milk jug and sugar bowl. Then there were the spoons which needed to be found, briskly polished with a dishcloth and laid out onto each saucer.

Finally, after another wait to ensure the tea had drawn properly, it was ready to be served.

'My, you sure don't get this kind of treatment where I'm from,' said Donald, carefully sipping from his cup.

Jan watched him, but couldn't contain himself a moment longer. 'Where did they take you? How did you get out? How did you get here?' His questions spilled out in a long stream, making Donald roar with laughter again.

'I can't honestly tell you where I ended up, but it was a work camp on the border of Germany. I suppose it wasn't too bad. I got some food and a bed to sleep in. But the days were long and we spent most of it outside. They made us get up in the middle of the night so we could march for hours till we got to the road we were repairing. Back breaking it was, but we had to keep on for hours till the whistle blew and then we'd trudge all the way back again.'

Jan's eyes grew wide. Both he and Sara stayed silent.

Donald sighed deeply and drained his cup. Sara nodded towards the teapot. He nodded back. After she'd refilled his cup he was ready to continue.

'I made friends with one of the guards. His father was from Ohio, y'see. I saw my chance, took it slow but got him on my side. Promised him he could come and stay with us up at the Lake. My old dad's got a cabin where we used to go every summer when I was a kid. Some days all we'd do is fish, just sittin' there watching the lake as the sun came up, then hours later we'd still be there watchin' it go down. With a bucket full of fish though! My old dad grew all his own stuff up there, tomatoes, grapes, he even had a small apple orchard. I'd help him bring those apples down each autumn and put them in the storehouse for the winter.' He came to a stop, staring into the middle distance, then shook his head. 'I'm not sure Georg would actually come. But hey, you guys should come. Would you like to?'

'Yes, yes, I want to come!' Jan bounced up and down, making Donald laugh. He liked it when Donald laughed, because most of the time he had an anxious look on his face and Jan noticed a slight tremble in his hands.

Jan jumped up and went to the bureau in the corner of the room, his father's desk that no one was allowed to touch. He lifted the lid and pulled open a little drawer where his father always kept a packet of cigarettes. Jan hesitated, shook out just the one and held it up for Donald to see. He knew his mother couldn't object.

'My father's, but he's not here now so he can't get angry.' Jan rummaged in the desk for matches and found a box under a stack of letters tied up with a dark red ribbon. He pushed them back into the compartment where he'd found them. 'Here you are,' he cried triumphantly, before turning anxiously to his mother. She smiled and nodded.

'Gee, you're really swell,' said Donald, once he'd lit the cigarette and taken his first deep inhalation. He sat back in his chair and seemed to relax.

Jan giggled, not quite understanding what he said but sure Donald was grateful.

Donald sucked greedily on the cigarette before stubbing it out on the saucer Sara provided.

'You may as well have the rest. I don't think my husband will be back for a while,' she said, taking care not to catch his eye.

'Well, thank you kindly. Are you sure?'

'I don't think he'll be back. The war's got to him. He's gone with his cousin to Maassluis. That's on the west coast of Holland.' Her voice trembled. 'He's been doing a lot of work with the underground as well. He was fine when we had the first pilot here. But recently, he became so angry at the Germans, the injustice of it all. I think he must have had a breakdown of sorts. And he said the only one who listened to him was Fanny. There, I've said it. He's gone off with his cousin and left me.' She lifted her face to look directly into his blue eyes. The lines fanning out on each side of his face gave a hint that he was a man who loved life.

'And me, but I don't care, 'cos he was always in a bad mood and telling me off,' said Jan. His mother didn't try to stop him from telling on Father. Donald was listening intently, so Jan plucked up courage to say what had been on his mind. 'He was always stopping me from going into the woods but the more he forbade me, the more I wanted to. Then when I came across you, I got so excited that you'd come home with me, just like Nigel did, I thought it'd make Father nicer to us again. But when I came back with the shovel, you'd gone.'

'I'm sorry for that. I guess I didn't really believe you'd be back. Then I heard the trucks patrolling the woods and couldn't stick around that spot. Truth is, I got lost, wandering deeper into the woods and by the time they'd gone I was probably a mile away with no idea how to get back. Then I stumbled upon Mr Hendrik's house at the crossroads. I was nervous he might be a sympathiser and would hand me over. It was his idea I should go to Berkenhout. He painted such a great picture of what had been achieved and how the Germans hadn't been able to find it. I had high hopes of hiding out there. Then when I got there, I found it empty, deserted. You and Oscar were the first people I'd seen for weeks.' He was telling his story for Sara's benefit, who sat quietly, watching him.

'The whole experience made me lose my mind. Maybe it was the lack of human contact, but you guys turning up made me want to get out, do something, even something as little as going to fill the water can. Looking back, I should've listened to Oscar. I'm sorry I dragged you two into all this.'

'Why? It was… fun,' said Jan, enthusiastically.

'Fun.' Donald said the word without smiling this time. 'I

suppose I would've thought that too at your age.' He leant forward and ruffled Jan's hair.

Sara smiled at the scene. She couldn't help thinking how different Max's reaction would have been if Jan had said that to him.

'What will you do now?' she asked.

'Well, I… was hoping…'

'Please. Stay here. We have a room in the attic. Max was always talking about giving people shelter, but he never properly finished it. Jan can help put the camp bed up and there is a little window you can prop open, but it's quite cramped.'

Donald stood up and held onto Sara's hand. 'You're so kind. Just till I can work out what to do next.'

'Max would have been able to help. But we'll just have to work something out between us.'

Jan began tugging on Donald's other hand. 'Come on.' He could hardly contain himself for excitement. 'I'll show you my room first. Yours is just above mine. You can have Oscar's blanket and pillow, he won't mind.'

Sara watched them creak up the narrow staircase and she smiled at the way Donald had to stoop to go through the door on the landing. She set about making supper for the three of them, listening to the muffled sounds from upstairs. For the first time since Max had left, she felt herself relaxing.

Chapter 36

The cold weather started to take its toll. First, one of the children didn't turn up to class after developing a temperature and hacking cough. Soon half the class were unwell. Sofie and Laura tried their best to prevent the spread of germs by handing round handkerchiefs and instructing the children to cover their mouths when coughing. When Pim and Wim succumbed, it was only a matter of time before Sofie and Laura went down with the illness. Since it had turned so bitterly cold, the huts were kept as warm as possible and the door openings closed, creating a perfect environment for germs to breed.

Laura soldiered on for a few days feeling unwell, before she and Sofie decided to cancel classes. Shortly after, Sofie took to her bed. So conscious was she of spreading germs that she refused to see Karl, making her even more miserable.

Corrie was the only one in their small family unit to remain well, fussing round the patients with cups of tea she'd made from herbs she'd dried the previous summer.

'Here, drink this,' she said, holding out a cup and a couple of aspirin to Sofie who lay propped up in bed. Smiling weakly, she waved at Corrie to put the cup down next to the bed. It was so easy to let herself be mothered but she didn't have the strength to ask how she was coping without Kees. He'd had been gone several weeks. Word had come through that his back was badly bruised but he shouldn't be moved. Each day the treacherous snow remained was another day when he wouldn't return. Corrie never complained but the strained look on her face revealed her feelings.

'You're so kind to me,' said Sofie, her hoarse voice no more than a whisper.

'I'm hoping if I fall ill, you'll do the same,' said Corrie with a wan smile.

'You know I would.' Sofie wriggled into a more comfortable position, no easy feat as the straw-filled mattress was so scratchy and lumpy. Inhaling the fragrant vapour, she took a sip of the hot sweet drink, which instantly soothed her throat.

'Do you hear that?' Corrie cocked her ear towards the sound. Sofie's ears were so blocked up she had no idea what she was referring to. But Corrie wasn't listening. She hurried to the hut entrance to take a look outside. Her face visibly brightened.

'Dripping. The roof is dripping,' she announced, triumphantly. Normally, this wouldn't be a reason for celebration but it could only mean one thing. 'It's definitely milder. I can sense it. There's a proper thaw on the way.' She began to tidy things away with an enthusiasm Sofie hadn't seen for a long time.

'I want our home to look nice and *gezellig* for when Kees comes home. It can't be long now,' she said happily.

Sofie struggled out of bed to assess the thaw. It was certainly dripping fast. She jumped at the sound of a huge thump on the roof of the hut. The trees were finally shedding their load.

The village came to life. The men took up their brooms and began sweeping the snow away in earnest. And every time there was another snow dump on top of a hut, they would race each other to shovel it off. It was part necessity and part game as they directed snow showers at whoever was standing below.

But still the snow lay on the ground. Although it thawed by day, night-time temperatures plummeted. Each morning, they awakened to a magical landscape. Icicles hung in banners from the underside of the roofs. The refrozen snow crunched underfoot and glinted in the brilliant sunshine.

The following morning, Sofie woke feeling much better. Laura and the boys were also more cheerful. They set about their normal routine again, but Corrie was the one who lay ailing in bed. Trying to remember the recipe for the herb drink, Sofie prepared a cup and took it over to her.

'Will he be home today?' croaked Corrie. Her eyes were dull and Sofie could see her forehead was damp. Perhaps tea wasn't such a good idea. She fetched a bowl of cold water and flannel. Without speaking, she began dabbing Corrie's brow, noticing how hot it felt.

'Bring him to me today, will you? He wants to be home. He's better, I know it. Why won't he come home?' She tossed her head on the pillow as if trying to push her thoughts away. Her eyes were opened and unfocused.

'Shh... Kees is coming home soon. Don't worry.' Sofie dipped the cloth in the bowl again and squeezed the heat out of it before spreading it out again on her forehead. She went over to the little cupboard where they kept medicines, but found their only box of aspirins empty. Corrie must have given her the last tablets the day before.

'I'm just popping out for a minute. I'll be back straightaway,' she told her, but wasn't sure she was able to hear. Hesitating, she looked back from the door of the hut, before hurrying over to the square looking for Karl. She found him repairing the roof of his hut which was letting in melt water.

'What a nice surprise! Hang on and I'll come down.' He slipped his tools into the belt around his waist and deftly lowered himself off the roof, landing with a bounce at her feet. 'You look as if you're better. You are, aren't you?' He leant in to kiss her but she kept him at arm's length.

'Much. But it's Corrie. I'm really worried about her. She's been so strange and quiet since Kees' accident and now she's caught the illness, she's become a lot worse. Really high temperature and I don't think she knows what she's saying.'

'Have you given her aspirin?'

'We don't have any left. We've all had the fever and I'm afraid I used the last of it.'

Karl hugged her tight. 'It's not your fault. You needed it. I'm sure someone's got some spare.'

They went round all the huts but no one was able to help. The illness had swept through the village and no one had given a thought to the fact they might run out of aspirin. Sofie suspected that some weren't letting on because they were anxious they might need it themselves.

'Petr. Surely he'll have some?' said Sofie, who was beginning to despair. Karl carried on calling on others for help, while Sofie went off to find Petr.

The entrance to his hut was still closed. Sofie pulled aside the bundle of straw and tried to adjust her eyes to the gloom within. 'Petr? Are you alright?' The hut smelled unaired and Sofie tried not to breathe too deeply.

The hunched shape on the bed was unmoving. A stab of fear shot through Sofie as she tiptoed over and tentatively touched it. Petr groaned and began coughing, a rasping, wheezing noise.

'How long have you been like this? Has no one been in to see you?' said Sofie, rearranging the covers in an attempt to make him more comfortable. She found a box of matches by the side of the bed. The match briefly flared giving her enough light to see the stub of a candle. The flickering flame gave Petr's face a ghostly appearance. Shadows played round the hollows in his cheeks. A box of aspirin lay discarded on the floor. Inside were two tablets.

'When did you last take one?' she urged.

'Today, I think,' he croaked, then began to cough again.

Fortunately, Petr had been careful about keeping enough water for his needs and the milk can beside the small stove was half full. Sofie poured some into a beautifully carved wooden jug, without a thought that this might be for one of his customers.

'Here, you must take some more.' Sofie tipped the two tablets out into the palm of her hand and held them out with a glass of water. He squinted up at her, but did as she said, before flopping back onto his straw pillow. 'Thank you,' he whispered.

'That's alright. Now, do you have any more packets of aspirin?'

'I'll be fine. Just need to sleep it off now.' He pulled the covers over one shoulder and rolled over away from her.

'I'm glad. But Corrie's in a bad state and we've run out because we've all had the 'flu. I was hoping you might have some to spare.'

Petr didn't respond. Sighing, she got up to leave.

'In the top drawer of the dresser. You can take a box,' she heard him say quietly.

She knew she could rely on him, but was surprised at the stash of medicines. No wonder he was reluctant to tell her.

'I promise I won't tell anyone,' she said, after taking one of the half dozen boxes and dropping it into her apron pocket.

Walking back to her hut, she almost slipped on a patch of ice. Karl appeared at her elbow and caught her as she stumbled.

'Any luck? If anyone has got aspirin, they're not letting on.'

Sofie patted her pocket with a smile. 'Petr let me have these, but please don't tell anyone. He's not that well himself.'

They stopped for a moment to sit on the bench under the tall beech tree. Feeling Karl's warmth as he pressed close against her, she laid her head on his shoulder. 'How much longer do you think this will last?'

Karl looked skywards and shook his head. 'It doesn't look as if it'll snow again, but…'

'No, this. Us being hidden away. Before, the visits from tante Else and the others were like a lifeline back to the real world. Now, I sometimes think this is the real world. And I'm beginning to hate it.'

Karl squeezed her shoulder, but didn't answer. For a while, they sat in silence, each staring at the icy slush. Sofie reluctantly slid away from his comforting arm. 'I need to get back to Corrie.'

Chapter 37

The days that followed were the happiest Sara could remember, even though the cold winter showed no signs of letting up. The three of them remained cocooned inside the kitchen round the *kachel* to which Donald had taken a shine, ensuring it was stoked up throughout the day. Eager to help, Jan sawed wood into small pieces and stacked them in the log basket next to the stove. Sara kept them fed and warm with soup made from root vegetables and dried beans. There had been no need to venture out, though Sara and Donald knew it had to end soon enough.

One morning, after Donald had been with them for almost a week, Sara was up first, lighting the *kachel* which gave off enough heat as long as they kept all the doors shut. Scraping the ice off the kitchen window, she peered out with a sense of relief that the snow still lay thickly on the ground. It was like a barrier between them and the outside world, separating them from the dangers that lay beyond. She could almost imagine there was no war, no threat of discovery, just the kind of bad winter which they were quite used to.

Sara always let Donald sleep late and had to restrain Jan from climbing into the attic to chat to him. Today, she'd come down and found Jan reading an English book from the bookcase. It was the first time Sara had ever seen him sit still for more than five minutes. She hoped that it wasn't just because of the weather.

'Is it good?' She laid a hand on his shoulder. He was reading her brother's copy of *Swallows and Amazons* he'd given her when the boys were small.

'Shh... I'm trying to read.' He traced the words across the page.

As soon as Donald came creaking down the staircase, Jan lost concentration. He started asking questions about the lakes Donald had described near his home town.

'Did your dad ever let you take a boat out on your own?' Jan's eyes glistened in anticipation.

'Well, of course, but not till we were teenagers. But we always went out with him. He knew those lakes so well we didn't want to go out alone.'

'But didn't you ever go with friends and have adventures?'

Donald laughed, sweeping his unkempt fair hair off his face. He looked so different to the clean-cut pilot Jan had found all those weeks ago. 'Now you come to mention it, I do remember one time when we thought we'd overnight on a little island way out on the lake. We must have been fourteen.'

'Who? Who were you with?' asked Jan eagerly.

'Steady on. I'm getting there. There were three of us, me, my best friend Chuck and his sister Louise. If I remember correctly, it was Chuck's birthday. My old pa agreed to let us take the motorboat out as long as we didn't go further than Beaver Island. Beaver Island's the nearest one on the lake which takes only 20 minutes to get to on a good day. But we lost our bearings, even though we'd had the island in our sights from the start. Out in the middle of the lake a wind whipped up. The water got so choppy we were more concerned with keeping the boat afloat than reaching the island. By the time it got calm we couldn't see it any more 'cos of the mist that had turned up. Louise was getting a bit panicky and Chuck kept telling her to shut up, which didn't make for a great atmosphere. I tried to remember what my old pa would have done in the circumstances. Probably he would've turned off the engine and just drifted along whilst smoking his pipe. The noise of those two bickering made me think I wanted him to be there.'

'It must have been so scary,' breathed Jan, eyes wide.

'Y'know, I don't think it was. My pa used to say if you were sensible you wouldn't come to no harm. So I hollered to the two of them to shut up. I kept on steering the boat toward where I thought Beaver Island was, and, d'you know what?'

'What? What?' cried Jan.

Donald guffawed, throwing back his head. 'We'd gone round in a great big circle and found ourselves back where we started.'

Jan's face sagged. 'Oh, was that all?'

'I'm sorry to say, yes. But we did once stay overnight on the boat,' said Donald, with a wry smile.

'When? What happened? Tell me more,' Jan gasped.

'Well,' Donald paused, his eyes on Jan's. 'We went out a few weeks later, just me and Chuck this time. Louise didn't want to join us which was a relief. I reckon if she hadn't panicked so much we would've found that island. So Chuck and I were better prepared that next time. Learnt a few tricks from my pa and set out on a perfect summer's evening. Not a cloud in the sky. The water was so still you could have dropped a stone from a great height and the ripples would have spread out all the way to the shore. We dropped anchor as far from the shore as possible and fished for supper. Chuck was better than me, pulling up two whoppers, so I pretended I didn't care and set about lighting the little gas cooker. It was the most delicious meal we ever had eaten. The fish got a bit burnt on the outside but was hot and juicy on the inside. We scooped up huge forkfuls and soaked up the juices with the stale rolls we'd brought. It was bliss.' Donald leant back in his chair, his hands clasped behind his head.

'Can we do that when we come and see you?' asked Jan, who hated it when Donald stared into space. It was like he stopped being in the room.

Donald flicked his eyes back onto Jan's and chortled. 'You really serious 'bout coming, ain't you,' he drawled.

'You bet,' said Jan in a convincing American accent.

For three more days, the three of them sat round the *kachel* exchanging stories and making promises. After the war, Sara would take Jan to visit Donald in Ohio. Jan would stay with Donald; he'd go to an American school. Donald would return to Holland, find a job and settle to be near Sara and Jan. At each suggestion, they'd laugh, none daring to voice what they all secretly hoped for.

Then the thaw set in. It was such a relief to Sara that Donald was still with them when the water pipe burst.

'I don't know what I'll do when you go,' she sighed, crouching beside him as he applied himself to the leak under the kitchen sink. He was so much more handy than Max, so much more willing. She knew the situation was a little unreal, but wanted to believe his easy manner and attentiveness meant something more than either were prepared to admit to.

**

Within a few days, she heard from the neighbours that the Germans were back on the streets, banging on doors and making surprise visits again. Donald had to retreat to the attic for most of the day and only come out when she was sure the coast was clear.

Climbing into the attic space one morning, she told him it was time to make plans for his departure. He pulled a face of mock sadness and sighed. 'This has been the best time, y'know.'

'It's crazy, but I feel that too. We should be in fear of our lives and worrying about how we're going to find food, but...' She couldn't continue and tried to swallow her emotions away.

Donald gently twisted a strand of her hair round his finger, tracing the contour of her cheek, making her catch her breath. Before she could think, he slid his hand round the back of her head and guided her lips towards his own. It didn't occur to her to resist. She let herself melt into his embrace, letting him unbutton her blouse so he could slip his hand inside against her warm skin. The attic space was barely enough for two, so he tucked her underneath him, covering her face and neck with tiny teasing kisses.

'Mum! Where are you?' Jan's voice shattered the moment. Sara froze beneath Donald, who attempted to roll to one side, whilst still clasping hold of her.

'I'm just giving Donald some tea,' she said in as normal as voice as possible, trying not to laugh. 'I've got to go,' she mouthed, adjusting her blouse and skirt as she stepped onto the ladder. Donald leant across for a last kiss before she disappeared.

Sara was about to scold him for shouting up when she saw the look on his face. 'What's happened?' A feeling of dread gripped her stomach.

'The *moffen* have taken Mr Visser. I saw it just now. There were two of them and they made him get in the back of a van.'

Sara's hand flew to her mouth. 'But why? He's done nothing wrong.' She hurried to the front door, looked out but the street was deserted.

'Mimi. He'll be distraught without her. I must go and find out. You stay. Tell Donald.'

She flew down the street to Mr Visser's house. The front door was open. No sign of the old man's little dog, or anyone. Catching her breath, she took in the chaotic scene before her. Overturned chairs, table tossed aside, carpets pulled up. What could they have been looking for in an old man's house? He wasn't a Jew, although he'd been stopped before because they thought he looked like one with his angular nose and black eyes. Without thinking, Sara set about straightening up the room, as if expecting him to turn up at any moment. He must have been sitting in his old armchair when they came, as there was no sign of any disturbance upstairs. But where was Mimi? Perhaps she'd escaped into the street and run away. Surely someone other than Jan had seen what had happened?

Sara knocked at his neighbour's door, an elderly woman she didn't know. The door opened a crack. 'What is it?'

'Mr Visser. He's been taken away. Did you see anything?'

The door opened wider. The little bent woman hung onto the

handle for support. 'Nothing, no nothing.' She fiddled with her ear, cupping it towards Sara.

'Mimi. They can't have taken Mimi. He'll be so upset.' Sara raised her voice so the woman could hear. The old woman merely shook her head, retreating back inside. I mustn't take it personally, Sara told herself, fighting back tears. Not sure if she was more upset about Mr Visser or Mimi's disappearance, she retraced her steps back home. There was nothing more she could do.

***

They said their goodbyes in the cramped attic space, clinging to one another. Donald wanted to send word as soon as he arrived in Spain, but Sara begged him not to make promises neither knew he could keep.

'Just think about the future when we'll all be together. Taking that little boat out on the lake and staying overnight on Beaver Island. This time I'll make sure I'll find it.' He smiled into her sad eyes.

They waited downstairs for Gerrit to turn up. He'd agreed to drive Donald to a village on the French border where a colleague would escort him on the next part of the journey. Gerrit said that was all he knew. No specific plans had been revealed.

The knock came. It was time to say goodbye.

Sara let Gerrit in. He waited in the narrow passageway.

'Hey, buddy.' Donald slapped Jan on the back.

Jan threw his arms round Donald's waist, pressing his head against his chest. 'I don't want you to go,' he whispered, his cheeks wet. Donald gently unclasped Jan's hands so they were forced to stand face to face. Crouching to Jan's level, he wiped away the tears with his thumbs. 'Neither do I.'

When Max left, there was no such scene, no emotion. He'd been so gruff, ordering Jan to be good for his mother. The way he went, without hugging or kissing her, he must have felt guilty. Once he'd gone, Sara had wept for the way he'd left suddenly. How could he have abandoned his family at such a terrible time?

This time, she let her tears run freely, careless that Gerrit would see and draw conclusions. 'Take care,' she whispered into Donald's ear, breathing in his scent.

'Don't you worry, I'll be fine,' he murmured back.

Gerrit cleared his throat.

'Come on, you must go,' urged Sara, pressing a small package of food into Donald's hand. As she did so, she wished she'd thought of giving him something more. Their memories would have to be enough.

Turning to Gerrit, 'Please come and share a meal with us when you come back. It's the best I can offer you.'

'Most kind. I will.' Gerrit bowed his head slightly, without looking her in the eye.

Pulling back the latch, she opened the door a little so she could check if all was clear. With a nod, she stood aside. The two men hurried down the path and away.

Chapter 38

Day by day the snow and ice slowly retreated, but were hampered by the harsh night-time temperatures. The ground remained slippery underfoot, but this didn't deter tante Else's team of helpers who, once again, were able to bring supplies to the village. However, life was far from normal. The 'flu had touched every family in the village, weakening the frail and causing concern for the elderly. Several were transferred to hospital, but only if Dokter Voss considered them strong enough to survive the arduous journey. He came twice a week to administer medicine and bring reports on the sick people who had been moved out.

He arrived one morning when Sofie was sweeping the leaves and dirt that had accumulated overnight at the entrance to the hut. Corrie was resting inside.

'Good morning, Sofie. You seem fully recovered.' The doctor touched his hat and inclined his head.

'Yes, thankfully,' she smiled, propping her broom against a tree. 'Corrie's still very weak, though,' she whispered, jerking her head in the direction of the hut.

Dokter Voss frowned. 'She should be better by now. How long is it? Two, three weeks?'

'At least. Would you take a look?'

'Of course.'

He stooped low so he could enter the hut. Sofie followed him in. Corrie lay on her bed, facing the wall and didn't stir when

Dokter Voss addressed her.

'How are you feeling today?' he said in a low voice, gently touching her shoulder.

She began to say something, but it came out as a racking cough, leaving her gasping for breath.

The doctor opened his bag and took out a small brown bottle. 'Can you bring me a cup of water please?' he addressed Sofie, who stood by, terrified that he might be about to tell her the worst.

After Corrie had taken the medicine, her coughing subsided and Sofie helped to prop her up against the lumpy pillow. The doctor pulled a thermometer from the inside pocket of his jacket, wiped it with a clean cloth from his bag and placed it under Corrie's tongue. Then he listened to her chest using his stethoscope which hung round his neck. After he'd finished he nodded and turned to Sofie. 'I'll leave this with you. She can have a few drops in water every four hours.' The doctor placed the bottle on the wooden stool beside the bed. 'Now, how are you feeling, Mevrouw Janssen?'

Corrie shook her head without answering.

'You no longer have a temperature and your chest is clear, though you will probably have a cough for some time. You'd start feeling a lot better if you get up and moved around.'

Corrie stared at him blankly as if she hadn't heard. He cleared his throat before speaking again. 'Kees is making very good progress and is in safe hands. You can be sure that the doctors are doing all they can to help him.'

'Will he...?' began Sofie, but thought better of it. It wasn't for her to ask, but Corrie continued to lie there without speaking.

'I'll be sure to bring you news when I can. Do try to get up. You'll feel better for it.' He closed his battered black bag and left to continue his rounds. Sofie followed him out but didn't speak till she was sure Corrie wouldn't be able to hear.

'Is she really getting better?'

'Oh, yes. There's not much wrong with her. It's Kees I'm worried about. I spoke to the doctors yesterday. They're not sure he's going to make a full recovery. He is making progress and can walk the length of the ward with two sticks, but it would be a risk to have him in the village now.'

'You mean he won't be able to walk properly again?'

'No one can be sure, but let's put it this way, he certainly wouldn't be able to run if he had to.'

'What about Corrie? What about the boys? Don't their feelings come into it?'

'I wish I could say yes, but we have to think of everyone's safety. A sudden evacuation could prove fatal to Kees. Also to Corrie if she was left trying to help him.'

'But that may never happen. So they have to remain apart just in case?' Sofie could feel the heat rise in her cheeks.

'Yes. I wanted to speak to you first. I'd of course be happy to tell her.'

'No, no of course I'll tell her. But not yet. Not till she's stronger.' Sofie struggled to stop the tears from coming.

'Good idea. For now, encourage her to get up and about. However awful it is out here.' He turned his palm up to catch the cold drizzle which had increased whilst they'd been standing there.

***

Sofie kept a close eye on Corrie, praying she would just pull herself together. So much was unspoken between them now. Sofie hardly dared mention Kees, knowing what she did. And there was little anyone could do to help Corrie in her weakened state. Her illness wasn't life-threatening, but dragged on for weeks. Sofie took over the cleaning and cooking with Laura. Corrie didn't even protest. It scared her to see Corrie so weakened, but she kept cheerful for the sake of the boys.

'I'm really worried about Corrie,' Sofie confided in Karl one morning before daybreak. It was too cold and damp to do exercises, but Sofie didn't care. Early morning was the only time the two of them had alone together before the village woke up.

'We can arrange for her to go to Kampenveld, then she'd be able to be with Kees.' Karl nuzzled her neck.

'Stop it. You're not taking this seriously. It's not just that she's unwell. She's been like this since Kees' accident. The boys notice it too. They're always bickering. She does nothing to stop them.'

The sound of water sloshing made them both look up. Corrie had come outside to empty a bucket of dirty water. She didn't look up, though she must have seen the two of them watching her. Pulling her thin shawl round her bony shoulders, she lowered her head to go back through the entrance to the hut.

Sofie and Karl looked at each other. 'See? See how thin she is?

She's giving up.' Sofie's eyes glistened.

'She's bound to be drained after all she's been through. At least she's up and doing something. She'll perk up when Kees comes home. Trust me.'

Sofie took a sharp intake of breath. 'He's not coming "home" as you call it. Dokter Voss told me. He's not strong enough to walk. They're not even sure if he'll be able to walk again. It's too risky if we have to evacuate again.'

'Has he told Corrie?'

'No. He told me because I'm living with her and the boys. But it's a hard secret to keep. The way she droops tells me she knows Kees isn't coming back anytime soon. Is it fair not to tell her?'

Before he could answer, they were joined by Laura, who had heard their murmurings. Yawning, she came to sit next to Sofie, pressing herself close. Sofie put an arm round her shoulders. 'It's freezing out here. Come in and have coffee. I've just put the pot on to boil,' said Laura.

'*Gezellig*! We'll be along in a minute.' Sofie smiled at her, until she got the hint.

'And then there's tante Else. She told me something else,' she said, after Laura had gone back in. 'She keeps telling me this stuff. I don't know why she wants to confide in me. It makes it so hard.' Sofie sighed deeply.

Karl took her hands and tried to rub the coldness away. 'She knows she can trust you.'

Sofie looked at him in surprise. 'But she could just as easily confide in other people here.' Her voice tailed off as she mentally ticked off all the people who might have fitted the bill. Corrie was vulnerable and pining for Kees. Kees was no longer here. Karl was German and, besides, hadn't been in the village long enough. Petr was solid enough but never one to put himself forward.

'But you're a school teacher,' said Karl, as if reading her mind.

'So is Laura.'

Karl smiled. 'Not like you, Sofie. You're special.'

'You're bound to say that.' She knew there was no way that Tante Else would have taken Laura into her confidence. It would have upset the girl too much.

'It's true. Others have said it. Now are you going to tell me what she said?'

'Maybe I shouldn't as I'm meant to be so trustworthy.'

The light mood between them darkened as she remembered the worried look on tante Else's face.

'I want you to keep an eye on Wouter,' tante Else had said at the end of a visit. Sofie had walked to the edge of the village to see her off. Jan had been waiting a little way away, keeping watch.

'He spoke to me recently about wanting to leave Berkenhout for good, but it would be bad for the morale of the village,' Else had said. 'I think I persuaded him to stay for now, by praising him for his good work but also because of Laura. He admitted he found it difficult to show her his true feelings all the time he was planning to leave.'

Sofie had been surprised at this. She hadn't noticed any problem with Wouter. He'd certainly been a lot quieter these days. She wondered if all was well between him and Laura. But then the fight had gone out of so many people recently. The relentless cold, the illness, the lack of any news on when the war might end. Perhaps it would be best not to mention it to Karl, who was looking at her, waiting.

'Tante Else just tells me stuff she's worried about. Mostly it's to do with running out of supplies. Now that we're up to 95, it's creating a huge strain on the system. She said that when there weren't so many of us, it was easy to disguise the extra few kilos of potatoes here and there. The shopkeepers in Kampenveld are still willing to help, but they don't like it when they're asked to put aside even more. There's a rumour that there may be even more coming to Berkenhout.'

'They'll only do it if the system can support it,' said Karl.

'That's what tante Else is afraid of. She has no control over the numbers. Without more support, she fears the system will break down.'

Laura stood at the door and waved them over. Karl gave Sofie an encouraging hug and they went to join her. It bothered her that she was keeping secrets from Laura, but she knew that nothing good would come of telling her.

Chapter 39

The temptation to ignore the sharp rap at the door was overwhelming. The repeated rap became a pounding that shook the door on its hinges.

Henk wasn't expecting any visitors, especially after dark, which came early. He'd only just returned home having completed a second trip in his dilapidated old van to Kampenveld where he'd left sickly patients at Dick Foppen's house. It made for an uncomfortable ride, hidden underneath suffocating piles of sacking, but the old van was unlikely to attract anyone's attention as it bounced along the pot-holed woodland tracks. Twice, Henk had been stopped by Germans on patrol, but they waved him on without searching his vehicle. They had no reason to suspect the head forester going about his business. Henk had made a point of being civil almost to the point of friendliness, giving them the occasional tip-offs about where they could find supplies. They came to rely on Henk, just as the Berkenhout inhabitants did. He knew it was an unusual set-up, enjoying the sense of power it gave him. If it hadn't been for the war, he knew there would have been little excitement in his life. He would certainly not have gained the respect he'd so craved.

A late-night visitor was the last thing he wanted. He didn't fancy a further trip out along the icy, rutted track. He'd only just managed to stoke up the stove which spluttered companionably in the corner. Sighing, Henk heaved himself up from his armchair, shouting: 'Are you trying to break down my door?' He flung it open and the young man on the other side of it almost fell headlong into the room.

'Ah, Dieter. *Wie geht's?*' Henk's shoulders relaxed as he pushed the door shut against the cold air. He could cope with Dieter, the nervous SS-er, who'd recently taken a shine to him. He'd confided to Henk that he was unhappy patrolling the woods day in, day out. It wasn't in his nature to kill and he was dreading the time he'd be forced into it. His *Oberführer* of course knew nothing of this and certainly had no idea that Dieter was friendly with Henk. Today, he wasn't in uniform, a trick the Germans tried to pull off when springing surprise visits. Henk had no need to worry after everything the young man had told him.

'I was passing and hoped you might have a little something for me.' Dieter clapped and rubbed his hands together as he stood over the *kachel.*

'Of course. A hot drink?' He waited for Dieter to shake his head. 'Or something stronger?' He went over to the dark oak cupboard his father had constructed many years ago and poured a finger of *jenever* into two small glasses. '*Proost!*' he said, handing Dieter one.

'*Proost!*' echoed Dieter, knocking it back in one. '*Ach,* that's better. I feel human again.'

Henk laughed. It was true, he was probably the most human of all the Germans he had met. But still he needed to be cautious.

'I never see your van parked outside when we patrol these parts. You must be busy.'

'I've work over towards Apeldoorn. It's about ten kilometres away.' It was the response Henk had prepared in his head in case he was stopped. Apeldoorn could only be reached by driving via Kampenveld. 'And you? How are you coping with the cold weather?'

Dieter blew out his cheeks. 'Tolerable. I suppose I'm lucky having a family to stay with, but some poor buggers are forced to camp.' He stared at the empty glass in his hand, which Henk took as a sign to refill. After downing a second shot, he frowned at Henk. 'Do you think we're wasting our time searching these woods? It's almost a year since we got the tip-off about the Jewish settlement. But, me, I don't believe there is one. You see, there are dozens of us swarming all over these woods and we've never found anything. Just a couple of pilots and local people out doing their business. There was that young boy we came across out playing where he shouldn't. That was fishy. But they couldn't find anything on him.' Shaking his head, he sighed.

Henk didn't answer, hoping Dieter had forgotten his question.

'If anyone would know, surely you would.' Dieter fixed his blue eyes on Henk, but didn't appear to be interrogating him.

'There are a lot of rumours. It's best you take them with a pinch of salt.' Henk steadily returned his gaze.

Dieter glanced at his watch. 'I'd best be going. Mr Foppen will be waiting up.'

Henk's stomach gave a little lurch. 'Dick Foppen?'

'Yeah. You know him?'

'Not really. He's well known around these parts for the work he does in the town hall. Well off he was before the war.'

'I can believe that. His house is huge and it's only him and his wife rattling around in it. Anyway, thanks for the *jenever*. And you will tell me if you hear of anything round these parts?' He pulled his hat down onto his head, but it didn't quite reach his ears which stuck out. Henk almost felt sorry for the young chap as he closed the door behind him.

Sinking into his chair beside the *kachel*, Henk felt unsettled by their conversation. Maybe Dieter had just been passing and decided to pop in for a sociable drink. It wasn't the first time. But the boy seemed more anxious than normal. Was he being used to get information out of Henk? It hardly seemed likely, the boy was so guileless. Then there was Foppen supposedly doing his bit for the Germans. Henk wished there'd been a way of warning Dieter not to say anything about his visits here without raising suspicion. Not that he had anything to hide, he thought, shaking his head. He was quite happy to help out wherever he was needed, as long as there was something in it for him, but he certainly didn't want Foppen suspecting he was doing anything he shouldn't be.

Chapter 40

Jan was excited. Dick Foppen had asked him to come round to his house for a meeting. It made him feel important. Greater involvement with Berkenhout. More responsibility. Jan made sure he didn't tell his mother that Dick Foppen had asked him over. This was one secret he hoped to keep to himself.

He crept into his parents' bedroom, where there was a mirror on the back of the door. Examining his appearance, he found that if he pushed his chest out and straightened his legs, he definitely looked taller. He wished he'd allowed his mother to cut his hair, as he pulled a comb through the unruly mess, looking for a side parting. Spitting into his hands, he flattened his hair as best he could. Not bad, he thought, peering into the tarnished mirror which had silver poking through in places. Surely he'd pass for thirteen?

The clock in the hall chimed two. Hastily tucking his shirt into his long trousers, the only pair he possessed, he tumbled down the stairs, grabbed his jacket and sped out of the door. He'd think of something to tell his mother later. With any luck she wouldn't notice he'd gone.

Suppressing the urge to skip, he forced himself to walk slowly with his chin up.

'Hey, Jan! What are you up to!'

Jan jerked his head round to see Nico creeping up behind him with a smirk on his face.

'Nothing. Just going for a walk,' he said, unconvincingly.

'What, dressed up like that? And what's the funny walk all about?' Nico slouched alongside him, hands in his pockets.

Jan felt himself redden.

'Don't tell me. You're off to see Henny!'

'Don't be so ridiculous.' Jan's cheeks went even hotter. Henny was the most popular girl in the class with white-blond hair that swung left and right when she walked, but she never looked in Jan's direction. That smarted. And it wasn't as if she'd ever given Nico a second glance either. It annoyed him that mention of her made him go red when he hadn't even been thinking about her.

'So who then?' Nico wouldn't leave off. He'd have to tell him.

'I'm going to discuss doing some work for... you know.' He glanced around, but the street was deserted.

'But you do already, don't you?' Nico was smiling broadly.

'Yes, but this would be more important work,' said Jan in an even more important whisper.

'Do they need anyone else? I can come too.' He hopped from foot to foot, impatiently.

'I don't know anything yet. That's why I'm going to...' He stopped himself from saying any more. This was his adventure and he didn't want Nico spoiling it.

'Besides, I thought you aren't allowed into the woods.'

'Nor are you,' Nico retorted.

'Well, I can now. I'm older.'

Jan pushed out his chest again. Nico burst out laughing.

'Shut up! Look, they've asked me to help, not you.'

It was ridiculous, but now his eyes started pricking for no

reason at all. He blinked fast to try and stop them. He couldn't let Nico see. But Nico had lost interest, distracted by Lex who had turned the corner and was walking towards them. He looked different, taller or something. Can it have been that long since he'd last seen him?

'Jan! Are you coming too?'

Jan shot a glance at Nico who didn't say anything. It then dawned on him. He pulled at the collar of his shirt which had suddenly begun to feel tight.

***

Dick Foppen's front room was packed. Packed with youngsters. Jan felt like leaving there and then, but then Dick winked at him. Maybe everything would be alright, after all. But he still felt let down and sat, arms folded, refusing to speak either to Nico or Lex. So they'd known about this all the time and hadn't bothered to consult him. Keeping his head still, he watched them out of the corner of his eye. Whispering together just like he used to with Nico. It wasn't his fault he'd barely seen Nico recently, what with Donald turning up and all the snow. So now he's taking it out on me, thought Jan, shooting a vicious glance in their direction.

He felt relieved when Dick finally got them all to shut up by tapping a spoon on the desk he was sitting behind.

'Are you wondering why I've called you all here today?' he began, with a knowing smile on his face.

'Yes!' the children chorused. Jan silently stared straight ahead.

'The first thing is we have to learn to keep our voices down. Shhh,' said Dick, placing a finger over his mouth. He was no longer smiling. 'I want your help, but it's essential that you take it very seriously. We are in the middle of a war. The Germans are the enemy.'

Jan fidgeted in his seat. Was it necessary for him to talk to them like this? They might not be grown-ups but they weren't stupid. Glancing over at the door, he considered leaving for a moment, but Dick kept looking at him as he spoke.

'Please, sir, will we get to fight them?' piped up Jaap, who was almost as gormless as his older brother. Except Lex no longer had that gormless look about him.

Everybody around Jan laughed, even Dick Foppen. 'I sincerely hope not,' he smiled. 'But as I say, this is a serious situation. Can you keep a secret?'

'Yes!' chorused the children. Jan shifted in his chair, unable to find a comfortable position.

'If you are ever approached by a German soldier, you must never tell them anything. Anything about coming here today. Anything about what we are about to tell you. You're doing nothing wrong, but they won't see it like that. They'll find any excuse to question you, question your family, even arrest members of your family. Just because you are young, this doesn't mean they won't pick on you. Children have been known to be sent away from home. We want to avoid that at all costs.'

The room was now quiet as a sea of serious young faces gazed up at Dick.

'Now, I don't want to alarm you.' Dick's face was no longer so serious as a plump, kindly-looking woman slipped in at the back. 'Let me introduce you to tante Else. Some of you might already know her.'

Jan felt himself relax and couldn't help smiling at her. But why had Dick asked him to come to the meeting knowing he already worked for tante Else? He made himself concentrate on what she was saying.

'Hello, children. Things will change for a lot of you over the coming weeks. Your families have been asked to have guests to stay, many of them young people like yourselves. If that happens, first and foremost, please make them feel welcome. They will have left their own families behind and will feel very homesick. If they seem unfriendly, give them time and you may find you make new friendships.'

'But how long are these guests going to stay?' said Mieke, a small girl of about ten with short blonde hair secured off her face with clips.

'No one really knows. It could be a few days. It could be weeks. We all have to be patient,' said tante Else, who kept smiling.

'Will everyone be hiding people?' Jan asked, impatiently. No point pretending they were 'guests'.

'Yes, well I was about to come onto that,' said tante Else, letting her smile slip a little. 'It's very important that if you have a guest you don't talk to anyone about it. That means even your best friend.'

'How ridiculous. Let's say Nico here has a "guest" staying in his house and I go round there, surely it's obvious they are there. We all know about it now, so how come it's such a secret?'

'I'm glad you brought that up, Jan. It's an important point. You might know your best friend has a guest, but you must avoid talking about them when you're at school or out in the street,' explained Dick. 'It's a very unusual situation, which is why we called you all here today. Some of you will have guests and others will not, but we must all help each other. So keep your ears and eyes open for anything that might arouse suspicion. Even if a friend or neighbour asks questions about who is staying with you, don't let on. Now is everything clear?'

Nobody piped up this time. The children began murmuring amongst themselves.

Dick tapped his spoon for quiet again. 'Now is everything clear?' he repeated.

'Yes, Mr Foppen,' they chorused with a lot less enthusiasm than at the beginning of the meeting.

'Children, I know it's an unusual situation. But if you play by the rules and stay out of danger, we'll all be helping each other.'

Chapter 41

Jan couldn't wait to get home to take off the stupid shirt he was wearing. What had he been thinking? Just because he'd helped tante Else pack a few boxes. Of course they weren't about to give him some amazing role.

He slipped out of Dick's house without the usual check to see that nothing untoward was happening. He could hear Nico and Lex's voices behind him, but the idea of them laughing at his foolishness propelled him away and towards home. As far as he was concerned their friendship was over.

His mother was in the garden digging up potatoes. It was a fairly fruitless task as she'd been going over the same patch for weeks in the hope that there might be a few small ones she'd missed.

Jan crept down the path, hoping to sneak in the back door before she saw him.

'Jan! Where have you been?'

Too late. Jan sauntered over to his mother as if he'd been intending to anyway. 'I bumped into Nico and Lex.'

'Wearing your best shirt? What were you doing?' She leaned on her spade and peered at him. When he didn't answer, she picked up the spade and jammed it into the ground. 'Come on inside. I want to hear this.'

Jan trailed after her wishing he could just forget about it. Instead he was in for another interrogation. At least it wasn't from his father, he thought with relief.

'So, Jan. What have you been up to?' Sara stood with her arms folded, but at least her face was kind.

'Mr Foppen asked me to his house. I didn't think the others would be there. But it wasn't just Nico and Lex. All the children from the village were there. I shouldn't have bothered.' Jan fidgeted with his neck collar.

'Ah, Mrs Janker did say something about this. Was it about having guests to stay?'

'You knew? Why didn't you tell me?' Jan was furious.

'Because it's only just been decided. It's about helping refugees from the west of Holland. Berkenhout can't take many more so we're being asked to house children who've been separated from their parents. We have the space. We have the hiding place. Don't look like that, Jan,' Sara laughed.

Jan was frowning, his bottom lip jutting forward. 'So it's all arranged then?'

'I have agreed and was going to tell you about it today, but you weren't around. What is it, Jan? You were quite happy to have Nigel and Donald here. I know it's not the same, but...'

'No, it's not the same. Some stupid kid forced on us. I found Nigel. I found Donald. That was different.'

For a moment, a look of sadness moved fleetingly across Sara's face. 'I wish things were different too, but we've got to be realistic. It would be impossible to refuse. Gerrit knows we have the attic. He also knows it's empty.'

'When's it happening?'

'Tomorrow.' Sara tried to lay an arm round Jan's shoulders but he shrugged her off. 'Look, it's all happened so quickly. It'll be fine. We know how to hide someone, don't we?'

Her smile failed to convince Jan, who rushed off upstairs, slamming the door of his room behind him. He tugged at the buttons of his shirt in his haste to remove it. A button burst free and bounced over the bare floorboards, disappearing under his bed. Jan ignored it as he struggled out of his ill-fitting trousers, relieved to get them off. Back in his usual scruffy shorts and jumper he threw himself onto his bed with a sigh. He realised he hadn't waited to find out anything more about the person who was to stay with them. He'd been so angry that everyone was planning things behind his back. Maybe it'd be a boy his own age, someone to replace Nico and Lex. He stretched out, relaxing a little at the thought. Then he remembered. His mission was to help fallen pilots, men like Nigel and Donald. There must be more. He just had to find them.

***

Gerrit arrived the next evening after curfew, knocking quietly at the door. Sara put down the socks she'd been darning and gave Jan a warning look. Scowling up at her, he went back to his *Swallows and Amazons*, which he was rereading for the third time. Sara shook her head with a sigh and went to open up.

A small fair-haired boy stood on the doorstep in front of Gerrit who pushed him forward gently. The boy looked up at Sara who held out her hand.

'Please come in. You are most welcome.' She smiled down at

him. Gerrit made a move as if to leave.

'You too, Gerrit. Come and join us for a cup of tea.'

Uncertainly, the boy stepped over the doorstep and caught sight of Jan sitting with his back to them. Sara noticed the flicker of a smile around the boy's mouth, though his big blue eyes remained fearful.

'Let me take your coat and your bag.'

'No!' The boy clutched his battered leather satchel close to his chest.

Jan jumped up and sidled up to the boy. 'I'm Jan. Who are you?'

'Jan! Ask him politely.'

'Arend,' the boy said, staring at Jan.

'Come upstairs and I'll show you something.'

Jan didn't wait for him to answer. Sara was about to scold Jan again when Arend trailed after him up the stairs, still holding on tight to his bag.

Gerrit removed his cap and smoothed down his hair. 'We're so grateful that you agreed to take on Arend. He's had a very traumatic few weeks.' He lowered his voice.

Sara waited for him to tell the kind of story she'd heard so often these days. Children sent away from their Jewish parents who feared for their lives but thought they could provide a better one for their sons and daughters. It worried her that she no longer felt sadness on hearing these tales. More a kind of dull complacency because these stories were becoming so commonplace.

Gerrit cleared his throat, but continued to speak quietly.

'Arend's parents were killed in a car accident three weeks ago. His father was driving the three of them in their old car loaded up with all the possessions they could fit in. They were heading for England. They think it was the steering that gave out. A van was coming in the opposite direction and Arend's father drove straight into its path. Arend was sitting in the back seat. Somehow he escaped injury.'

'What a terrible thing to see his parents die like that. Has he no relatives to go to?'

'That's the sad thing. They were on their way to England to be with them. Fortunately for Arend, the policeman who picked him up was a non-sympathiser. He removed him from the scene before the Germans could find out and send him off to a concentration camp.'

'What happened to the parents after the accident? Surely Arend would have wanted to know?'

Again Gerrit cleared his throat. 'They were taken to the mortuary at the big hospital in Rotterdam. We weren't able to find out any more details.'

Sara felt chilled at the thought that this boy, who looked younger than Jan, was not only an orphan but had lost his parents in such cruel circumstances. Somehow it seemed worse than the story she'd been expecting to hear.

She went to the sink to fill the kettle, her back turned, so Gerrit couldn't see her face. Placing it on the *kachel* to boil, she regained her composure enough to turn back and smile at him. 'You won't need to worry about Arend. Listen.' She cocked her ear at the sound of voices from upstairs 'Jan's a bit of a handful, but he's a good boy. Always wants to help, even if it sometimes lands him in trouble.'

Gerrit didn't answer and she felt an awkward silence open up between them. She didn't know him well and began to wonder how much he knew about her circumstances. Sipping his tea, he seemed to relax a little.

'I've taken twelve children to their host families today. Tomorrow I've been told there will be twenty.' His face looked drawn. Sara remembered he had a young daughter who must be Arend's age.

'We have to remember it's the best solution, even if it doesn't seem like it right now,' she said quietly.

Gerrit nodded but didn't look convinced. She began to wish he'd finish his tea and leave. But he kept sitting there, nursing his cup, staring ahead. Humming to herself, she busied herself clearing the dishes out of the drainer, every so often catching a look at him. Only when she straightened up after stacking some plates in the cupboard did she notice he was standing up, turning his cap over in his big hands.

'We've had news about Max,' he said, out of the blue.

'Oh. How is he?' Sara carefully laid the tea towel she'd been holding over a chair. It must have been nearly four months since he'd left. She'd had no news during that time.

Gerrit coughed into his fist. 'He's not been well these past cold weeks. They've almost nothing left to eat, just tulip bulbs. He wanted to know how you and Jan are. I think he regrets going.' For the first time since he arrived he gave Sara a little smile. Sara didn't smile back. Her first thought was that it served Max right, rushing off with Fanny to live near Maassluis. Of course she'd heard how hard the people had it there, but somehow didn't think that Max would be affected. He'd always seemed so robust and able to brush off difficulties.

'He should have thought about that before leaving so suddenly,' Sara said brusquely. 'Sorry, Gerrit, but he shouldn't have abandoned us they way he did. You do see that, don't you?'

Gerrit dropped his gaze. She could tell he was embarrassed by her comment. 'Of course, but he was such a good organiser of people. Don't get me wrong. Dick's doing the best job he can, but he doesn't have Max's contacts. With Max gone, I worry that the work we do will get found out, then we'll all be for it.'

'But you managed to get Donald out, didn't you?'

'Yes, that was different. We still have our contacts to get people out if we have to. It's dealing with the flow of people coming in that worries me. There's no control and they just keep coming.'

'You never said, but was there ever any word from Donald?' Sara hardly dared ask.

'Once they move down the line, that's the last we hear of them. Your best bet is not hearing any news.'

Sighing she said, 'Thanks for telling me this. If you can pass a message onto Max, tell him that we're doing fine.' She went to the pantry where she rummaged for some scraps to wrap up in an old newspaper. 'Here, it's the best I can do. I have an extra mouth to feed now.'

Gerrit took the parcel. 'I'll do my best to see that he gets it. I'm sure he and...I'm sure he'll be thankful.' He put his cap back on, dipped his head towards Sara, and left.

Jan came clattering down the stairs followed by Arend before she could give the matter any more thought.

Chapter 42

It wasn't bad having Arend around, but Jan wished he wasn't so quiet. How could anyone willingly stay up in that small space day after day? Jan did his best, crawling through the narrow opening with milk and biscuits, when his mother had enough ingredients to bake any. He even let him borrow a few of his prized comics, which he stored in a box under his bed, but only on condition that he didn't tear the pages or spill anything on them.

The only one Arend was not allowed to touch was the one Donald had given him just before he'd left. Jan kept it covered up in an envelope and hardly dared look at it himself in case he damaged it. It was already in a pretty tatty state as Donald had forgotten he'd had it and only discovered it when fiddling around in his coat for something else. He'd pulled it out, all crumpled, and laughed out loud at his discovery. Jan had begged Donald to show him. It had a picture of Superman on the front cover riding a bomb destined to wipe out the 'Japanazis'.

'Here, why don't you have it? I've no use for it now,' Donald had said with a wink. Why he'd had it, Jan never found out, because his mother had turned up at the moment and Jan had quickly slid it behind a cushion before she could see. Later, he'd transferred it to his comics box, underneath his own stash. At first he'd rationed himself, reading only one or two pages at a time, but once he'd come to the end he would go back to the beginning and consume it greedily again and again. For him, it represented a glamorous, far-off existence where any dangers were swiftly dealt with by Superman. He knew it was fantasy, but couldn't help believing that all Americans were good and all Germans were bad. Sometimes, lying in bed, he would dream up his own comic stories in his head which always featured a Superman/Donald hybrid who was impervious to evil forces and rescued Holland from the Nazis.

Since Donald had left and Arend arrived, Jan spent a lot of time lying on his bed thinking. Sometimes it would be about Donald and how he wished he were still sitting in the attic space above him. Or the times he, his mum and Donald had sat around the kitchen table, usually after curfew, drinking cups of tea chatting late into the night. They never talked about the war, just normal things that made them laugh and feel happy. Even when they all knew Donald's time had come to leave, none of them ever let their sadness show. Occasionally, his thoughts turned to his father and this inevitably made him feel sad. His mum hardly ever mentioned him these days, as if she'd scrubbed him out of her life. Jan couldn't explain it, but he missed having him around, even though his presence had so often made him feel as if he'd done something wrong. Maybe that was it. Jan had overstepped the mark once too often and driven his father away. The thought made him squirm inside. What made him squirm even more was knowing that the life his father had chosen was a hard one. Why didn't he just come back? *Because of you, you jerk,* a voice spoke in his head.

He jumped off the bed as if trying to escape his thoughts. A slight scraping noise above him made him look up. He called out, not expecting Arend to answer but more to alert him that he was on his way up. Climbing up the wooden ladder, he heaved himself up through the hatch.

Arend was stretched out on the mattress, much as Jan had been moments earlier on his own.

'*Hoi*, Arend. Aren't you cold in here?' Jan knelt on the mattress and pulled the window shut. The noise Jan had heard must have been Arend opening it.

'Leave it. Please.' Arend said in a voice Jan hadn't heard before. Arend reached out and pushed it open again.

'Do you want to be seen?' Jan was irritated now and yanked the latch from him. What did Arend think he was doing, drawing attention to himself?

From the road, a passing soldier could easily have heard the creak and looked up.

Arend started crying, making Jan feel he'd been too hard on him. He tried to imagine what it must be like stuck up there day in day out. He knew it would drive him mad.

'I used to go out whenever I wanted into the woods with my friends. But my mother won't let me go there now. Too dangerous, she thinks. So I'm stuck here too. Yeah, I know it's not the same as for you, but don't think I enjoy it either.' Jan squinted over at Arend.

Arend wiped his eyes on his sleeve. 'But you can still go out to school, see your friends. And your mum.'

Jan didn't know much about what had happened to Arend before he'd come to them. Only that he'd lost his parents and had to be sheltered because he was a Jew.

An idea came to him. Quite a stupid one, he knew, but he'd

missed the feeling in the pit of his stomach he always used to get when setting out on a new adventure. He wouldn't say too much to Arend just yet, in case he took fright and told Jan's mother.

'It won't be forever,' said Jan lamely. His mind was on his new plan, one that would involve Arend and allow him to become his new best friend.

Arend grunted and still looked miserable.

'I'll see if tante Else would allow you to meet my friends.'

'What, leave here?' Arend looked scared.

'No, I'll get them to come over. My birthday's next week, Mum always lets me have my friends over for tea. One more won't hurt.'

'But what if they tell on me?'

'They won't. I'll make sure of it. Now, come on, it's nearly dark. You can come downstairs now. You do want to, don't you?'

But Arend kept staring at the darkening sky through the window.

***

Sara went down to the shops nearly every day, as she always had. These days, she often returned with nothing, but still kept up her routine, just in case. The greengrocer was her best bet, as she could usually pick up a few turnips or carrots or whatever Mr Vogel had been able to lay his hands on. Everyone knew that so much was now siphoned off to feed Berkenhout that it left most shop shelves bare.

'It's not right that they get it all and we're virtually starving,' grumbled old Mevrouw Stock. Sara bumped into her more often than she cared for. The old woman stooped over the meagre pile of roots, picking them over disdainfully. 'Have you been over to the butchers? Nothing. Not even a sausage,' she continued, talking to no one in particular.

'What do you expect after nearly four and a half years of war? We're doing the best we can under the circumstances,' said Mr Vogel, shaking his head in Sara's direction. 'Haven't you heard how hard they've got it over in the West? Nothing, they have. The shops are shut and people are dying in the streets.'

His words made Sara shudder as she was reminded about Max and Fanny. She'd had no news since the time she'd given those few scraps to Gerrit to pass on. No doubt someone down the line had taken them for themselves. People would snatch the food from others' mouths, they were so desperate.

'Hmmph,' grunted Mevrouw Stock, who for once had nothing to say. She shovelled three knobbly turnips into her bag and handed over a few coins, before leaving.

Sara was left alone in the shop with Mr Vogel, who set about rearranging what was left of the pile into something that resembled an attractive display.

'What else have you heard?' asked Sara, watching him. She felt safe he didn't know about Max.

'They have coupons for either one bowl of soup a day or for some potatoes. But it's a joke. The greengrocers are all shut so there are no potatoes. And the soup is nothing more than a bowl of hot water. I've heard that some people are digging up tulip bulbs as there's nothing else.'

'Tulip bulbs? What on earth can they do with them?'

'Boil them and eat them like a potato. At least they're nutritious.'

'Can't we do anything to help?' Sara was close to tears.

Mr Vogel probably wasn't much older than Sara, but he had deep lines on his forehead. 'Believe me, we've tried. The Germans always manage to intercept any supplies. You see, it's not just the Dutch who are suffering from hunger.'

Sara felt anger well up inside her chest. 'It's all so pointless. Why don't they just go back to Germany?'

Mr Vogel gave a short laugh. 'Can you see Hitler agreeing to that? The man's a lunatic and as long as he's in power it can only get worse.'

They both looked guilty as the door of the shop opened with a loud tinkle of the bell. It was only another grumpy customer, who would be sure to complain about the paucity of goods.

'I'll take a couple of your turnips, Mr Vogel,' said Sara in a normal voice.

Clutching her shopping bag in her arms, she walked a little unsteadily over to the grocers. There was nothing she could do.

'Good morning, Mevrouw Mulder,' said the grocer cheerily. 'I've managed to get you a little something. He bent down and pulled out a bulging brown paper bag from under the counter. Sara peered inside and her eyes welled up. She hadn't seen eggs and sugar for months.

'Are you sure?' she said, her voice breaking.

'Well, of course. You told me it's young Jan's birthday and he has to have a cake, doesn't he?'

Sara could have hugged him, but instead gave him a broad smile. 'I'll keep you a slice, you can be sure,' she said happily. She began to fish in her purse for some coins, but he would have nothing of it. 'Your Jan has been doing some great work for...' he jerked his head in the direction of the woods. 'It's a little thank you. Let's leave it at that.'

***

She liked the feeling of a little weight in her shopping bag as she returned home. There was bound to be some flour stored in the cellar, but no butter, a luxury she hadn't seen since Max had left. He'd always been able to get hold of various essentials for the family. Poor Max, she thought, walking a little more quickly. He'd well and truly messed things up.

Instead of walking straight home, she took a small detour to Gerrit's house. She hadn't wanted to ask him, but surely just the once wouldn't hurt.

'Sara. How nice to see you.' Gerrit hurried her in, a gesture she'd grown used to amongst those working for the underground. 'How are you and how's the Jewish boy?'

'As well as can be expected. He's very quiet, which is probably a good thing.'

Gerrit waved a hand towards a chair with a rumpled blanket over the back of it. It looked like his chair.

'No, I won't stop for long. I just wanted to ask you a favour.' Sara stood awkwardly, clutching her shopping bag. 'It's Jan's birthday tomorrow and I want to bake him a cake. It would cheer us all up, especially Arend. Would you have any butter or margarine? I wouldn't normally ask, but with Max gone...'

Gerrit looked uncomfortable. 'Butter? Margarine?' He experimented with the words as if he'd never heard of them. 'Ah, let me go and ask Betje. She may have some.'

'*Schatje*? Sara is here,' he called out. His face lit up when she came through from the kitchen, wiping her hands on her apron.

Sara felt she was intruding and half turned to leave.

'Do we have a little butter to spare?' Gerrit asked his wife.

Sara now felt as if she'd come begging. 'Really, if doesn't matter if you don't.'

'It's Jan's birthday. She wants to bake him a cake,' explained Gerrit.

'Ah, if it's for Jan, then of course. Wait here a moment,' beamed Betje, hurrying back into the kitchen.

'She knows Jan?' asked Sara, puzzled.

'Of course. Everyone knows Jan!' laughed Gerrit. 'I don't know what we'd do without him. You do know about his work with us, don't you?'

'Yes, of course,' lied Sara. She'd have a few words with Jan when she got home. How could she have not noticed?

Betje came back in with the butter which she'd wrapped up in greaseproof paper and handed it to Sara.

'That's far too much. Are you sure you can spare it?'

'Jan's a good boy. Always willing to help. Just think of it as a small present from us,' smiled Betje.

'Why, thank you very much. I'll let him know.'

Gerrit showed Sara to the door. Before letting her out, he hesitated a moment. 'I heard the news yesterday. He's managed to get through to England and should be on his way back to America now.'

'Donald?' Sara gasped, relieved and sad in equal measure. 'How did you know?'

Gerrit shook his head. 'Intelligence. But good intelligence.'

'That's wonderful. I can't thank you enough.' Sara wanted to kiss him, but held back. After all, he was one of Max's best friends. She wanted to ask if there was some way she could contact Donald. Instead, she shook Gerrit's hand and left.

* * *

Jan hadn't really been looking forward to his birthday, then he woke feeling shivery and his throat was sandpaper. His mother made him a scalding hot cup of tea but as soon as he'd finished it, the nasty scraping sensation when he swallowed was back.

'I feel terrible. And it's my birthday,' he moaned, pulling a scarf off the hall rack and winding it round his neck. 'I'm going back to bed.'

Feeling sorry for himself, he stayed upstairs dozing till lunchtime when the smell of pea and ham soup lured him down. He banged on the attic door and mumbled at Arend to come on down too, but got no answer.

His mother had gone to the effort of making a 'birthday table', laying out her best chequered blue and white cloth and china crockery. Arend was fixing the last of the lilac he was holding onto the frame of Jan's chair. He stopped when he saw Jan and smiled. 'Happy birthday, Jan.'

Jan grunted and slumped onto the chair opposite. 'My throat,' he croaked.

'Here, this should help', said Sara, placing a bowl of steaming soup in front of him.

'Don't you want to sit in your birthday chair?' Arend had finally finished rearranging the blooms to his satisfaction.

Jan wasn't in the mood for any of this, least of all to sit like some old woman on a floral throne. It was one Dutch tradition that his mother had never adopted and he'd always been pleased about that.

'You've got a natural talent for that. You must have done it lots of times,' said Sara, beaming at Arend.

'It wasn't really me. It was my mum. She used to have a flower shop and I'd help her making up the bouquets.' Arend was smiling and his eyes shone.

Jan's spirits seemed to revive a little after he'd eaten his soup and he spied a wrapped parcel on the sideboard.

'Are you ready for your birthday then?' said Sara, placing the parcel in front of him. It didn't look much; the wrapping was a little torn and faded with pictures of *Sinterklaas* riding his horse. 'Try not to rip it, then I can use it again.' Sara pushed it towards him.

The paper was so thin, that it tore as soon as Jan gingerly lifted a corner. He lifted up the parcel and shook out a blue sweater with a white band knitted across the middle. 'Oh. That's nice.' He wasn't sure what he was expecting. Holding it up against himself he tried again. 'That's nice, Mum. When did you knit it?'

'Every evening after you'd gone to bed. I got the white wool from the haberdasher. It was such a surprise to find any at all. I suppose white's not a colour many want, but looks fine when knitted into a sweater like that. You don't like it, do you?' she said with an uncertain smile.

'It's fine. Like I said, it's nice.' He leant over to give her a kiss, but the action made him cough.

'Better keep your germs to yourself.' Sara jokingly warded him off with her elbows.

They were finishing their soup when there was a loud knock on the door, making Arend flinch.

'It'll be for Jan, don't worry,' said Sara, hurrying a little too anxiously to see who it was. 'Gerrit! How nice to see you. Do come in.'

Gerrit followed Sara into the kitchen, his hands behind his back. 'I've come with birthday wishes from tante Else and Mr Foppen,' he said, producing a better-wrapped parcel than the one Jan had just opened, from behind his back.

Jan's face lit up at the prospect of more birthday presents. 'What is it?'

Gerrit laughed. 'I have no idea. Open it.'

The parcel was square and quite heavy. Jan shook it and it rattled, making them all laugh. It reminded him of when he was little and his presents would be wooden train sets or building bricks. He peeled back the blue paper to find a shabby box with a metal clasp. The lid creaked as he lifted it releasing a musty smell of old wood and metal. The box contained a couple of screwdrivers, spanner, chisel and a small wrench along with a selection of nails and screws. 'They're brilliant!' breathed Jan, fingering each of the tools in turn.

'Else saw you have an aptitude for hard work. The tools belonged to her husband,' said Gerrit.

'Mum, you'll let me go round there to help now, won't you?'

'Looks like I don't have much choice,' laughed Sara. 'I must say I feel much happier you'll have a reason to stay out of those woods.'

It wasn't how Jan saw it, but he didn't say. His mind was full of possible projects involving Henk and Berkenhout.

Soon after Gerrit left, there was another knock on the door.

Arend jumped up and made for the stairs again.

'It'll be for you again, Jan. Stay downstairs, Arend,' said Sara, once again opening up.

'Nico? Lex?' Jan looked furious. He was still smarting since their last humiliating encounter.

'I invited them over to help eat the cake,' said Sara.

Nico and Lex didn't seem to notice when Jan pointedly ignored them and were immediately drawn to Jan's new toolbox.

'My mum would never allow me loose with those,' said Lex.

'My uncle lets me use his tools. I'm really nifty with a screwdriver. You'd let me help too, wouldn't you?' said Nico.

His interest piqued, Jan tried to suppress a laugh. 'Depends what the job is. I'd have to consult with Mr Foppen,' he said importantly.

'Boys, let's wish Jan a Happy Birthday,' said Sara fetching the cake she'd made when Jan had been ailing upstairs on his bed. The cake was nothing like the Victoria sponges she used to make, all soft and jammy with a dusting of sugar on the top. With the ingredients she had available, she'd made a kind of fruit cake, containing mainly raisins and a little spice she'd found at the back of the larder. The elderly baking powder obviously hadn't worked as the cake was fairly dense. However, it was the first cake any of them had had for months and they fell upon it with gusto. The sugar rush made Jan feel a little warmer towards his friends and soon they were joking and joshing just like the old days. Nico was particularly kind towards Arend, explaining in-jokes and patting him on the shoulder now and again. Jan felt himself relax in his chair. It felt good to be talking about silly stuff again. When Nico and Lex finally got up to go, he almost asked them to stay longer, but his old pride prevented him from doing so.

'Come over again soon, will you?' he found himself saying.

'Yes, will you?' piped up Arend, his face animated at last.

'I'll bring my cards over and we can make up a four,' smiled Nico, clapping Arend on the shoulder, making him beam even more.

After they left, Jan realised his throat didn't feel quite so sore.

PART 6

BETRAYAL

Twelve was better than eleven, but not much. His mother kept saying how much more grown up he was now, but she still questioned him whenever he went out. From his more grown-up standpoint, he supposed he really should have let her in on some of his forays, but then she would probably have stopped him anyway. It annoyed him that Nico and Lex didn't get the same stick from their parents. But then, they hadn't saved two pilots. Nor had they spent time in a police cell, Jan smiled to himself.

'Mother! I'm going over to see tante Else. She's got a job she wants me to do. With the tools,' he called out, waving the box as he was going out of the door.

'Wait a minute.' Sara stopped pummelling the clothes she was washing in the sink and wiped her red hands on a cloth. She peered at him before speaking. 'You will come straight back after, won't you. Tell me you won't go into the woods. I've heard they've got more soldiers patrolling now the weather's improving.'

'Yes, mother. I'll be fine. I can't say exactly when I'll be back, but it'll be in time for tea.' He gave her a winning smile and slammed the door behind him.

Whistling as he sauntered along, he felt quite pleased he'd told her nearly all the truth. All part of growing up, he convinced himself. That's it. A visit to tante Else as promised, then he should have enough time to...

'Oh, hello, Nico. Where are you heading?'

Jan quickened his pace a little, hoping Nico might not fall into step beside him.

'Same direction as you by the looks of it.' Nico began whistling his own tune. Jan fell silent.

Their friendship had taken a different turn since Nico had befriended Arend, coming round regularly in the evenings to teach him card games and tricks. They rarely played as a four, as Lex didn't care much for cards and it wasn't the same with three. Nico and Arend were equally matched and would sit at the kitchen table, playing fast games that had them collapsing with laughter. Jan became increasingly po-faced and began retreating to his armchair where he pretended to read his English books. Jan knew he should be grateful, but felt as if Nico had come and snatched his friend away, even though Arend could never be considered to be a friend. Why couldn't things go back to how they used to be, he thought, walking a little faster.

They arrived at tante Else's, checked no one was following before slipping down the path towards the outbuilding at the back. On the dusty floor were three large hessian sacks of carrots and potatoes waiting to be loaded into crates. Tante Else was writing in an exercise book, ticking columns of numbers. Her face brightened when they arrived and she set them to work.

'Henk will be along in half an hour. There's a lot to do today.'

Liesbeth came out from the kitchen weighed down by several bags. A delicious smell of freshly baked bread filled the space.

'Can I help with that?' said Jan, sniffing noisily, sidling up with a cheeky look on his face.

'If you work well, there'll be a slice for each of you when you've finished,' said tante Else with a smile. She took the bags and dumped them on a trestle table. Spurred on by the promise of a reward, the boys worked quickly side by side with Liesbeth overseeing that the crates were filled correctly.

'Can I come over and play cards tonight?' said Nico, out of the blue.

Jan bristled. He was fed up with Nico, who never used to be that friendly. Perhaps he was jealous because his family hadn't been selected. Everyone had made a big fuss of Arend on Jan's birthday, which had annoyed Jan, but he'd managed to hide his feelings. If Jan had any say in it, he wouldn't have asked him round. He was still annoyed with Nico, especially now that he was trying so hard to become tante Else's favourite.

'No point.'

'What?'

'You coming round.'

'Maybe Arend would like it.'

What, and Nico become his best friend? 'I don't think so. He's boring and just sits upstairs.'

'Boys, hurry up and stop chatting. Those crates are only half full,' chided tante Else.

No one heard Henk arrive, the way he liked it. He'd developed the knack of blending in, despite his large frame. His van he parked in a side street round the back, accessed by an alley. Making friends with all the neighbours, he sometimes dropped in for coffee or brought them a bottle of beer. In exchange, they always kept an eye out for anybody suspicious.

'All ready?' said Henk, filling the doorway, surveying the scene.

Tante Else looked up from her book-keeping and greeted Henk with a wave of her hand. 'Boys, come on now. Don't keep Mr Hauer waiting.' Under his gaze, she became flustered, her cheeks reddening. 'Will you stop for coffee?'

'Not today, thanks. The coast is clear, so I'd best get on with it.' He didn't mention that he'd already had coffee with one of the neighbours. 'Jan, will you come with me?'

'Me? Yes, I'll come,' he said, without hesitation. He glanced at Nico who was pursing his lips.

'Nico, you come next time. No need for both of you. Now, let's load the van.'

'Can I have my slice of bread first?' Jan asked tante Else, who had gone back to her calculations.

'Go and help yourself. Cut one for Mr Hauer too. You'll find there's a little margarine in the crock in the pantry.'

Jan went into the kitchen where he found a large loaf on the cutting board. Making sure no one was looking, he cut four slices, wrapping two in a separate piece of paper which he stuffed into his jacket pocket. Smearing the remaining two slices with the margarine, he began eating his immediately. He hadn't tasted fresh bread like that in ages. Looking quickly round the kitchen for anything else, he helped himself to a couple of apples too. Any more and they wouldn't have fitted into his pockets without being obvious.

When he came back out, he found only tante Else and

Liesbeth.

'Where's Nico?' he said in a panic.

'Helping Mr Hauer load the van.' Tante Else gave him a strange look.

Jan darted out of the door and down the alley. Nico and Henk were standing by the van talking, but stopped when they saw Jan.

'I'm ready to go,' panted Jan, skidding to a halt. He held out the slice of bread he'd cut for Henk.

'No thanks. Give it to Nico,' said Henk.

Nico smirked, took the bread and began stuffing it into his mouth, his eyes on Jan.

'Let's go. Bye, Nico. Tomorrow, huh?' said Henk, opening the driver's door and getting in.

'I'll be there,' said Nico, holding up his hand to say goodbye.

Ignoring Nico, Jan scuttled round to his side and jumped in as Henk was starting up the engine.

'Has Nico been helping you long?' asked Jan after they'd been travelling along in silence for a few minutes.

'Now and then,' said Henk, concentrating on the road ahead.

The crates in the van began to rattle as they took a bumpy side road off in the direction of the woods. Soon the road ran out and they were onto the rutted track. A combination of the harsh winter and army vehicles had left it in a terrible state. It was a miracle Henk's old van was still able to make these daily trips.

Today's trip was routine. Drive to the crossroads, a quick wave to old Mr Hendrik, who was out digging in his front garden, then turn right down the horse track to the end. Henk parked the van off the track a little way under the trees where it couldn't be spotted. Jan jumped out and ran off in the direction of Berkenhout, whilst Henk began to unload the crates.

It was a wonderful feeling of freedom being back in the woods after all this time. As he pelted along, dodging the tree roots, he thought back to the time he'd come across Donald hiding in the village. If Donald hadn't insisted they'd go off to the water pump, would he still be there?

Wouter and Karl were already walking towards him as he careered through the familiar undergrowth and almost bumped into them.

'Steady on! What's the hurry?' laughed Wouter, grabbing hold of Jan by the arms.

'I came to get you,' said Jan indignantly. 'Wouldn't have bothered if I'd known you were coming anyway.'

'Henk told us to get down to the meeting place at eleven. Didn't he say?'

'No. Henk doesn't tell me anything,' said Jan sullenly.

Wouter ruffled his hair. Jan tried not to pull away, but wished he could do something to show he wasn't a little boy any more.

The three of them walked in silence back towards the van. The only sound was the birds singing in the leafy trees high above them and the swishing of their feet through the dead vegetation.

Jan heard it first and put out an arm to stop the other two. Putting a finger to his lips, he stared intently towards where he knew Henk was standing. The sound of voices, one of them Henk's, speaking German. He couldn't make out the words and glanced over at Karl, who shook his head. The sound of footsteps which got fainter was the signal that whoever was there had gone. Jan gestured to the two men to wait, whilst he went to investigate.

Henk was still moving the crates into the undergrowth, as if nothing had happened.

'I heard voices,' said Jan, appearing from a thicket.

Henk raised his head and frowned. 'Can't say I did. Now, did you fetch the others?'

Jan was about to say something, but only nodded. He looked at the stack of crates. Were there fewer than when they'd left tante Else's? He couldn't be sure, nor could he read Henk's blank expression as he turned back to the task. Hesitating, Jan walked slowly back to the thicket, wondering what to do next. He certainly couldn't say anything to the other two with Henk standing there. But they knew. They were also witnesses to the conversation.

Jan simply jerked his head to inform them it was safe to come out.

Henk looked up. 'Good, there you are. Can you take two each? Jan, you take one. We should be able to take them down in one go.'

Wouter and Karl didn't question him and merely carried on with the job in hand. Jan wished he'd counted the crates, but he'd had no reason to. Had there been seven or eight, or even nine? They trooped back to Berkenhout, concentrating on their heavy load. Even Jan, normally so chatty, fell silent, weighed down by the unspoken words between them.

Sofie was there to greet them, cheerful as ever. The arrival of food was always a big occasion and soon the reception hut was filled with volunteers who'd appeared to divide up the spoils. Henk waited at the perimeter, smoking.

'Come on Jan. Show us what you've got,' said Sofie, looking at him quizzically. 'Are you alright?' she whispered.

Jan nodded vigorously and stepped forward. 'The loaves are fresh this morning. Baked by Liesbeth.'

'They must be good, then,' said Sofie, handing loaves out for each hut.

Jan waited till the food had been distributed and everyone had gone back to their huts. Henk would be expecting him to leave, but he had to say something to Sofie, at least.

'Something odd happened on the way here,' he began in a low voice, with an eye out for Henk. 'I think Henk was doing a deal with some Germans when I was off fetching Wouter and Karl. I definitely heard him speaking German and when I got back I think a couple of crates were missing.'

A look of concern crossed Sofie's face. 'Did you say anything to him?'

'Yes, no. Not really. He had a strange look on his face as if to say "don't challenge" me. Said he didn't hear anything.'

'Well, perhaps you imagined it then…'

'No!' said Jan in exasperation. 'Wouter and Karl heard. I'm sure they did.'

'So didn't they say anything?'

'No.' Jan looked miserable.

'I'm sure there's a reasonable explanation. Henk's a good man. He's done so much for us. Still does. Why would he jeopardise that? You'd better go. Best you don't say anything more, alright?' She patted him on the shoulder, forcing a smile.

Between them, they carried the empty crates back to the van. With Henk silent, Jan was left with his thoughts swarming through his mind. Was he making more of it than he imagined? Of course Henk knew many people, so it wouldn't be surprising if he also knew the Germans patrolling these parts. It was in his interests to keep on good terms with everyone. But those missing crates. If Henk was passing food over to the Germans that was meant for Berkenhout, that would be a massive act of betrayal.

By the time they reached the van, Jan was bursting with indignation. He waited till they were on their way before he spoke.

'I heard you speaking in German. You gave them two of our crates. That's wrong.' Jan's heart thumped painfully.

Henk sighed and glanced quickly at Jan. 'You are right. But I had to. You see, if I'm to have the freedom to move about in these woods, then I have to play their game. They know I have access to stuff and demand that I supply them. If I don't...' He drew his finger across his throat.

'But they saw you had a van full of crates. What did you tell them?' Jan felt scared.

'I didn't tell them anything as they didn't ask.'

'They must have suspected you were up to something?'

'There was nothing to see. By the time they'd arrived, I'd hidden the crates for Berkenhout in the bushes.'

'Wasn't it risky that we'd turn up?'

'Yes, so I made sure you could hear our voices. I knew you'd be sensible enough to hang back.'

'But you denied it.'

'And tell Wouter and Karl. In broad daylight?' Henk snorted. 'They're not stupid. What would they do? Go and tell Dick Foppen? Then what? Cut me out? Berkenhout wouldn't last five minutes.'

Jan hated the smug look on Henk's face. It was obvious he thought what he was doing was completely acceptable.

'When you're older, you'll understand that nothing's as straightforward as it seems. Driving through these woods is a dangerous business. It's my business and I can't risk making any mistakes. One slip and Berkenhout will be discovered. For now, it'd be best if you just forget what you saw.'

Jan's earlier excitement had evaporated. He went quiet as the van jolted onto the horse track, left the woods and returned to Kampenveld. By the time they were back, he'd convinced himself that maybe Henk was doing the right thing.

Chapter 44

Sara was worried about Arend. He was so pale and listless, even more than after he'd first arrived. He had to be missing his parents terribly, but there was nothing she nor Jan did that seemed to help. She made a point of inviting him to come and join them round the *kachel*, but he never stayed for long, sitting on the edge of his chair, as he nervously glanced towards the stairs.

One day, she said, 'I've something to show you,' and went to the foot of the stairs, where there was a faded patterned rug. She pushed it to one side and lifted a couple of floorboards. Arend couldn't contain his curiosity and came over to look. Sara shone a torch she kept in her apron pocket so he could see into the small space. It wasn't much to look at, but that wasn't the point. A scattering of sand lined the bottom keeping it dry.

'We haven't had a raid for ages and if we do, you can squeeze down there and we'd pull the rug over the top. No one would know you're there,' she told him encouragingly.

'No, no. I won't go in there,' said Arend, his blue eyes rounder than normal. He stood with his hand on the banister, ready to bolt up to his safe haven.

'Jan, you show him. You're taller than Arend but I'm sure you'd fit in.'

Jan grinned at Arend, then folded himself into the cramped space. Sara secured the floorboards over him and smoothed out the rug over the top. 'You're alright in there, aren't you?' she said brightly.

'Mmm,' came a muffled sound.

Sara took Arend's hand and led him to an armchair. 'Now, this is what it would be like,' she said. 'See? No sight and no sound from Jan.'

At that moment there was a loud knocking on the door. Arend fled up the stairs as if chased by a tiger. Sara hissed at Jan to be absolutely quiet.

Before opening the door, she glanced in the mirror in the passageway and rearranged her hair a little. If the Germans were making a surprise visit, she didn't want to give them any reason to suspect anything.

But it was only Gerrit.

'Gerrit. Come in. You gave me a fright,' she said, standing back to allow Gerrit to step inside.

Gerrit had an anxious look on his face. 'I'm sorry to impose on you like this. I wanted to warn you that they've caught wind of what we're up to. They've been conducting raids and ransacking houses.'

'Has anyone been found out?'

'Thankfully not, but I'm calling on all the recent arrivals to make sure that the hiding places are secure.'

'You don't need to worry about us,' said Sara with a smile. 'I'm confident that the attic room is well concealed.'

A coughing came from the floorboards.

'Ah, yes, and our extra space right here.' Sara was annoyed at Jan that he couldn't keep quiet. She felt obliged to show Gerrit the hiding place she'd told no one else about.

Coughing more loudly, Jan popped his head out. 'It's a bit

tight in there,' he said, rubbing the dust out of his hair.

'Perhaps not such a good hiding place after all then,' said Gerrit, looking amused.

'Oh no, I'm sure it's fine once you get used to it, though I wouldn't be so keen on hobnailed boots walking over the top of me,' laughed Jan.

Sara frowned as something occurred to her. 'Do you think someone has tipped them off?'

'Who knows? It's strange that the houses they've raided are all hiding young children. It might just be coincidence. But we have to be vigilant, all the same. Now, I must be on my way.' Gerrit bowed his head and went on his way.

'Jan, pop upstairs and see that Arend's alright. I don't suppose we'll get him down for ages now,' said Sara, shutting the door behind Gerrit.

Later, whilst darning a pile of socks and stockings she would once have considered past repairing, she began musing over the possibility of integrating Arend within the family. The boy had fairish hair and blue eyes, so didn't have the dark features that singled out so many Jewish people. He would have to change his name and take on a new identity. She glanced over at Jan, who was reading *The Pickwick Papers* and burst out laughing whenever he came to an amusing passage. He rarely asked her to translate for him now. Who would have thought that he would become such an avid reader of English books?

'I'm thinking of adopting Arend,' she said quietly.

Immediately he looked up. 'What?'

'I thought that would get your attention,' laughed Sara. 'Not literally. But I want us to lead a normal life which is impossible with Arend concealed upstairs. We would need to construct a believable story that we all stick to. I was thinking that Arend could be a cousin who has come to live with us because his parents have died. At least part of that would be true.'

'Let's get him down and tell him,' said Jan, jumping up.

'Wait. It's not that simple. I need to tell Gerrit first and perhaps you should speak to Nico and Lex. In fact, there are a lot of people who need to know.' Sara sighed.

'But we should talk to Arend as it's about him.' Jan didn't wait for her reply and took the steps up to his room two at a time.

Sara began to regret her thoughts. Jan was so impetuous. It could all go horribly wrong. To her surprise, Jan soon came down with Arend in tow, looking animated.

'So Jan has told you about my idea?'

'Does it mean I don't have to hide in the attic?' Arend's eyes shone.

'Eventually, yes, but there's a lot to sort out before I can allow that to happen.'

Arend's eyes dropped to stare at the floor. She wished she hadn't been so quick to tell Jan before she'd thought it through.

'I don't see why it can't work. But you will need to learn to lie. Do you think you can do that?'

Jan was fidgeting around, eager to get on with the new adventure. Sara knew he'd have no problem with lying.

'My parents always told me I must never lie. What must I do?'

'Of course they were right. But this is about your safety,' said Sara, not wanting to spell out the dangers too clearly. 'We will need to change your name, for a start, if you are to be Jan's cousin. You will have to become Arend Smit.'

Jan wrinkled his nose. 'That's not very original. Can't he have an English name and we pretend he's from your side of the family?'

Sara had no brothers or sisters, so any name they chose would have to be an invention. 'No, let's keep it simple for all our sakes,' she said.

'Arend Smit.' Arend tried the words out a couple of times and smiled for the first time.

Sara had a knot of tension in her stomach before they made their first trip out to the village. She would walk slightly ahead of the two boys, who would chat like friends. That was the hard part, although she'd made them practise enough times. Jan was no problem, easily adapting to his role, but Arend had a habit of letting his fear show if he stumbled over his words.

'I can't do this. They'll guess I'm Jewish,' he cried, one day.

'There's no reason why they would. Now come, I want you to look at yourself in the mirror.' Sara shooed him upstairs. 'There, tell me what you see. Apart from a frightened boy.'

Arend blinked through the tears he'd been trying to hold back.

'Nothing to suggest you're Jewish, is there? You have lovely fair hair and blue eyes and dress like any other boy your age. Alright, you and Jan don't look alike, but you're meant to be cousins, not brothers. Remember, a lot of your story is true.'

'Are we going, then?' called Jan impatiently from downstairs.

'Come on. Let's get this bit over with. When people see you walking with us, with Jan, they'll start to get used to seeing you.'

Sara wished Gerrit had been a bit more supportive of her idea. She'd invited him round one evening so she could explain her plan.

'I'm not sure it is wise. If all the other families did the same, it would seem very suspicious.'

'We're not any other family. Arend is suffering. I want to give him a better life.'

'Well, if anything happens, you must be prepared for the consequences.'

So that was that. He'd meant she was on her own. Nothing different to the way things were anyway.

As she took her coat down from the peg in the hall and slipped it on, she wondered what Max's reaction would have been. Probably the same, only it would have been harder to go against his wishes.

Walking down to the shops, no one took any notice of them. Just three ordinary people out shopping. She'd instructed Jan and Arend only to speak if spoken to. Any explanations would be left to her.

There was a small queue at the greengrocer's who had turned up because there had been a delivery of potatoes and cabbage. They joined the end and edged forward until it was their turn. Sara was thankful she didn't recognise anyone. No one glanced in their direction. When it was their turn, Mr Vogel glanced from Arend to Sara, but said nothing.

'Good morning, Mr Vogel. I'd like a kilo of potatoes and a

large cabbage, please.' She cleared her throat. 'Jan's cousin has come to stay,' she said as explanation.

He nodded, weighing out the potatoes before tipping them into her shopping bag. He took an extra large cabbage from the back of the pile and slipped that in too. Sara allowed herself a little smile as she handed over the money.

'Come on boys,' she said loudly, as she marched past the queue of waiting customers, out of the shop and onto the next one. In each shop it was the same and Sara began to relax. Arend also looked happier than when they'd started off down the street.

'I want to see if the haberdasher has any thread. Would you like to wait on the bench by the church while I do that?' she said.

Jan was off like a dog off the leash, with an uncertain Arend behind him.

'Now, wait there till I'm back,' she warned, walking off quickly with a brief backwards glance.

She disappeared down the little side street, hoping they would be alright.

***

A German army vehicle drew up in the square and three soldiers jumped out. Anyone in the square melted away into doorways and away from the square.

Jan and Arend were left sitting on the bench under the big spreading oak tree.

The driver of the vehicle swaggered across adjusting his belt, his pistol visible. 'What are you doing here?' He spoke in German.

Jan was sure he knew him and was relieved that the soldier didn't recognise him. 'Waiting for my mother who's shopping,' he said.

'And you?' The soldier fixed Arend with a stare.

'*Ik begrijp U niet*,' Arend said. I don't understand.

'He doesn't know German,' explained Jan.

'And you do? You're the same age. Aren't you in the same class?'

Jan's mind was working fast. Suddenly the story they'd concocted didn't sound plausible. Why would the soldier believe him?

'He missed a lot of classes because he's been ill,' Jan made up on the spot. 'He's much better now.'

The soldier continued to stare at Arend, who was examining his hands in his lap.

'What was wrong with him?'

Jan tried to think of an illness that would mean he missed lots of school. Then he remembered, Robbie, the boy who had been off school for a whole year with something to do with his legs.

'It's his legs. He wasn't able to walk. We still need to take a rest when he comes out.'

The soldier spat on the ground. 'You'd better go home then. Unless you want to come with us?' His smile was a smirk, but he turned back to his colleagues who were leaning against the vehicle, finishing off their cigarettes.

Jan's stomach lurched as he recognised one of them. It was the

Dutch-speaking German soldier who had taken the cigarettes off him the first time he'd met Donald. Jan turned to go, but knew he'd been spotted.

'Hey, you!' The man sauntered over. 'You're that boy who's been sniffing around the woods, aren't you?'

Jan declined to answer.

'Well, aren't you going to answer me?'

Once again, Jan's mind worked fast, recalling all the events in the woods and wondering just how much this German knew. 'I visit an old man at the Tongeren crossroads from time to time. He's all alone...'

'Shut up! I'm not interested in you. Who's this?' The soldier circled the boys, clearly enjoying their discomfort. 'Are you Jewish?' He pushed his face close to Arend's, who looked as if he was about to cry.

'No,' said Arend in a wavering voice.

'Come on Jürgen. Leave these two alone. We need to get on with our arrests,' said the first soldier, who was getting bored with the encounter.

'I'll be watching you,' smirked Jürgen, turning his back on them and walking off with his colleagues.

Jan didn't like the way he looked back. He knew there was unfinished business.

Chapter 45

It was almost nine months since Kees' accident. Corrie was so much quieter these days and seemed to go about her daily chores with an air of resignation. Rarely did she talk about him, yet his absence always hung heavy in the air. Even the boys stopped mentioning their father. Sofie just hoped they hadn't forgotten him.

One morning, Sofie was whisking up batter for pancakes for the family when there was a commotion outside.

Corrie, who was pouring out the tea, almost dropped the kettle and ran outside. 'Kees!' she cried. 'You're back!'

Kees almost lost his balance as she threw herself into his arms, heedless of the walking stick he was holding. The twins ran out, shouting, 'Papa! Papa!' and danced round the couple, tugging on their father's coat.

'Shh, shh. Not so much noise,' laughed Kees, shooing his family into the hut.

'Breakfast?' smiled Sofie, who was piling a plate with warm pancakes and honey.

Kees sat down heavily on a wooden stool and let himself be served. Corrie pulled another stool close up to him and began eating off his plate. 'Did you walk all the way?' she asked in-between mouthfuls.

'Henk drove to the end of the track and walked with me. It was slow, but he was patient. He's a good man.'

'Didn't he come into the village with you?'

'No, he had to get back as he's got to make a delivery of materials. I don't know how we'd all manage without him,' he said, wistfully.

After they'd eaten breakfast, Kees told them about his time in hospital, which had been bleak and lonely. Patients came and went, but they always had visitors. Kees said he came to dread visiting times when he would be forced to listen to the conversations in the beds around him, usually about leaving the hospital. It became clear that Kees was the only patient who wouldn't be discharged. After a couple of months, he became determined to return to Berkenhout. He began working at the exercises to strengthen his legs which had become wasted after so many months lying in bed. His progress was noted by the doctor, who had first told him to have no expectations of a return to full fitness.

'As soon as I heard him say those words, I thought, right, I'll disprove you. I didn't think much of the exercise programme they'd given me, so I used to double, treble the length of time I did it. As long as I didn't have any pain, I just kept on. After a while I could walk the length of the ward without that wretched contraption.'

'They told me they wouldn't allow you back because you'd be a liability if we were forced to flee again,' said Corrie.

'I kicked up such a fuss, that they were forced to discharge me. I know I can get away quickly if I need to, even though I'll always have this damned limp. This is home to me now, however basic it is.' He surveyed the gloomy hut fondly. 'I hope the others will allow me to work again. I couldn't stand not pulling my weight.'

Corrie stiffened. 'Is that wise after what happened? I don't think I could go through the worry again.'

Kees gently stroked her cheek. 'Now, let's put that behind us. I'll be extra careful, promise. And if it makes you feel any better, I won't go up on the roof,' he said, his eyes twinkling.

***

Corrie blossomed, now that Kees was home. Although much thinner, she resumed her household chores with vigour, even becoming more attentive to the boys who loved the novelty of having their father back home again. They followed him around like puppies and scrapped over whose turn it was to sit on his lap. He would indulge them, even though it hurt his legs to have them clambering over him. 'Boys, leave Papa alone,' said Corrie, noticing him wince.

'We're playing a game,' said Wim, bouncing up and down.

'We're playing a game,' echoed Pim, tugging at his father's hand.

'Your mother's right. It's time to stop.' Kees struggled to his feet. Mornings were the worst, when his legs refused to move the way he wanted them too. From experience, he knew that he needed to get up and walk about. 'I'm going over to Petr's to see if I can help. Now be good. Help Mama.'

He ruffled each of their hair in turn and winked at Corrie.

Kees was keen to become useful to the village again. He was unable to do any heavy work, but chipped in with hut maintenance. Petr taught him basic woodwork skills. They would work side by side in

Petr's hut, Kees repairing wonky table legs and smoothing off rough edges, while Petr carved intricately designed cupboards and chairs.

'We make a good team,' said Petr, assessing Kees' handiwork. 'We could set up a business selling high quality furniture we'd made ourselves.'

'Are you asking me to go back to Russia with you?' joked Kees.

For a moment, Petr looked startled. 'Russia? Oh no, I could never return. My family is here.' Unsmiling, he thumped his chest.

Petr had never spoken about his experience after escaping from a German work camp. All Kees knew was that he'd been picked up by the side of the road by the greengrocer on the road to Almelo. Like so many refugees, he'd been taken to Dick Foppen who was in the early stages of populating Berkenhout.

'Is there no one back where you came from?' Kees asked tentatively.

Petr's face clouded over and he sunk onto the chair he'd just completed. 'My father died of a heart attack when I was fourteen and my mother never recovered. She was in poor health anyway, something to do with her lungs. I was seventeen and on my own, no brothers, no sisters. I went to live with my aunt who encouraged me to take up a trade. That's how I became a carpenter. It meant I was able to avoid conscription. It was a wonderful time. I was young, no responsibilities and doing something I knew I was good at. After qualifying, I was taken on by a local furniture workshop in my hometown and was soon promoted on account of my skills. My boss was a patient man, but very keen to pass on his knowledge. I learnt everything I know from him. The war put a stop to it all and I got my call-up papers. My aunt said I should join, but all I could think of was losing the job I loved. Fighting a war filled me with horror. When is it ever justified to kill a man?' Petr paused for a moment, shaking his head. 'I was young and foolish. Didn't think I'd be caught, but I made a stupid mistake which cost me my freedom. Anyway, I don't want to talk about that now.'

'Well, Russia's loss is our gain,' said Kees, in an attempt to get Petr to lighten up. 'And yes, I would love to work with you in the future.'

Petr's face brightened and he fetched a bottle he kept under the mattress. He only had the one shot glass, which he offered to Kees, while he splashed a generous amount into his only mug.

'*Proost!*' they both cried and threw back the burning liquid.

'Where did this come from?' coughed Kees, examining his empty glass.

Petr narrowed his eyes before answering. 'You won't tell, will you? Everyone will want some.'

'I'm not sure they will,' said Kees, still coughing.

'Alright. It was Henk. In exchange for some woodwork. Seems fair.'

'Ah, Henk. You know, I sometimes worry what would happen if anything happened to him.'

'Oh, I wouldn't worry. He can look after himself. King of the woods, he is. And I reckon he has those Germans wrapped round his little finger. He gets what he wants and if we're lucky, we get what we want.' Petr slopped some more *jenever* into his cup, then waggled the bottle towards Kees.

'No thanks. I'd best be going now.' Kees stood up a little clumsily and grabbed onto the back of the chair. 'I'm not used to drinking and especially this early in the day. Let me know when you need some more help.'

Kees stepped out into the bright sunlight and steadied himself by clinging onto the doorpost. He breathed in deeply, savouring the sweet scent of blossom from the hawthorn bushes on the breeze, something he'd missed so badly when cooped up in hospital. For a moment, he forgot the ache that fanned out from the small of his back and down his legs. It only slowed him down a little, as he traversed the yard. With a little bit more time and exertion, he was determined to get back to full fitness.

Chapter 46

She hurried along as fast as she could, trying not to draw attention to herself, whilst dread gripped her. She'd only been gone five minutes and in that time the square had cleared of people as the two German vehicles patrolled up and down. Hoping that a small blond woman, wearing a dark green headscarf and carrying a shopping bag on either side, would be of no interest to those brutes, she lowered her eyes to the ground. If only she could catch a glimpse inside the vehicles, but she resolutely kept her head down as she hastened past.

It was Arend who filled her with panic. Jan, she knew, could look after himself. The thought that he'd already emerged from several scrapes unscathed reassured her. He will have avoided a confrontation and they will be back home, she repeated to herself, as she turned into her road. Her heart in her mouth, she unlocked the door and immediately called out after pushing it to behind her. The only sound was the tock, tock of Max mother's *stoeltjesklok* in the hallway. Dropping her bags, she ran upstairs, still calling for Jan and Arend. *They were in that truck,* a voice hammered in her head.

The attic. They're hiding in the attic. She slid open the false door, careful to shut it behind her. The attic was empty. Her legs could hardly support her as she retraced her steps downstairs. The only sound was the clock which began to strike the hour, making her flinch.

Breathing heavily, she weighed her options. Waiting at home was unbearable. She had to speak to someone. She scribbled a note for Jan, careful not to say anything that could be interpreted wrongly and set off for Gerrit's house. It's the one thing she didn't want to do, but what else was there?

It was almost a relief that Gerrit wasn't home. Her mind racing, she settled on tante Else. Of course, they would have gone there.

'Sara, whatever is the matter? Come in,' said Else, standing aside to let her through. The smell of baking bread filled the warm kitchen. Liesbeth was at the sink, washing dishes.

'Is...is Jan here? And Arend?' Sara gripped the back of a chair.

'Jan said he'd be round today, but hasn't arrived yet. And Arend?' Else drew her eyebrows together.

'So they're not here. Where can they be?' said Sara, her voice rising. 'I left them in the centre, only for five minutes, and when I returned the *moffen* had arrived. I fear they may have taken them. I shouldn't have. It's my fault.' Tears spilled down her cheeks.

'Liesbeth, can you make us all some tea? Now, please sit down and let's talk about this calmly. You were shopping with both boys?' She shook her best chair with the tapestry cushion on it until Milo, her tabby cat, jumped off, protesting.

Sara could only nod.

'And where were you when they disappeared?

'Buying thread from the haberdasher. You know how small the shop is. It would have been crowded if they'd come too. And everything had gone so smoothly up to then. No one took any notice of us, of Arend.'

Else leant over and touched her arm. 'May I ask why you'd taken him out?'

Sara retrieved a hanky from her coat pocket and blew her nose. 'I see it was wrong, now. But he doesn't look at all Jewish and he's been so unhappy cooped up in the attic.' She accepted the tea Liesbeth put before her. Shakily, she took a sip. 'I made sure he understood the dangers before going out, but you never really know, do you?'

'Let's not jump to conclusions. You've been home...'

'Yes, of course. I've come straight here.'

'So you haven't tried anywhere else?'

'Only Gerrit, but he wasn't in. Nico! Why didn't I think of him?' Sara jumped to her feet.

'I'm sure you're right. Liesbeth, you go with her. Bring them back here and we'll decide what to do next.'

***

It was a relief to have Liesbeth with her, who became quite animated as she spoke about Jan and the work he did for tante Else.

'We always look forward to when he comes. He makes us all laugh and then it doesn't really seem like work. I can't resist slipping him a cookie, just to see his face light up.'

Sara did her best to smile, but wasn't really listening. Her chest was tight with dread as they hurried through the streets, now devoid of any Germans.

'Look, he's there!' Liesbeth caught sight of him first, outside

Nico's house. He was bending over his friend's bike, while Nico stood by watching.

'*Hoi* Liesbeth! Mum? Where did you get to?' said Jan, straightening up and stretching with a yawn.

'I've been all over looking for you. What happened? Where's Arend?'

'Inside, chatting to my mum,' said Nico. 'Do you want to come inside?'

Sara's anxiety turned to rage at her son's nonchalant attitude. Did he not realise the seriousness of the situation? She swallowed hard, determined not to make a scene.

'Good morning Mevrouw Muller. I see the boys have descended on you. Arend, are you alright?' She said, forcing a smile.

'Oh, yes. Mevrouw Muller's been telling me she grew flowers before the war and sold them at the market. Isn't that wonderful?'

'Arend has quite a knowledge about the different varieties of tulip. It's such a shame they aren't grown for their blooms anymore.' She shook her head, as if pushing any dark thoughts away.

'Arend, Jan. Time to go home. Thank you Mevrouw Muller, for keeping an eye on them. I was quite anxious about their whereabouts.'

'I'm so sorry. I had no idea. They turned up here about half an hour ago to visit Nico, at least that's what Jan told me. Shouldn't they have come?'

'Jan, tell Mevrouw Muller what happened. I'd like to know too.' Sara stood, arms folded.

Jan recounted the episode in the square, leaving out some

details about the questioning and the soldier he'd recognised. Hearing his version made Sara feel slightly foolish.

'I asked you to wait for me,' she said quietly.

'They were asking what we were doing. I thought it best we didn't hang around. Sorry, mum.'

'Let's go home now, shall we?' said Sara, thanking Mevrouw Muller.

'It's no trouble at all. Jan and Arend are welcome any time. Nico likes the company and so do I.'

'Yes, well we'll have to think about that. We don't want anything like this happening again.'

Sara felt torn. The episode had obviously enlivened Arend who chatted away to Jan as they walked back. If she forbade him from going out again she feared he would retreat into his own dark world again, which wouldn't do any of them any good. She resolved to do things differently, to be better prepared.

When they arrived home, Jan unearthed his old chess set from the back of the dresser and spent the rest of the afternoon locked in friendly rivalry with Arend. It helped that they were evenly matched, the scores swinging back and forth as they outwitted each other with clever and surprising moves.

Sara was able to get on with her plan at her writing desk, where she composed a letter to Oscar. It meant being complicit with Gerrit, but as he was involved with the relocation of Jewish children, she was sure he'd agree. About to close up her leather writing folder, she pulled out another sheet, which she covered on both sides with small, neat handwriting. Slipping it into the envelope, she hesitated before deciding to leave the addressee blank. Gerrit would know what to do.

Chapter 47

Sara had mixed feelings about Oscar's visit, the first for many months. He'd arrived with the help of the underground, turning up late one night about two weeks after Sara had written to him. She knew she could rely on him. Of course she was delighted to see him looking so grown up and well. His shoulders were broad, he sported a decent stubble and was a full six centimetres taller than her. She had to remind herself that he was heading towards seventeen years old.

'Ma, are you looking after yourself? You're a lot thinner than when I last saw you.' He clasped her bony shoulders and gazed down into her eyes. She wriggled away, uncomfortable that he had noticed. 'Is it Father?' he said.

She had a sudden urge to cry. No one had shown any concern for her for so long. Swallowing down the ache in her throat, she said, 'Oscar, there's so much I should have told you. Come and sit next to me and I'll try to explain.'

She spoke in a low voice, telling him about how she'd become close to Donald. How the three of them had stayed cocooned during the cold snap.

'It was unreal, the three of us cooped up together. Even Jan was upset to see him go, not just because he saw Donald as his "prize". The days, weeks after were very hard.'

'Why didn't you say anything before? I would have come.'

'It all happened so quickly and I was scared he'd be found out.

Anyway, it's over now. Arend's been more of a concern. I took him in on a whim, really. I suppose you could say he filled a space.' She smiled weakly.

'Didn't you think about the risk?'

'It seemed a lot less risky than hiding an American pilot on the run. And I thought it would be company for Jan, though I'm not sure he needed it. He's so independent.'

Oscar grinned, jumping to his feet. 'Can I go and wake him? He does know I was coming, doesn't he?'

Sara shook her head. 'I thought it best not to say. He would have kept on at me. You know what he's like.'

Oscar took the stairs two at a time. Seconds later, Sara could hear the muffled sound of the brothers' familiar sparring. It felt good having Oscar back in their midst again.

Later, she and Oscar drank tea, while he recounted life in Hilversum. It seemed a world away, though still fraught with the dangers they all faced. The house he now lived in was huge, owned by a kindly retired doctor and his wife, both members of the underground. The surgery and waiting room had been converted into two large living rooms, which served them well for their clandestine meetings after dark. Upstairs in the sprawling attic, where Oscar bedded down with three other boys of his age, was a printing press, paper, ink and all the necessary tools needed to produce false documents. Whenever there was even the hint of a raid, the four boys would roll the press away behind a false wall, before clambering into the cramped space directly above.

'The funny thing is that we can't take it seriously. Michael's always cracking jokes about the *moffen* and their clumsy attempts to search the house. It's happened twice now. We hear them clumping around downstairs making stupid remarks. Up there, we dare not look at one another in case it sets us off laughing. You should see us, Ma, four grown men crouching with our knees up to our ears.'

'But what about the doctor and his wife? It must be frightening for them.' Sara wished she could be more like her son.

'They're used to it. The *moffen* only search his house because they're told to. They're actually on pretty good terms with the doctor, who always offers them a *jenever*, which of course they decline,' Oscar pretended to cough. 'Whilst this is going on it gives us time to scarper before they do their "search". It's all a charade, you know.'

'Oscar. Please be careful. It might seem a game to you, but if they were to discover you, you do realise what the consequences would be?'

'Ma, you don't need to worry. I've got my story all worked out. Plus any identity to fit the situation.' Oscar crushed her with a hug, before opening the battered black folder that lay on the table. He'd arranged everything. A new identity for Arend, who was now officially Jan's cousin from Rotterdam. The official stamp neatly clipped the photo which bore a passing resemblance to Arend, even though Oscar hadn't met him. Sara's description of Arend must have sufficed. The photo was even slightly dog-eared and faded. No one would suspect it had been newly minted. Oscar had also brought a sheaf of extra coupons, which he handed to his mother with the instruction to keep them hidden under the floorboards until she needed them.

All at once he was on his feet, sweeping his papers back into the folder. 'I'm so sorry, Ma, but I have to go.'

'So soon? I thought you might stay a few days…'

'You know I'd love to. And I will, but Gerrit's organised a lift with Henk. He'll take me to the edge of Hilversum. Ma, don't look like that, I'll be fine. Now, remember what I told you about the coupons? And take care of yourself and those two.' He scooped her into a hug, and was gone.

Tried as she might, she was unable to push the image of Oscar walking along dark streets back to a life she found hard to envisage. He seemed so confident, but all it took was one stray German to bump into him. She shuddered as she remembered the episode in the village. Mechanically, she tucked Arend's ID into the drawer with the others and hid the coupons under the floorboards. There was nothing more to do, except wait and hope.

***

Jan was setting off for school the next day when he turned the corner and almost ran into the two soldiers leaning against their vehicle. His heart thumped painfully as he recognised them. He knew at once they had too. If he hurried past, head down, perhaps they'd let him go.

'*Hoi*. So you live round here?' said the Dutch-speaking one, sucking on his cigarette before blowing the smoke noisily towards Jan.

Better not ignore them.

'I'm on my way to school. Good day.'

The Dutch-speaking one put his foot out. Jan could either side-step it or stop. He stopped.

'You didn't answer my question.'

'Sorry, yes I live round here. I'm going to be late...'

'Would you like to show us?' The man said with mock politeness.

He had no time to warn his mother and Arend, who would still be sitting eating breakfast. Unlike a raid, they would have no chance to hide anything suspicious before opening up. Jan could only hope that Arend would remember his story.

Jan fumbled with his key, whilst the soldiers waited impatiently behind him on the path. As he turned the lock, the door flew open. His mother had heard the commotion and come to see. Panic crossed her face.

'Good morning, mevrouw. We've come to pay you a visit,' said the Dutch-speaking one obsequiously.

She had no choice but to let them in.

'We have a few questions we'd like to ask.' The soldier helped himself to a seat and waited for the others to do the same. 'Your son. We met him the other day. With another boy. Where is he?'

Jan kept his face expressionless and looked to his mother to answer.

'He's upstairs. Getting dressed. Why do you want to know?'

'Well,' said the man, making a charade of tapping a cigarette out and striking a match, then lighting it. 'He should be going to school, shouldn't he?'

'He's been ill. I told you that,' said Jan, a little too quickly.

'Ah yes. You did. Perhaps we could meet him again?'

Sara nodded and went to the bottom of the stairs. 'Arend! Can you come downstairs please?'

They waited. The other soldier grew impatient and muttered something to his companion. Eventually, Arend appeared, timidly stepping down the stairs as if they were burning the soles of his feet.

'So, you're the boy who hasn't been to school. Been ill, have you? Tell us your name,' grinned the Dutch-German.

'I'm Arend. Arend Smit,' he said in a hesitant voice.

'Papers! Show them,' barked the other soldier, moving menacingly towards Arend.

'Tante Sara. She has them.'

Sara fingers fumbled, as she tried to retrieve Arend's ID from the drawer.

The other soldier snatched the card from her and began to scrutinise it. He kept looking from the document to Arend, who stood white-faced and silent. The soldier began shaking his head slowly.

'What is it? It's regular ID, can't you see?' Jan burst out.

The soldier feigned surprise. 'Perhaps we can look at yours to compare. Mevrouw?'

Sara handed over Jan's papers and kept a neutral expression on her face.

The soldier jabbed his finger at Arend's photo. 'It doesn't much look like you. Hmm?'

'He's been ill!' said Jan indignantly. 'The photo was taken a while ago. Surely you can see that?'

It was true that the boy in the photo looked a lot healthier than the one standing before them.

'You boy,' he said, turning to Jan. 'You've been arrested once before, haven't you? How do you fancy another trip in our van down to Amersfoort? You can bring your friend.'

'He's not my friend! He's my cousin.' Jan had the sense not to say more.

'Let me explain,' said Sara in a calm voice. 'My nephew, Arend, is staying with us while he gets better. His mother, my sister, has six other children and was afraid they would fall ill too. He's only recently become well enough to be up and about. You can see that, surely?'

A slow grin spread across the Dutch-German's face. 'Very convincing. But not convincing enough.' He slapped his hand on the arm of his chair, making Sara, Jan and Arend flinch. 'I have it on good authority that Jewish children are being hidden in houses in Kampenveld. We know it's happening, but now we know it to be true.'

'What authority? That's ridiculous! You've seen his ID. It's in order. You heard what my mother said. It's all true. You have nothing on him,' Jan spoke so forcefully, spit flew from his mouth.

'That is none of your business. Come on, boy, *los!*'

Arend had no option but to walk in front of the two soldiers to the door. Sara moved to intervene, but one had his hand on the gun in his waistband. She stopped.

'Here, Arend, take your ID. Try not to worry,' said Sara, pressing the card into his clammy hand. He kept his eyes on the floor, as if in a trance.

'Move! We haven't got all day,' said the Dutch-German, roughly pushing Arend forward and out of the door. The man briefly looked back at Jan and smirked.

'How could you let them do that?' Jan burst out as soon as the door banged shut.

'Shh! Keep your voice down. We were lucky it was just Arend. I know it seems harsh. They got what they wanted, but Arend won't be the last.'

'So why didn't they arrest you for hiding a Jew?'

'Not enough evidence. Perhaps I should have tried to prevent them but didn't you see how he kept fingering his gun?'

Jan paced up and down as he processed this information. The Dutch-German one was definitely out to get him, that much he knew. Why else would they have forced him back home like that? Arresting Arend was simply out of order. His papers could not be faulted. There was absolutely nothing to suggest otherwise. Jan knew he must do something about it.

'Mum. I'm going to tell Gerrit. He's got to help us.'

Sara opened her mouth to object, but Jan had already pulled on his jacket and was leaving by the back door.

He kept well away from the street, jumping over fences and skirting round the village through back gardens. He knew the neighbours wouldn't complain. They were used to Jan's clandestine antics.

Gerrit was just leaving his house as Jan skidded to a halt, out of breath.

'It's urgent,' Jan gasped, then in a whisper, 'They've taken Arend.'

Gerrit calmly unlocked the door and they both went in. He listened without interrupting as Jan spilled out what had happened. Gerrit sighed deeply.

'I warned your mother not to take him out. You're sure they have no proof that he's Jewish?'

Jan nodded.

'Then as long as the boy doesn't confess, they will release him. There's nothing more I can do.'

Jan stared incredulously at Gerrit. The man who had helped both his father, then Donald and now all these Jewish children. How could he be so dismissive?

'You think I can magic the situation better, don't you? I wish I could, but there are lines beyond which I'm not prepared to go.'

'But if you can't, isn't there someone else who can? Tante Else, Dick Foppen, Henk?' Jan searched desperately for all the people he thought likely to help.

'No, Jan. No. The safety of Berkenhout is more important. Ninety lives are at stake there. You are talking about one boy, whose papers show that he's not Jewish. I suggest you go home and be there for your mother. In case they come back.'

Burning with anger, Jan left without saying another word. He didn't head back home. He set off rapidly in the direction of the woods.

Chapter 48

It was a glorious warm summer's day. The sun glinted through the leaves in the tops of the trees, throwing dappled shadows across the woodland floor. Apart from the pure sound of the birds engaged in their morning chorus, the wood was perfectly quiet. Normally, Jan would stop and listen, breathing in the damp earthy scent, but today he hurried on, head down without pausing until he reached Henk's cottage. Coming through the clearing, he was relieved to see Henk's van parked out front, but held back when he heard voices. He shrunk himself behind a tree so he could observe. It was like the last time. Henk was moving crates from the back of the van and another man was piling them up on the side of the path. This one wasn't in uniform, so Jan couldn't be sure if he was German. Suddenly, the idea of asking Henk for help didn't seem such a good idea.

Henk slammed the van doors shut and slapped the other man on the shoulder, who grinned, saying something that Jan couldn't quite pick up. A loud scuffling noise made Jan shrink back further and hold his breath. From behind Henk's cottage, three men in SS uniform came bounding out of the trees over to where the two men were standing.

Jan tried to work out from their body language what was going on. They all seemed to know each other, for there was much shaking of hands and laughter. Then, incredibly, the three newcomers went over to the crates, heaved them onto their shoulders before setting off down the road in the direction of Berkenhout. The first man shook Henk's hand and walked round to the back of the cottage, where Jan could hear the sound of a motorbike starting up. Henk watched and waved as his companion moved off onto the road and disappeared in the direction of the others. As Henk turned, Jan caught the satisfied expression on his face as he went back into his cottage and closed the door.

Jan slumped down against the tree and hugged his knees. Surely this was proof that Henk was working hand in glove with the Germans? And he thought he could trust him. Now the last thing he wanted to do was to tell Henk about Arend. What about those Germans? They were actually walking off in the direction of Berkenhout. To do what? Help them with supplies? Jan shook his head vigorously and screwed his eyes in concentration. When he opened them, he saw Henk was coming back out, whistling softly, before getting into his van and driving off in the direction of Kampenveld.

Pulling himself up to standing, Jan decided he had better find out what was happening. He set off at a jog, avoiding the path and staying close to the trees. It was a short-cut he knew well and gave him the advantage of arriving at Berkenhout before the three Germans, if that was where they were heading. After a while he relaxed, sure that he was on his own. Back in his beloved woods, he almost forgot about others who must have been some way behind him. He even began to whistle, but desisted when he remembered how it would draw attention to himself.

The route took him past the place where he'd first found Nigel. It seemed such a long time ago, but Jan remembered the wave of excitement he'd felt on discovering his first fallen pilot. And the fear when they'd emerged from their den to find Henk standing there. Yes, even then there was something a bit shifty about Henk. Jan had liked Nigel and wished he could have stayed hidden with them at home a bit longer. But after he'd disappeared through the network, they'd never heard from him again.

A small detour took him past where he'd found Donald. He smiled at the memory of Donald calling out: 'God Save the President!' and how he'd teased him with his Camel cigarettes. Even then, Jan had felt a huge respect for the tall, handsome man in uniform who'd become a sort of best friend to him. Jan sped up as he resolved to travel to Ohio in search of him.

The woods had turned eerily silent, even though he knew those Germans couldn't be that far from him. He slowed, skirting the trees and listening hard for any unusual sounds. If only the twigs wouldn't snap so loudly underfoot. Each popping sound seemed to echo through the whole wood.

Not far now. He took a deep breath, confident that he was ahead. With any luck, there would be time to alert Wouter who would instigate the escape plan to evacuate within minutes. Jan had heard about the plan to put Wouter in charge when eavesdropping one day as he was helping with food supplies over at tante Else's. He'd been so excited, almost wishing he could have been part of one of the dummy runs Wouter had been planning. Now he had his chance for the real thing.

Determined to beat the men who must be closing in, Jan broke into a run and took another short-cut he knew would save him precious seconds. It meant crossing a track that ran through a clearing with no tree cover, but it was a risk he had to take. Stepping out, something hurled him right onto the track before he had a chance to look left or right. As he regained his balance a loud cracking noise ripped through his head as he dropped to the ground.

It all happened so fast, that he had trouble remembering the sequence of events. The pain in his foot was excruciating. At first he thought he must have turned it on a hidden tree root or something beneath the leaves. Or perhaps it was the loud crack that made him stumble and twist his ankle. After falling to the ground, and clutching his foot, he became aware that the three Germans were rushing towards him from the trees. They were no more than fifty metres from Berkenhout. Then he saw blood pouring from his foot. He'd been shot.

Two of them hoisted him by his armpits, shrieking urgently to one another, all the while dragging him closer and closer to the village. Jan tried to struggle free, but he could only think about protecting his foot which had gone completely numb. Then without warning they dropped him, as if he were an object to be discarded.

It was Karl. He must have come to investigate the noise, thinking it was Henk arriving with supplies. He stood, blinking rapidly, then looked as if he were about to turn and run, but must have thought better of it. Three guns were trained on him. Simultaneously, the three soldiers barked out the command for him to stop.

As quietly as he could, Jan crawled behind a thorny bush, which snagged at his clothes, scratching his arms and legs. It felt like nothing compared to the searing pain in his foot. His sock was soaked red, but he didn't dare try to pull it off. Then to his horror, one of the soldiers took aim at Karl's feet. The noise was deafening. Jan couldn't be sure if the soldier had shot once or more times. Jan clapped his hands over his ears and ducked his head. He could no longer see Karl and wasn't sure if he'd been hit or had managed to escape.

All at once, the air was rent with screaming and more gun shots. More Germans appeared, jubilant at their discovery as they tore through the village. It was pandemonium. In their haste to escape, people left their possessions, even their shoes. There was no time to count heads. It was each to their own, clutching onto their nearest and dearest. The escape route, so meticulously planned in endless meetings, would take them deep into the woods, but quickly became clogged as they tried to flee. The Germans moved in, pushing the weak and elderly aside, training guns on them.

Jan stared at the scene unfolding, powerless to do anything. He was forced to witness the executions, each shot thumping through his chest as if he were the victim. Unable to cry out, tears coursed down his face as he recognised first Kees fall to the ground, followed by Corrie who had run screaming from her hut and straight into the line of fire. *Please don't let them get Sofie*, he whispered in a shuddering breath. There was no sign of her. He prayed she'd escaped.

He lay still, listening to the yells and screams until they subsided. Surely most had managed to get away? He counted the bodies, the ones he could see. There were seven. He couldn't be sure, but was one of them Karl? Two were young children, he could tell by their small huddled shapes, but he was sure they weren't Kees and Corrie's twins. And all the time Jan had been watching he hadn't seen Sofie. Good news, surely, but he had a niggling feeling that would not go away. Sofie, of all people, would have been out there, fired up with anger and herding the children to safety, wouldn't she? Still he didn't dare make himself visible, waiting until he could be sure all the Germans had left, strolling away from the village, laughing and banging each other on the shoulders, without a backward glance. Only then did he allow himself a long shuddering sigh, grateful that they hadn't gone in pursuit of those who had made it into the thick woodland. He stared down at his swollen foot that filled his blood-soaked sock. His injury seemed futile compared to what he had just witnessed.

As he lay there, the first drops of water pattered on the leaves, making a rat-a-tat sound like soft continuous gunfire. Within minutes, it grew louder and louder as if someone was trying to wash away the carnage. Despite the hissing and spitting of raindrops, it was deathly quiet, just Jan and the bodies before him. But there was nothing he could do. He knew he had to raise the alarm and get back home, somehow, even though he couldn't put any weight on his foot. Unable to resist the great wave of tiredness that surged over him, he drifted in and out of consciousness. At one point, he heard a noise. Opening his eyes, he thought he saw Henk standing over one of the bodies but couldn't make out what he was doing. It seemed he was prodding, then leaning in closer and examining the clothing, perhaps the pockets. It was too tiring to watch, so Jan let himself fall into sleep again. Next time he came to, he tried to remember what he'd seen, as there was no sign of anyone. The bodies were still lain where they had fallen. It grew dark, but at least the rain had stopped. Jan had managed to shelter quite successfully, but the dampness was now accompanied by a fall in temperature. On and off he dozed, but kept waking stiff and cold. At least his foot didn't bother him as much. He must have slept eventually, because the next time he woke he could make out grey shapes of trees all around him. A bird started up its morning song and for a moment, Jan felt his spirits lift, until he peered through the leaves. The bodies were still there. It hadn't been a dream.

Noticing a hazel tree close by, he crawled over and snapped off a branch for a makeshift walking stick. He dragged himself to standing and tentatively put his weight on his swollen stiff foot. Slowly, he began his journey back home.

***

He heard the voices first. Jan stopped to stare. It was a sight the likes of which he'd never seen before. A forest of umbrellas moving about and bursts of joyful laughter as people spoke rapidly and excitedly. Then he spotted his mother, holding hands with Arend who was also laughing. What could they be celebrating?

Jan hung back. They couldn't possibly have known what had happened at Berkenhout, but all this jubilation could mean only one thing. Shaking his head in disbelief, he turned away from the square and hobbled through the side streets back to his own house. He would tell his mother everything all in good time.

A folded sheet of paper with his name on it lay on the kitchen table. He knew she wouldn't have left a note out if she'd been worried about it being found. First, he settled himself down with his foot raised on a kitchen chair. This big swollen thing didn't look like it belonged to him, but it throbbed like hell. Sighing, he picked up the note and scanned it.

> *Lieve* Jan,
>
> Where have you got to? I've been so worried. Everything happened so quickly after you left. We just heard the news that the allies are on their way to free us!! Then Arend arrived back home. The Germans must have known and let him go. I'll tell you all very soon. We've all gone to the square to celebrate.
>
> Love and kisses, Mama.

He had no time to consider what it meant as the door flew open. It was Sara, with Arend and Gerrit. Sara rushed up to Jan and hugged him hard, oblivious to his injury.

'Where have you been? You're injured! What's happened?'

Jan flinched as she bent over his foot, tentatively touching it. Nausea enveloped him. He had to catch his breath. 'I was shot. The *moffen* got me,' he gasped. 'There must be dozens hiding in the woods. They gunned down seven. That's all I could see.'

Gerrit crouched beside Jan, his hand on his arm. 'They found

Berkenhout? Have you just come from there?'

'It happened yesterday afternoon. I managed to hide in the undergrowth, but the pain was too much for me to move at first. It was terrible.' His voice gave out as tears streamed down his face. 'I'm sorry, mama.' He hadn't called her that in years but now all he wanted was for her to speak in her soothing voice like she used to when he was unwell.

'I can't believe it's happened now, right at the end. All this time we managed to keep them safe and now this. We need to help them get out to safety. I must go and tell Dick.' Gerrit left, his face grim.

'It's my fault. I know it is,' said Jan desperately. 'I should've listened and not gone into the woods. But it's always been fine, well almost always. I just thought Henk would help.'

'Henk? You went to see Henk? So he was there too?' said his mother, frowning.

Jan explained the scene he'd come across at Henk's cottage and how he'd set off to try and avert the Germans from finding Berkenhout. How this wasn't the first time he'd suspected Henk of helping them.

'So it was his actions that led to the discovery of Berkenhout, not yours,' said Sara quietly. 'Dick needs to know.'

'No!' shouted Jan. 'I know he was doing wrong but it wasn't like that. He just wanted to help everybody.' He wasn't sure why he was defending Henk after all he'd seen. All he knew was that if he hadn't gone back to Berkenhout at that point, things would have turned out differently. He should never have taken that shortcut running straight into the Germans' path. Over and over the images came back into his head. If only he could start from the beginning and change the course of what happened.

'Jan, this is too serious. You don't know for certain what Henk was up to. Even if it wasn't deliberate, he will be accountable.'

Chapter 49

It was deathly quiet. No songbirds singing or low chatter signifying the start of a new day. No warmth from the fire Corrie would light without fail on waking. How long she'd lain on the floor of the hut, she couldn't be sure. Stiffly, she turned towards the dim light visible through the opening of the hut. It must be day.

Sofie unclasped her knees and used her palms to ease herself to standing. Everything hurt. Nothing made sense. Where was everyone? What had happened? She edged slowly towards the daylight, but the brightness hurt her eyes, making her turn away. Defeated, she groped her way back to her bunk to lie down. But she couldn't sleep. Disjointed images kept flashing through her head. Had they been real or had she suddenly fallen very ill, leaving her unable to distinguish these nightmares from reality?

Sporadically, harsh images and sounds jumped through her head: gunfire, screams, crying, thuds, loud voices, silence. Then it had started up again, this time more shouts, laughter, German voices, huge shapes filling the hut. She was on her back, pushed down, unable to cry out, unable to move. The weight of something on her was unbearable. That sharp pain starting somewhere in her body before travelling all over and tipping her over into welcome blackness.

She woke with a raging thirst. Relieved that the blood and pain had subsided, she hoisted herself to sitting and focused on the milk can lying on its side on a damp patch of floor. Were those footprints?

She couldn't be sure. Picking up the empty can, she shook it and felt a little water swishing from side to side. Too tired to find a cup, she drank greedily and some of the water escaped, trickling onto her blouse and making her shiver. Revived, she knew she must investigate the eerie silence. Corrie, Kees, Karl, where were they? A gnawing dread clutched at her insides.

At the sound of voices, she shrank back, her heart pounding. Were they coming for her again? The same images flashed across her brain – looming dark shapes filling the hut, leaving no space for her, almost suffocating her.

'Sofie! You're still here... are you alright?'

The voice was familiar, but fear shot through her causing her to scrabble to the furthest corner so her back was to the wall.

'Sofie, *schatje*. It's fine.' It was Dick Foppen.

Sofie relaxed a little but stiffened again as she saw someone with him. She wanted to speak but couldn't think of the words. What was happening? Why did it hurt so? What were they doing here?

Dick was crouching beside her and spoke in a low, soothing voice. 'You've been by yourself but everything is fine and we've come to take you home.'

Home? Wasn't this home? Perhaps he meant her old home and that her parents were back. Sofie shook her head in disbelief. That couldn't be right.

'Come, you'll be staying with me for a while where it's safe. Look, Gerrit's here, you remember him, don't you?'

Sofie stared at the silhouette. If Dick said it was Gerrit, it must be so. She gave a tiny nod. How could she even begin to say what had happened.

Outside, her eyes gradually accustomed to the bright light. The place was deserted, no sign of anyone. Of course. Now she knew. There'd been an evacuation and she'd been left behind. She looked into Dick's face but it was blank, his lips drawn into a thin line.

'Over here, just a little way to the car. Then I'll drive you home.'

Sofie stumbled a little as she walked across the yard. She caught sight of a several dark patches on the ground and caught her breath. Surely it wasn't? But the village was empty. No sign of any people. She had to stop still to let the images of her friends mown down by gunfire, which coursed through her head accompanied by a roaring sound. She was dimly aware of Dick and Gerrit whispering in low voices while she stood taking deep breaths. Then, with one on either side of her holding her arms, they gently led her away from Berkenhout for the last time.

***

The journey back to Kampenveld took an age. Bumping and rattling over the rutted tracks, Sofie kept her hand to her mouth to prevent herself being sick. Dick and Gerrit talked to one another in falsely cheerful voices, but she wasn't listening. Gradually, it dawned on her, the reason they'd come and were being so kind to her. The crack of gunshots that kept repeating in her head could only mean one thing. Berkenhout had been discovered and somehow, she had no idea how or why she'd been left behind.

The jerky movements of the car soon made her sleepy. She'd been digging for vegetables a few yards behind the hut. Hearing the shouts and shots, she'd hidden herself in a bush, paralysed with fear. Of course she should have joined the others and fled deeper into the woods, but what if those she loved needed help? But she hadn't gone to see. It wasn't until nightfall, when she could be sure that the Germans had left, that she'd stirred herself and crept back to the hut. All her nerves had been on edge as she'd strained at every little sound from outside. The hoot of an owl, the creak of a tree branch, any little sound had sent a new shockwave through her body. It was properly dark when she'd heard the approach of the men, the thud of their hobnailed boots as they came nearer. Unable to stop herself, she'd let out a cry. It was enough to alert the men, who, with whooping voices, crashed through the entrance to the hut and stood over her, laughing and jeering. They'd talked rapidly amongst themselves, as if they were having an argument. There'd been one, tall, very blond, who seemed to be in charge. At his command, the group had left the hut. He'd turned to Sofie and had begun speaking in a softer voice, but she'd been unable to understand him. That'd seemed to make him angry and he'd grabbed her by the shoulders, kissing her roughly and yanking up her skirt. Rigid with fear, she'd been unable to put up any resistance as he'd pinned her down so he could thrust himself inside her. The pain had been excruciating, as if she'd been torn in half. It couldn't have been more than a few seconds, but the memory of his sour breath, feeling of suffocation and agonising pain kept washing over her. After he'd tossed her aside and hurried away to join his collaborators, she'd felt a warm trickle between her legs and been horrified to discover it was blood. Convinced she would die, she'd pressed a cloth against her and prayed for mercy.

'That's the worst bit over,' smiled Dick as they finally reached the main road towards Kampenveld. He patted her hands which she was clasping tightly in her lap. Staring ahead and barely blinking, she didn't feel like smiling. She knew something truly terrible had happened back there, far worse than being separated from her family and the long drawn-out years of hiding from the enemy. She didn't want to hear that she would never see her dearest friends again and all because she hadn't gone to help. She could have changed things, but she didn't and now she was the only one left. It had all been for nothing. She'd lost everything. Taking a slow breath so the others wouldn't notice, she moved her hands towards her belly and let them rest there. *Please don't let it be*, she prayed silently.

Chapter 50

News about the fateful discovery of Berkenhout swept through Kampenveld. How ironic that *Dolle Dinsdag*, Mad Tuesday, came to mean something quite different from the original joy they'd all experienced when they believed they were about to be liberated by the Allies. One short day in September 1944, when all the worries of the previous five years disappeared before cruelly returning with the realisation that the Germans were far from ready to give up. And the double blow as so many were connected in some way with the inhabitants of Berkenhout. For many people, *Dolle Dinsdag* became etched on minds as the day after Berkenhout was raided. Hidden from the Germans all those years, only to be discovered at the very moment everyone believed the war had ended. That day, joy turned to terror, as houses, barns and outhouses filled up with Jews who had fled in panic. Pandemonium ensued over the following days and weeks as Dick Foppen and his trusted helpers had struggled to accommodate so many evacuees and kept them safely hidden from the prying eyes of any passing Germans. It was a miracle the majority remained undiscovered for so long, thanks largely to the incompetence and growing disillusionment of the German soldiers, who themselves had hoped the war would soon be at an end.

Sofie, the last to be evacuated after being found by Dick and Gerrit in a deserted Berkenhout, was given a safe haven with Sara, Jan and Arend. For weeks, she stayed up in the attic, once Arend's hiding place. Arend moved into Oscar's old room, assuming his new role as Jan's cousin with growing confidence. Sara arranged for the doctor to come and check out Sofie. Apart from the trauma she'd suffered, he decreed he could find nothing physically wrong with her, so prescribed only warmth and bed rest to help her recover. Sara wasn't convinced. The change in Sofie was so profound, from bubbly and chatty teenager to this subdued young woman, who seemed much older than her years. Something must have happened to change her and Sara found it hard to believe it was solely being the last one left behind was the reason. But Sofie refused to open up. Nothing gave her pleasure and she answered in monosyllables only when spoken to. Jan, too, was much more subdued, having lost his innate liveliness. Maybe there was a connection, wondered Sara, knowing they had both witnessed that terrible event. Whereas Sofie clammed up, Jan brushed off any of Sara's questions. So she resorted to sharing her concerns by enquiring about his foot. The bullet had badly damaged his foot, but it was healing, leaving a livid red scar and a limp. 'It's nothing,' he'd say, wincing as he put his weight on it. 'Serves me right, I suppose.'

Often he'd sit up in the cramped attic space, squeezed next to Sofie. He'd take a book and read passages out to her while she listened, staring out of the tiny window. One time, he came up with an Agatha Christie mystery, which he'd found in his mother's bookcase. Sofie seemed to like hearing him read to her in English and refused to let him leave if he tried to break off. Their friendship seemed to do her good and occasionally she'd smile when he deliberately put on a funny 'Hercule Poirot' accent. Little by little, he coaxed her to speak again, although she would never refer to the terrible things that had happened to her that night after everyone else had gone.

Over the coming weeks, the nights became much colder so the risk of raids was greatly reduced. Liesbeth was a frequent visitor and much practised in the art of evading the Germans in the event of a raid. She persuaded Sofie to come and sit downstairs with the family by the *kachel*. Endlessly upbeat, she'd crack jokes and discuss her plans to go to University, which, of course, included Sofie. It was as if she didn't notice that Sofie failed to answer as she chattered away. But the effect on Sofie was marked and she always seemed more relaxed in Liesbeth's company.

One day, after many weeks, Sara was in the kitchen preparing soup for lunch, when she heard a creak on the stairs. She turned to see Sofie creeping down, step by step, as she held onto the wooden banister. Her face still looked pale and drawn and she seemed thinner, except for the unmistakable swelling of her abdomen.

'Sofie... how nice to see you up and about. Come and sit down and I'll make you a cup of tea,' said Sara, holding a chair out to her. Sofie managed a small smile and sat herself down.

'How are you feeling?' asked Sara, trying hard to keep her eyes on Sofie's face.

'I don't want to be up there all the time.'

'Well, it's a good thing to stretch your legs a bit. It can't do you any good being cooped up like that,' said Sara brightly, placing a cup of tea in front of her. 'Would you like the doctor to come and make sure you're quite well?'

'No! I'm fine,' said Sofie forcefully, instinctively cupping her hand over her belly.

Sara pulled up a chair and sat beside her. 'You know it'll be for the best and he'll be able to suggest how to keep yourself well.'

Sofie bowed her head as the tears rolled down her cheeks. 'I can't hide it any more, can I? What am I going to do?' she said in a high thin voice.

Sara patted her arm, at a loss what to say. It was unimaginable what the poor girl had endured and her reluctance to talk about it made it only harder. She spoke in a low voice so as not to alarm her. 'You can stay here for as long as you want, but you must let the doctor come and examine you.'

'No! I can't let anyone know,' sobbed Sofie, standing up and gripping the edge of the table. 'It's so unfair. Why did it have to happen?'

'Sofie, it's not going to go away, so you'll have to face up to it sooner or later. I'm sure we can work something out.'

'I don't want it, this... thing. Can't you see that?' The tears were streaming down her face.

'Shh, don't speak like that. We'll find a way, I promise,' said Sara, desperate to provide some kind of reassurance.

It was Sofie, who finally saw a way out of her misery. She was nearly seven months pregnant when she approached Liesbeth, asking to speak to her privately. Sofie led her friend up to the attic where they stayed for a long time, their low voices only faintly discernible to Sara who was working in the kitchen. Eventually, Liesbeth came down and quietly told Sara about Sofie's intentions. It was something that would change the two friends' lives forever.

Chapter 51

One spring morning, just weeks before the end of the war, Dick Foppen was visiting Liesbeth, Wouter and Laura at tante Else's. Everyone was in high spirits as news was filtering through about the progress of the Allies. It could only be a matter of days and weeks before this terrible war was at an end. It was Laura's birthday and tante Else was determined to make the day as nice as she could. They sat around the kitchen table sipping *ersatz* coffee and nibbling on tiny slices of a cake Liesbeth had managed to magic up out of virtually no ingredients.

'*Hartelijk gefeliciteerd!*' Happy birthday, they all said, raising their cups to Laura, before kissing her on both cheeks. Wouter gathered her into his arms and whispered in her ear, 'You look beautiful today,' making her blush.

Tante Else smiled at the couple, pleased to see them together after all they had endured. On more than one occasion, Wouter had been on the verge of leaving Berkenhout, only to be dissuaded by tante Else. She'd made him believe in himself and become the leader they'd all needed. And since the break up of Berkenhout, he'd continued to work on behalf of those who'd been forced to flee, helping to keep the community alive at places like tante Else's house, where people could meet safely and have a little bit of normality and forget there was still a war on.

'Delicious, considering it doesn't have any ingredients normally found in cakes,' said Dick cheerfully, licking the last crumbs from his cake fork.

'I'm not sure I even remember what a normal cake tastes like any more. Do you really think the war will be over soon?' asked Laura, her eyes dark and intense. Wouter squeezed her hand as they waited for Dick to reply.

'Yes, I do. Now, don't you worry. The Germans have no more appetite for this war. And when we're sure they've well and truly gone, we're going to have the biggest party Kampenveld has ever seen. This time, it'll be for real. Celebrations like we've never seen before. Brass bands, fireworks, eating, drinking, dancing till we all drop…'

'Hot doughnuts dipped in sugar!' sighed Liesbeth.

'Beer!' shouted Wouter, lifting his empty coffee cup and pretending to drink deeply from it.

Laura smiled too and leant her head against Wouter's shoulder as the laughter in the room became more raucous.

Tante Else shook her head, but was laughing along with the rest of them. It was a welcome break from the anxieties they all now took for granted and couldn't quite believe would ever be a thing of the past.

Cheeks ablaze, Dick got up and announced that he had to be on his way.

'Please stay for one more coffee. Don't break up the party yet,' said tante Else, pushing her chair back as well.

'I wish I could but I have an arrangement to meet Gerrit. There's still business to be done,' he said.

'Then come again. Let's not wait for another birthday. You've been a real tonic.' All at once, tante Else gave him a peck on the cheek and the rest of the group cheered. Dick held her hands and solemnly promised to come back soon.

***

He left by the back door, always careful to look around him before leaving. It was perfectly quiet, no passing cars, and the only sound were the sweet strains of a robin practising its song from a chimney top across the road. Dick looked up and smiled. He lifted the latch on the low gate, which creaked as he opened it. The robin stopped singing. Dick carefully shut the gate behind him and began walking away down the road. The robin began singing again.

The crack of gunfire ripped through the air, too loud to be a backfiring car. Dick had only walked a few yards. He had no time to react. Targeted from behind, Dick was gunned down by two SS-ers who had been waiting in their army vehicle parked out of sight a little way up the road. They must have known about tante Else and the others, but it was Dick, the leader of Berkenhout, they had come for. Their job done, the soldiers jumped back into their vehicle and tore off in the direction of the woods.

Alerted to the loud gunfire, tante Else rushed to the front window only to see two soldiers running back to their vehicle. She was the only witness. Not that any was needed. Can it have been chance they'd been passing and seen Dick walk into her house? Or maybe someone had tipped them off.

Chapter 52

After Dick Foppen was killed, the Kampenveld community became extremely nervous, fearing that one of their own would be next. Someone must surely have told the soldiers stationed near Kampenveld about Dick's renewed efforts to move Berkenhout evacuees to safe houses. Fingers were pointed at Henk, who strongly denied any involvement, but made himself increasingly helpful in continuing Dick's work. Through his contacts, he helped Berkenhout inhabitants to find more secure hiding places and, in doing so, gradually won over people's trust. In doing so, many were prepared to overlook his murky negotiations in obtaining black market foodstuffs and drink. Being able to drink coffee sweetened with sugar again was too hard to resist. The long war had sapped their resolve and Henk was seen as the only way to get hold of those long desired small luxuries.

With Dick gone, it fell to Gerrit to hold the community together, but it was a role he was loathe to take on. What if he were next? He was profoundly affected by the death of his friend and feared for his own safety, but knew he couldn't just ignore the threat. He decided it was time to pay Henk a visit to try and discover the truth.

'Come in, my good friend,' said Henk, opening the door of his cottage in the woods. He was a big man and filled the doorway. Stepping aside, he ushered Gerrit in. 'Would you like a *jenever*?' He already had the bottle in his hand and started pouring two glasses before Gerrit had a chance to answer. Gerrit noticed how well Henk looked. His cheeks had colour and he had a sparkle in his eye.

'Just a small one,' said Gerrit, embarrassed to refuse the glass Henk held out to him, but he knew he mustn't allow himself to be deflected from his purpose. 'I've come to discuss a serious matter and hope you'll be frank with me.'

'Of course. Now, what is it that's bothering you?' Henk knocked back his *jenever* and straightaway poured himself another.

'This business with the Germans. Now, we all know that you're on friendly terms with them.'

'I don't know what you mean,' interrupted Henk. 'It's true I had a few negotiations but only to obtain essentials we've been denied for so long. Like this *jenever*,' he smiled and held up the bottle.

'I understand, but wasn't it more than that? Young Jan tells me that he saw you handing over crates of goods, not the other way round.'

Henk shook his head vigorously. 'No, he's mistaken. The only time anything was handed over was when I obtained these *jenever* bottles for hard cash. Tell Jan that's what it was.'

Gerrit sipped at his *jenever* as he considered how to reply. Perhaps Henk was telling the truth. Sara had said that Jan often became overexcited and was prone to exaggeration. But something in Henk's manner suggested he was not telling him the whole story. Henk, normally so monosyllabic, seemed to be making an effort to be more chatty, perhaps as a way of covering up. His manner made Gerrit determined to push on. So he told him what Jan had seen that fateful day.

'Jan followed the soldiers he saw heading in the direction of Berkenhout. Unfortunately for Jan, they caught sight of him and that's what precipitated the raid on the camp. Are you saying you didn't tip them off?'

Henk stood up and his chair fell to the floor with a loud clatter. 'Enough of these accusations! I admit I became friendly with one or two young soldiers who couldn't stand serving for the German army. But that doesn't mean I was tipping anyone off. I was the one who got Karl a place in Berkenhout, don't you remember?'

Henk towered above Gerrit, but Gerrit knew it was bravado. He wouldn't dare do anything to him. 'And a lot of people were unhappy about it,' said Gerrit in a quiet voice. 'There's talk that you and Karl had been planning the attack on Berkenhout for some time.'

Henk loomed over Gerrit, who kept his gaze steady. He needed an answer, but he sensed he wasn't going to get one. Henk looked momentarily uncomfortable before replying. 'That's just not true. After Karl joined Berkenhout I never spoke to him again. He may have had his own contacts, but no one ever spoke to me about that. I only ever wanted to help people. It doesn't matter what side they're on. We're all the same and we're all trying to get through this terrible war as best we can. I may have made a few errors along the way, who doesn't? But why would I willingly hurt my own people?'

Was that a tear in his eye? Gerrit couldn't decide whether or not it was genuine. He sighed. If Henk were telling the truth, then it was more complicated than he'd first thought. Maybe Henk didn't realise the consequences of his perceived good intentions.

Henk went back to his bottle but seemed to think better of pouring himself another glass. 'See this? It's the only thing that keeps me going these days,' he said. 'I want this war to end as much as the next man and go back to living a peaceful life. You do see, don't you?'

Gerrit did see and decided not to pursue the matter further. He reasoned that the amount of good Henk had done surely outweighed any errors of judgement, however dire the consequences had been. After all, he was unable to prove anything.

'These are strange times, Henk, and with Berkenhout disbanded and Dick gone, we must all pull together. I suggest you keep your distance from the Germans. It can't be long now.' He politely finished his *jenever* and stood up to go.

'I never meant any harm,' said Henk, placing a large hand on Gerrit's arm.

'No, I don't believe you did,' said Gerrit, who left with a heavy heart.

Chapter 53

Twenty years later

Liesbeth held out the square black and white photograph for Marieke to look at. Marieke peered at the two laughing girls: the smaller one with short dark hair she could make out as her mother. The other girl looked more confident with her halo of wiry chestnut hair and head thrown back in laughter. 'Who's she?' She narrowed her eyes to get a better look.

'That's Sofie, my best friend. Before the war we were inseparable. That photo was taken at the end of the Easter holidays and we were so looking forward to the summer term. Of course, everything changed just after that photo was taken. All because of those terrible Germans.' Liesbeth's face became contorted as she spoke. Marieke could see real hatred in her eyes.

'What happened to her after the war?' Marieke knew that Liesbeth's best friend had been in Berkenhout right to the end of the war, but her mother had never said anything more than that.

'She went back to live in Kampenveld. Not her own home, of course. The Germans had requisitioned it and the memories would have been too painful. You see, that's what I wanted to talk to you about.' Liesbeth stared at her hands twisting a handkerchief in her lap and trying to find the right words.

'It must have been really hard for her adapting to normal life again,' said Marieke. 'She looks such a cheerful girl. Is she happy now?'

'I don't know. I hoped she would find some happiness and

maybe she still will. Marieke, I'd like you to meet her. Will you come with me?'

'Yes, sure, if you like. If you think she'd like it. Mum, look, I have to go now. I'm late. Let's arrange something later.'

Marieke swung her bag onto her shoulder and leant over her mother to give her a quick kiss. Hurrying out of the door, she spotted the bus approaching the stop and sprinted down the road to catch it. Out of breath, she managed to hop on before it pulled away, flicking her student pass at the driver, who nodded. From the back seat, her friend waved and Marieke swayed down the bus, steadying herself pole to pole.

'*Hoi* Griet,' she said, and they kissed cheeks three times, the Dutch way.

When Marieke let out an enormous sigh Griet asked her if anything was the matter.

'It's Mum, she was acting a bit odd just now. Nearly made me miss the bus.' She tossed her dark brown curls from her face and settled into her seat. 'She wants me to go and visit her old friend from before the war. Don't know why.'

'Didn't you ask her?'

'No, 'cos I knew I'd miss the bus if I did. But I feel guilty rushing out like that. She looked really upset.'

'Forget it for now. You'll find out sooner or later. Guess what? Piet van Beenstra phoned me last night,' said Griet, triumphantly.

'No! Tell me all.'

But Marieke's mind wasn't on Griet's latest conquest. Something was bothering her about the picture and the way her mother had reacted.

***

By the time she got back home after college, it was as if the episode that morning hadn't happened. Liesbeth had made one of her amazing Indonesian *nasi goreng* dishes for supper, and announced that Johan would be joining them.

'That's the second time this week. And you're telling me there's nothing going on, hmm?' teased Marieke, helping to chop up the cucumber for one of the side dishes.

She liked Johan. In fact he was the first of her mother's boyfriends, if you could call it that, she really got on with. And he took a genuine interest in her, unlike all the others. She wondered if that was what having a dad would be like, then decided he was more like a proper grown-up friend. She listened to him when he dished out advice on trying for Leiden, in a way her own mother hadn't done when discussing her options for university. Johan was a doctor himself, not the medical kind, and taught history at Utrecht, so he must know a thing or two about what universities were looking for.

Liesbeth put her arms round Marieke's waist resting her chin on her shoulder. 'It was his idea to get in touch with Sofie and he's offered to drive us to Kampenveld.'

Marieke twisted round to face Liesbeth. 'Whatever for? Does he know her?'

'Didn't I tell you? We all knew each other quite well during the war.'

'Was he in Berkenhout during the war?'

'No, oh no. Ah, there he is.' Liesbeth's face brightened at the sound of the doorbell.

Marieke went back to her chopping. She could hear by the tone of Liesbeth's voice that she was pleased to see him.

'Look, a lovely chrysanthemum plant, my favourite.' She placed it on the little telephone table by the front door.

No one mentioned a word about the war or going to visit Sofie until the end of the meal.

'Johan, are you still able to take us to Kampenveld sometime?' asked Liesbeth, pushing the dishes into an untidy pile.

'I've got a day free on Saturday if that's any good,' he said, draining his glass of beer. 'Liesbeth's told you, hasn't she?'

'Yes, she wants me to meet Sofie.' Marieke gave Johan a quizzical look but he didn't seem to pick up on it.

'I should have been to see her earlier but somehow things always get in the way,' said Liesbeth.

'You can't blame yourself. I'm sure she'll be pleased to see you,' said Johan, absentmindedly stroking her hand which lay on the table.

***

Marieke had better things to do than give up her free day. The weather was particularly gloomy for May, foggy with a wet sheen on the pavements. Kampenveld was only three quarters of an hour away by car. Johan and Liesbeth spent all their time reminiscing in the front while Marieke stared out at the endless wide green polders dotted with black and white cows.

'Look! The church!' exclaimed Liesbeth, leaning forward in her seat as they approached the centre. 'Nothing's changed a bit,' she said, with obvious relief.

They parked with difficulty round the back of the church as there was the weekly market on in the square. The place was heaving with people despite the dreary drizzle.

Johan led the way to Sofie's tiny narrow house two streets away from the centre and rang the bell. The door opened immediately and there stood a woman the same age as her mother. She looked straight at Marieke, as if the others weren't there. 'Marieke,' she murmured, half behind the door as if she was about to shut it again.

'Sofie! How lovely to see you. Aren't you going to let us in?' Liesbeth pushed forward over the step and into the house to kiss her friend on the cheeks.

Unasked, Marieke and Johan followed her in and Sofie seemed to remember her manners, leading the way down a dark, panelled corridor to a large room at the back. It was part kitchen, part living room with an enormous picture window facing a tiny patio covered in pot plants. Marieke wondered if she ever sat outside, the patio was so crowded.

Liesbeth chatted away as if she'd only seen Sofie yesterday, while Marieke stood awkwardly, wondering why she'd been asked to come along. Johan was no help and was inspecting the bookcase, pulling first one, then another book out and examining them intently.

Marieke watched Sofie, who gradually came to life as she and Liesbeth exchanged stories as children. Johan butted in every so often and soon the three of them were laughing at shared jokes. It seemed that Johan, the younger of the three, used to get up to all kinds of pranks as a way of drawing attention to himself. You wouldn't have guessed that from Johan's serious demeanour, probably developed from years of research and teaching.

All the while, Sofie kept an eye on Marieke who sat sipping her tea and listening. It was nice enough meeting her mother's old friend, but Marieke couldn't make out why she'd been included on the trip. Racking her brains, she tried to remember what her mother had mentioned about Sofie, but failed. Yet there was something familiar about her speech and her gestures that Marieke couldn't put her finger on.

Looking back, she couldn't quite remember what happened next and how she'd reacted at Sofie's revelation. She did know that all eyes were on her.

'Why didn't you tell me this before?' she asked Liesbeth, although it would have been logical to ask Sofie.

'Jan, you tell her what happened,' said Sofie in barely a whisper. She no longer kept looking at Marieke but at her hands which she held clasped tightly in her lap.

'It was because of me that the village was discovered by the Germans. I'd grown suspicious about some Germans I'd seen heading in the direction of Berkenhout but misjudged where they were when they ambushed me. It wasn't my first encounter with them, but on every other occasion I'd managed to talk my way out of it. They must have followed me from the path and towards the village. They were waiting for me. You see, the last time I ran into the Germans they bundled me, my brother Oscar and the American pilot we'd found, into a van and we spent three days in custody.

'They'd been looking for the village for nearly two whole years, but never got close to it. Then I went and gave the game away. I should never have tried to outwit them. They might never have found Berkenhout if it hadn't been for me.' Johan... Jan, was shaking his head. 'I'm sorry, Sofie.'

Marieke furrowed her brow. Why did she call him Jan? 'But you managed to escape, didn't you?'

'No, I didn't,' Sofie finally picked up the story. 'It all happened so fast. I don't know how many stormed into the village. It was such a shock as I was round the back of our hut digging vegetables. We'd always been told to be quiet, so when the screaming started it was so deafening. People trying to grab their shoes so they could run. Lots did manage it, running in the direction of the thickest part of the woods, where they hid for days until it was safe to come out. But some of them couldn't run, because they were too old, too ill or too young. It didn't occur to me to run too. No one had spotted me and I was too scared to. In the panic that followed, seven were shot dead. I heard the shots and knew then that they were killing my friends.' Sofie began to cry at this point and began dabbing at her eyes with a handkerchief.

'Kees and Corrie looked after Sofie all the time she was in Berkenhout. They were like family,' whispered Liesbeth.

'The men came back later and found me hiding in my hut. I

don't know why they didn't just shoot me as well. Perhaps because I wasn't trying to escape. I realised then it was just me left. Everyone had managed to get out, apart from those poor people who'd been shot. For the first time I felt fear, real fear, alone in the presence of those German officers intent on murder. But when they saw me all by myself the mood changed and they were laughing and saying things I didn't understand. It was so dark in there and something seemed to make one of them angry. What happened next I… daren't say. It must have happened quickly but I lost all sense of time. I must have lain there for hours before Gerrit and Dick Foppen turned up. I couldn't move it hurt so much. It would have been better to shoot me and be done with it.'

Liesbeth stroked her hand. 'Come, don't talk like that. Look what you have.'

Sofie lifted her eyes, swimming with tears, to gaze straight at Marieke again, who squirmed a little in her seat. No one said anything. It was like they were waiting to let it sink in.

'My daughter. I'm so sorry. I just wanted to forget about it all. The only thing I could do was ask *lieve* Liesbeth to take you. Do you forgive me?' Sofie said at last.

Marieke wasn't sure what to say. Forgive her for what? For giving her away to her best friend?

'Mum, can we go?' she said pointedly in Liesbeth's direction. But she didn't wait and left the room and walked out of the house and into the crowds still filling the market.

'Cheer up, *schatje*. Don't look so sad.' The man standing behind the mound of shiny red-green apples had terrible teeth but had no shame exposing them in a wide grin that joined up with the creases in his eyes. He held out an apple and she began to fumble in her purse for a few coins. 'Go on. You can have it if you give me a smile.'

But she couldn't even manage that and pressed 25 cents in his hand and quickly walked away.

She wandered down towards the canal where it was less chaotic. Everything was the same as before, but she viewed the strip of water with houseboats moored along the side with different eyes.

The sound of footsteps made her swing round. It was Johan, hurrying towards her with that familiar limp of his. Without saying anything he enveloped her in a hug, causing her to drop her half-eaten apple that bounced away and into the canal.

'Come back. We were worried about you,' he said. She let him steer her round so that they faced the way they'd come.

'Why?'

'It wasn't easy in those days. Lots of women had babies by German soldiers which they gave up for adoption. Sofie couldn't do that as she couldn't bear the idea of never seeing you again. She did what she thought would be best for you and for her and Liesbeth didn't think twice about having you as her own daughter.

'But she never tried to contact me in twenty years. Why?'

'I can't say for sure. Guilt, but also shame. It was a terrible thing to have a baby under those circumstances. But I do know that Liesbeth always kept in touch with Sofie with news as you were growing up.'

'But never told me she was doing it. I feel they were both

hiding this secret from me. What good can come of that?'

'People don't always behave in the way you expect them to. You shouldn't blame them. They did what they thought was right.'

'What a mess,' she sighed.

'I wouldn't say that. You haven't lost anything. In fact, you've gained another mother,' he said, in an attempt to be light-hearted. 'And maybe a father, if you want.'

'You mean...?' Marieke stared at his profile for a moment. They were almost back in the square where the market traders were packing up. The last stragglers were picking over the stalls and hoping for bargains.

'Shh. You'd better not say anything yet. I haven't even asked Liesbeth and she could always turn me down.'

'Oh, she won't,' said Marieke, a little too quickly. 'I mean, it's the best thing that could happen to her. And to me.' She linked arms. Then she remembered what she meant to ask. 'Why did Sofie call you Jan?'

'It's the name I was known by when I was a boy. I changed it after the war and took my uncle's name. There was so much I wanted to forget. My mother took me to England to make a fresh start. That was before we both moved to Ohio and she remarried a wonderful American I'd introduced her to during the war. But you don't want to hear all that now.' Jan put his arm round Marieke's shoulders.

'Liesbeth calls you Johan, though.' Marieke looked pensive.

'Yes. I met her by chance in Utrecht a few years ago. I'd just landed my job at the University which brought me back to Holland.

She was cycling over the *Oude Gracht* and I recognised her immediately. She only stopped, because I called her name. We laugh about it now. You see, the last time I'd seen her was when I was about thirteen and I suppose I'd changed quite a bit. Fortunately, she looked just the same, otherwise we would have passed each other and that would have been that. My foot never really recovered after I'd been shot and I suppose my limp was what made her recognise me. But Liesbeth says I'm so different from that little squirt she knew and that she preferred me by my new, more grown up name.' He roared with laughter at the memory. 'Come on, I can see them.' He dropped her arm and hurried over to where the two women were standing outside Sofie's house.

Marieke followed more slowly, watching as he kissed Liesbeth and slid his hand around her waist. Sofie didn't notice. She was gazing across the square at Marieke, and smiled.

Glossary of Words & Phrases

Dutch

Appelmoes	Apple sauce
Boslaan	Wood Lane
Dolle Dinsdag	Mad Tuesday
Gezellig	Cosy
Hoi	Hi
Hartelijk gefeliciteerd	Happy Birithday
Heel lekker	Really delicious
Jenever	Dutch gin
Kachel	Stove
Lieve	Dear
Mevrouw	Mrs
Moffen	Derogatory slang for Germans
Onderduiker	Someone in hiding
Proost	Cheers
Schatje	Darling
Sinterklaas	Annual celebration on December 5th
Stroop	Syrup (used as a topping on bread and pancakes)
Stoeltjesklok	Antique clock from Friesland
Tante	Aunty
Waar ben je?	Where are you?
Warme maaltijd	Hot midday meal
Wat is er gebeurd?	What happened?

Voorzichtig, meneer Visser Take care, Mr Visser

German

Alles in Ordnung	Everything is in order
Ersatz	Substitute
Halt	Stop
Hände hoch	Hands up
Heil Hitler	Hail Hitler
Komm	Come on
Los	Hurry up
Oberführer	Nazi party member in charge of a group of Paramilitary units in a region
Papiere	Papers
Sofort	Immediately; get on with it
Wie geht's?	How are you; alright?

Pictures

One of the three reconstructed huts of the hidden
village near Vierhouten.

The interior of one of the huts.

About the Author

Imogen Matthews lives in Oxford, England and is the author of two romantic fiction e-novels. The Hidden Village is her first foray into historical fiction. Born in Rijswijk, Holland, to a Dutch mother and English father, the family moved to England when Imogen was very young. She has always enjoyed holidays in Holland and since 1990, has gone regularly with her husband and two children to Nunspeet on the edge of the Veluwe woods. It was here that she discovered the story of the hidden village, and, together with her mother's vivid stories of life in WW2 Holland, she was inspired to write her next novel...

Made in the USA
Middletown, DE
02 July 2019